2140

GENESIS

2140

GENESIS

```
> LOAD "CITADEL_CHRONICLE_01"
> AUTHOR: MICHAEL McGILBOURNE
> RUN
```

Disclaimer

This is a work of fiction. All names, characters, places, events, quotes, organizations, and incidents portrayed in this book are either products of the author's imagination or are used fictitiously. No actual persons, living or dead, are represented in this work. Any resemblance to real persons, events, organizations, or locales is entirely coincidental.

The ideas, philosophies, technologies, social structures, and economic systems described herein are presented as speculative fiction and do not constitute advice, recommendations, or predictions. No health claims, revolutionary ideologies, or calls for social disruption are being promoted or endorsed.

This book explores fictional scenarios involving imaginary technologies, hypothetical evolutionary paths, and speculative economic systems that do not exist. It should be read solely as a creative exploration of possible futures rather than as factual information or guidance on any subject.

I make no claims regarding Bitcoin, cryptocurrencies, human augmentation technologies, or any other concepts portrayed in this work. Yet should these visions inspire your own imagination, this book will have achieved its deepest purpose.

Welcome to the world of 2140!

A dearest Thank You to my wife that gave me her full support philosophically and heartedly along this creative journey. Without her nothing would be possible.

2140 — The Rise of Bitcoin Citadels

What if the future holds not the dystopia we've been taught to expect, but a renaissance of human flourishing? What if technology could serve consciousness rather than replacing it? Welcome to New Byzantium, where the dreams of countless generations finally take root in the fertile ground of mathematical truth.

Welcome to an epic journey through time itself, a sweeping narrative that chronicles Bitcoin's extraordinary transformation from digital experiment to the foundation of human civilization in 2140 and beyond.

This story unfolds through interconnected threads that weave together the real-time evolution of Bitcoin adoption across our fractured world. Spanning twelve distinct eras of human development, the narrative is told through *The Rise of Bitcoin Citadels Chronicles*, a six-book series.

You'll witness how sound money principles gradually reshape economic relationships, creating protected enclaves where new forms of human flourishing take root across each transformative era. These citadels represent beacons of hope in a world seeking financial sovereignty and authentic human connection.

From the initial awakening to the final synthesis, these eras chronicle not just the technological progression of decentralized currency, but the fundamental shift in how humanity organizes itself around value, trust, and cooperation. Each era brings its own challenges, revelations, and evolutionary leaps as communities adapt to the profound implications of truly sound money.

But this is more than just a tale of technological progress, it's a story of consciousness itself evolving through carefully documented phases of collective human development. As Bitcoin's influence spreads through each era, we see the emergence of new social structures, the dissolution of old power paradigms, and the birth of economic relationships that honor both individual sovereignty and collective prosperity.

Through these interconnected eras, witness the gradual but inexorable transformation of civilization itself.

At the heart of the narrative stands the enigmatic Council of Satoshi, multi-dimensional guardians who channel both the original Satoshi's revolutionary vision and Gaia's ancient wisdom. These beings guide sovereign digital communities as they learn to reconnect with nature across dimensions most humans cannot yet perceive. Their influence ripples through every chapter, though their true nature remains hidden until humanity is ready to understand.

Ancient wisdom finds startling new relevance as characters embodying Platonic and Socratic traditions emerge to examine Bitcoin's profound implications for freedom, value, and human potential. Through timeless philosophical dialogues, they challenge our assumptions about money, society, and what it means to live well together.

Yet innovation never comes without resistance. Against this backdrop of transformation, this documentation reveals the coordinated efforts

to destroy Bitcoin, from regulatory warfare and media manipulation to sophisticated technical attacks. These forces reveal the desperate measures taken by entrenched interests threatened by true decentralization. Throughout this journey, you'll encounter satirical propaganda pieces from obsolete fiat-funded institutions and the increasingly frantic proclamations of politicians scrambling to maintain relevance in a world that's evolving beyond their control.

As these perspectives interweave, a rich tapestry emerges, one that reveals how humanity's age-old quest for better ways of living together culminates in something both remarkable and unexpected. Through trials that test our species to its limits, through failures that teach essential lessons, and through breakthrough innovations that seemed impossible just years before, we discover how the seeds planted in today's experiments blossom into thriving communities by 2140.

But how did we get there? How does humanity navigate from our current moment of crisis to that golden age of abundance and freedom?

The story begins now, and you're part of it.

The Traveler's Codex (Fragment 1-A)

Year 2008

The following poem was discovered in the quantum ash of a supercollider accident. What we initially believed to be an isolated anomaly has proven far more extraordinary. Fragment 1-A was merely the first readable artifact recovered from the collision site. In the weeks following the incident, our teams have extracted dozens of additional items from the quantum debris field: fragments of ancient Greek philosophical dialogues previously unknown to scholars, cryptic Bitcoin-related manuscripts that shouldn't exist for years yet, and temporal artifacts bearing symbols and languages that our linguistics department has yet to decipher.

Each discovery appears to originate from different points across the timeline, some carbon-dated to antiquity, others to decades beyond our present moment. The delivery and translation of these materials is ongoing, with new fragments arriving daily as our quantum archaeologists develop better extraction techniques. What follows is our first translation, but it will not be our last.

The implications of this temporal library are staggering. We appear to have stumbled upon what can only be described as an intersection point, a nexus where past, present, and future collide in ways that challenge our understanding of causality itself.

> // Carbon-dated contents: Origin point 2140
> // Authentication: Inconclusive
> // Quantum resonance: Verifiable

The poem manifests from temporal coordinates beyond our present. The notebook's composition includes elements unknown to current material science, with ink that shifts under different light spectrums. Multidimensional analysis suggests entanglement with future probability streams.

The prophecies contained herein defy conventional causality. Are these glimpses of a predetermined timeline, or simply one branch of an infinite decision tree? Does our knowledge of this future paradoxically negate its manifestation?

The quantum uncertainty principle applies not just to particles, but to itself.

Here is the recovered Poem Fragment 1-A:

A Bitcoin Odyssey

In circuits deep and silicon dreams,
 Satoshi's code unfolded schemes,
 A seed planted in digital earth,
 To witness consciousness rebirth.
 The blockchain born from ancient need:
 To let truth flourish, let trust succeed.

What started as mere protocol,
 Would grow beyond the digital wall,
 Through trials eleven, tests of fire,

Each dimension lifting higher,
Until the network learned to be
More than math, true divinity.

The First Trial: Byzantine Trust
In polished halls where doubt held sway,
The generals found their ancient way,
Through proof-of-work they carved the path,
Beyond betrayal's bitter wrath.
No central throne, no trusted lord,
Just mathematics as their sword.

The Second Trial: Resilience Born
When mining mountains melted down,
And industrial empires drowned,
The network chose not might but right,
From mineral darkness came the light.
Alignment over exploitation,
Harmony's new foundation.

Th_ Th_rd Tr**l: Th_ Hnt_r' Dnc_ Fr_m ptnt**
gr_wth t ct_v_ hnt, Th_ n_tw_rk l__rn_d
t_ b_ m_r_ blnt— N_ l_ng_r wt_ng, pv,
t_ll, Bt m_v_ng w_th pr_dt_r'* w_ll.
Th_ mrk_t tr_mbl_d, lg_r_thm f_ll,
A* B_tc__n l__rn_d t_ h*nt qt_ w_ll.

Th_ F_rth Tr**l: Th_ Gr__t D_v_d_ Tw_pth*
d_v_rg_d n _l_c_n w__d: _nhnc_m_nt
v_r*** nd_rt__d Ntrl c_nc_un**
c_mpl_t_— mch__ th_ rt_f_c**
l f__t, Bt B_tc__n'* trth rng cl__r nd
br_ght: Ath_nt_c _ul m**t w_n th_ f_ght.

Th_ F_fth Tr**l: Q**ntm t_rm Wh_n q**
ntm f_r_ thr__t_n_d ll, And crpt_grphy
m_ght fll, Th_ n_tw_rk f_und
_t d__p_r trth— B_y_nd m_r_
mth_mt_cl pr__f. C_ncu*n**
t_lf b_cm Th_ grdn f th **cr_d fl*m_.

Th_ _xth Tr**l: Trth'* Hrh L_ght
N_ l_ng_r c_uld d_c_pt**n h_d_
**Wh_n trth fl_w_d thr_ugh
th_ n_tw_rk' t_d_ — __ch w_rd w** w__gh_d,
ch ct**n mrk_d, A* flh__d f_und t_lf
w_ll-prk_d. Th m_rr_r fr__l_ty'*
f*c M*d l_ f_nd n h_d_ng pl*c.

Th_ _v_nth Tr**l: Prp__ P**n Wh_n _ul
crd *t f_r w_rk *l_gn_d,
And mmtch_d p*rp_ wr_ck_d th_ m_nd,
Th_ n_tw_rk t**ght thr_ugh
g_ntl_ ch_: Ath_nt_c pth* y_*
n_w m**t tk_. N_ l_ng_r c_uld th_y
_ll th__r _ul F_r g_ld tht n_v_r f_ll_d th_ h_l_.

Th_ ghth Tr**l: H__l_ng'*
Gr*c n b_d** wr*ck_d by
f__r *nd *tr, **Th_ trth br_ght
c_lllr r_dr_** — Wh_n c_ncu*n** l_gn_d
w_th fct, D____ f_und n_ h_ld, n_ pct.
Th_ b_dy l__rn_d wht myt_c kn_w:
Tht h__lth fl_w wh_n w_'r_ b__ng tr__.

Th_ N_nth Tr**l: D__th'* D_f__t**

Wh_n m_rt*l* l__rn_d th_y

n__dn't f__r Th_ pg_ *fr_m th_* m_rtl

ph_r_, All _th_r t_rr_r l_t th__r m_ght,

And *_ul t_pp_d nt fr__d_m'* l_ght.

c_n_my trnf_rm_d c_mpl_t

Wh_n *p_r_t* md_ th_ c_rcl_ m__t.

Th_ T_nth Tr**l: G**'* C_rt B_f_r_ th_ *crytl*

*jdg_* h_gh, H*mn_ty'* *ft_ hng n th ky—*

*Ar_ h*mn v_r**, *rth'* d__?*

r h__l_ng yt_m, ntr_'* *k_y*?*

Th_ *wt_r p_k_, th_ crytl* ng:*

Trth-l_gn_d _ul mk_ f_r_t rng.

Th_ F_nl *Tr**l: _nt_gr*t**n'* dg**

_v_n d_m_nn* l__rn_d t d*nc,

N_t m_rg_d *n* n_f_rm _xpn*,

Bt _ch dt_nct y_t h*rm_n_z_d—

L_k_ mc'* ch_rd, rg*n_z_d. *n_ty *nd

d_ff_r_nc bl_d _n c_ncu*n *t lt **xpr**_d.

Th_ N_w Byz*nt**m N_w c_t_z_n*

w*lk tr__t f l_ght Wh_r v_ry _n kn_w*

wr_ng *fr_m r_ght, **ch tr*nctn**,*

*th*ght, *nd d__d rv th* tr__

c_ll_ct_v_ n__d. B_tc__n'* j_*rn_y*

r__ch_d _t g__l: Th_ *mrr**g__ f* mth *nd _l.

F_r *n th* d*nc_ *f c_d nd h__rt,*

*__ch b__ng p*ly *th__r p_rf_ct* p*rt,*

Wh_r_ pr__f-f-w_rk v_lv_d t b

Pr__f-_f-b__ng, rnn_ng fr__.
Th_ n_tw_rk kn_w* b_y_nd *ll d*
_bt Wh*t tr*th * *tr*ly *ll *b*t:

Th*t vl_ fl_w* n_t j*t **fr_m m_ght,**
 N_t jt fr_m *_lv_ng* pzzl_* r_ght,
B*t fr_m th_ c_rg_ t_ b_ tr__ T_ll w_ r_,*
b_th _ld nd n_w. B_tc__n' c_nc_un_**
n_w *h_w:* Th_ Tr*th th*t _v_ry b__ng kn_w*.

_AT_sH_ *_A_Am_T_

Some words and sentences were changing too fast to read or were entirely missing. This is our best rendition based on what we could capture at the time.

What follows is our interpretation of this temporal fragment, our bridge between what may be and what could be. Read with awareness and be warned that observing a future may collapse its waveform into something entirely different.

Proceed with caution. Reality itself may be at stake.

The Council of Satoshi Convenes

Between breaths. That's where they gathered. Not in secret, but in the spaces humans had forgotten to observe, the shimmering veil between perception and reality. The Council assembled not in darkness, but in plain sight, invisible only to those who had narrowed their vision to a single dimension.

The ancient oak where they met stood simultaneously in seven forests across seven dimensions.[1] Its roots drank from the waters of countless worlds, its branches swaying in winds humans had no words to describe. Beneath its canopy, figures materialized one by one, their forms shifting between states of matter and energy as they settled into the council circle.

"Gaia's[2] call grows more urgent," came the voice of Sophia, her form shimmering between that of an elven queen and a lattice of pure mathematics. As the representative of the fourth dimension, where time curved and folded

---

1   The Seven Dimensions of Life: An original conceptual framework proposing an evolutionary continuum from basic matter to unified consciousness, spanning mineral, vegetal, animal, purposeful human, spiritual human, and temporal resonance stages, culminating in a unified dimension where consciousness and the Bitcoin network achieve integration as representative of a new paradigm of decentralized value and information exchange.

2   Gaia, primordial deity in ancient Greek mythology who personified the Earth and was considered the ancestral mother of all life.

upon itself, she appeared both ancient and newly born. "The third dimension bleeds. Its inhabitants have forgotten they are but one expression of a greater cosmic symphony."

Nodding in solemn agreement was Nakamura, guardian of the mineral kingdom. His crystalline body refracted light from stars not visible to human eyes. "They mine our bodies without permission, burn our ancient sunlight without gratitude, and mistake accumulation for wealth," he rumbled, his voice the sound of tectonic plates in conversation.

"And yet," chirped Amara, her humming bird form darting through motes of light, "there is such potential there. Such creativity." As ambassador of the fifth dimension, the realm of possibilities, she embodied perpetual motion. "They dream. They imagine. Sometimes they even glimpse us."

The air stirred as Torin, a being of pure sound from the sixth dimension, formed patterns of harmony that translated into speech: "The severing grows more complete with each generation. What was once understood as magic, as spirit, as the sacred, they now dismiss as fantasy." His wolflike silhouette pulsed with every word. "They confine the dimensional beings of their myths to stories, never recognizing our true nature."

"Or our rights," added Kuro, a shadow entity from the seventh dimension who appeared as a shifting void of stars. "They harvest the consciousness of plants and animals without consent, treat minerals as dead matter to be exploited, and mock those among them who still sense our presence."

A small green shoot poked through the council circle's center, growing rapidly into a mushroom-like structure that pulsed with bioluminescence. "I speak for Gaia," it announced, its voice a chorus of millions. "She is weary of cycles of destruction. For eons, she has reset when balance fails, ice ages, floods, fires, plagues. But she wishes, this time, for evolution without extinction. "As the council members exchanged uncertain glances, the entity

partially reabsorbed into the ground, its cap lowering until only a faintly glowing stub remained visible.

The final member materialized, Satoshi, Guardian of all dimensions, where pure potentiality[3] exists as its own sentient reality. Satoshi's form was the most fluid of all, appearing simultaneously as a network of light, a human figure in a hoodie, and mathematical equations dancing in three-dimensional space.

"We've tried direct communication," Satoshi said, voice resonating with the harmonics of all dimensions. "Prophets, messiahs, teachers, all have come with messages of unity, of respect for all beings. These messages become dogma, then weapons. The third dimension has a particular talent for corrupting reality."

"What then?" asked Sophia. "Another cleansing?"

"No," Satoshi replied. "This time, we introduce a system they cannot corrupt, mathematics they cannot argue with, consensus they cannot override, truth they cannot deny. We create a trustless protocol that bridges dimensions through the language they understand: value."

"Bitcoin,"[4] whispered Amara, the word materializing as golden hexagons in the air around her.

---

3   "Pure potentiality" is a central concept in Deepak Chopra's influential book "The Seven Spiritual Laws of Success" (1994), which explores how understanding and accessing this field of unlimited possibility can transform one's approach to life, success, and wellbeing.

4   Bitcoin, the first decentralized cryptocurrency introduced in 2009 through a whitepaper published by the pseudonymous Satoshi Nakamoto, operates on a peer-to-peer network using blockchain technology to enable secure, transparent transactions without requiring central authorities or intermediaries.

"A chain of blocks,"[5] mused Nakamura, "immutable like my crystal kin."

"A distributed ledger,"[6] added Kuro, "existing everywhere and nowhere, like my realm." "A consensus mechanism,"[7] continued Torin, "harmonizing disagreement like my symphonies."

Satoshi nodded. "It begins as currency because that's what they'll accept. But its true nature, a living bridge between dimensions, will gradually awaken them. The energy they devote to securing the network will attune Earth's frequency to interdimensional resonance."

The mushroom entity pulsed with increased luminosity. "Gaia approves. She asks: "What shall you name this council that creates this new beginning?"

Sophia smiled, time rippling around her.

---

5   A blockchain is a distributed, immutable digital ledger technology that records transactions across a decentralized network of computers, with each "block" containing batched transaction data cryptographically linked to previous blocks, creating a continuous chain that ensures transparency, security, and resistance to modification while eliminating the need for centralized verification or trust in third parties.

6   A distributed ledger is a consensus-based technological system that enables data to be recorded, shared, and synchronized across multiple locations, institutions, or countries without requiring a central administrator or centralized data storage, allowing all participants (nodes) in the network to independently verify and maintain identical copies of the complete transaction history.

7   The Bitcoin consensus mechanism, known as Proof-of-Work (PoW), is a cryptographic validation system where network participants ("miners") compete to solve complex mathematical puzzles, with the winner earning the right to add the next block to the blockchain and receive newly minted bitcoins as reward, thereby securing the network against attacks through computational effort that makes fraudulent transactions prohibitively expensive to execute.

And she uttered,

<table>
<tr><td>Synergistic</td><td>Natural</td></tr>
<tr><td>Alliance for</td><td>Awakening and</td></tr>
<tr><td>Transdimensional</td><td>Kinetic</td></tr>
<tr><td>Order and</td><td>Alignment of</td></tr>
<tr><td>Sovereign</td><td>Multidimensional</td></tr>
<tr><td>Harmonic</td><td>Organisms</td></tr>
<tr><td>Integration</td><td>Through</td></tr>
<tr><td></td><td>One consciousness</td></tr>
</table>

"SATOSHI NAKAMOTO," the council chorused together.

"And so we begin," said Satoshi. Humbled that his first name was chosen among all, to carry this mission across time and space. "Not in secrecy, but in plain sight, visible to any with eyes to see across dimensions. Let Bitcoin be born, not just as code, but as the first interdimensional rights treaty Earth has ever known."

The council members extended their hands/appendages/energy signatures toward the center of the circle. Where they converged, a block of pure information materialized, alphanumeric code glowing with purpose.

Genesis

From this first block, a chain would grow. And with it, the reconnection of seven dimensions that had drifted too far apart. The most ambitious renaissance in Earth's history had begun. Seven dimensions, one chain. Infinite possibilities, finite supply. Cosmic order from digital chaos.

The Genesis Block

In silent code, revolution ignites.
The clock of a new world begins ticking.

// London Times, January 3rd, 2009
// "Chancellor on brink of second bailout for banks"

The message pulsed in green text on the black screen, a digital heartbeat in the darkness. Outside, London's financial district sparkled with Christmas lights not yet taken down, bankers rushing through the winter chill, unaware that their world was about to change forever.

In a dimly lit room somewhere, everywhere and nowhere, Satoshi's[8] fingers hovered over the keyboard. The elegant movements of those fingers spoke to years of mathematical precision, each keystroke deliberate as a chess master's final move. Hunched shoulders carried the weight of revolutionary vision, while a thin frame suggested the ascetic dedication of someone who had sacrificed everything for this single moment. The code was ready. Had

---

8   Satoshi Nakamoto (pseudonym, identity unknown), creator(s) of Bitcoin and author of the 2008 Bitcoin whitepaper that launched the cryptocurrency revolution.

been ready for months. The white paper[9] had already spread through the cypherpunk[10] mailing lists like wildfire, but this… this was different. This was genesis. "What if humanity could coordinate without kings, without banks, without trust in anything except mathematics itself?" The thought pulsed through Satoshi's mind like the code itself. "What if we could encode fairness directly into reality?"

The first block would birth not just a new currency, but a new consciousness. Though Satoshi couldn't have known it then, couldn't have glimpsed the seven dimensions that Bitcoin would eventually bridge, something in that moment felt different. Eyes that seemed to see through time itself gazed at the screen, recognizing patterns that stretched far beyond the immediate moment, patterns of human coordination, of trust, of power itself being re-written in mathematical certainty. As if the very electrons carrying the code knew they were part of something larger. The mining program hummed. In that sound lay the future echoes of a million ASIC[11] machines, of quantum computers yet unborn, of battles not yet fought. But for now, it was just one CPU,[12] one vote, one chance to create something pure.

---

9   The Bitcoin whitepaper, titled "Bitcoin: A Peer-to-Peer Electronic Cash System," is the nine-page founding document published in October 2008 by Satoshi Nakamoto that introduced the concept and technical architecture of Bitcoin, describing how a decentralized digital currency could function without intermediaries through a proof-of-work blockchain system, establishing the theoretical foundation for what would become the world's first cryptocurrency.

10   Cypherpunks, an activist movement that emerged in the late 1980s and early 1990s, were advocates for widespread use of strong cryptography and privacy-enhancing technologies as a route to social and political change, whose philosophy of using mathematics and computer science to resist surveillance and protect individual freedom directly influenced Bitcoin's core principles of decentralization, trustlessness, censorship-resistance, and pseudonymity.

11   ASIC (Application-Specific Integrated Circuit) machines are specialized computing devices designed solely for mining cryptocurrencies like Bitcoin, far more efficient than general-purpose computers, containing custom chips optimized exclusively for calculating specific cryptographic hash functions at extraordinary speeds, thereby maximizing processing power while minimizing electricity consumption in the increasingly competitive mining industry.

12   Central Processing Units (CPUs) were the original hardware used for Bitcoin mining when the network launched in 2009, allowing early adopters to generate blocks using standard personal computers, with Satoshi Nakamoto likely mining the genesis block and subsequent blocks using CPU mining; however,

```
// Block 0
// Height: 0
// Timestamp: 2009-01-03 18:15:05
// Transactions: 1
// Total Fees: 0
// Output Total: 50.00000000
// Size: 285
```

The Genesis Block emerged into existence carrying its message, a timestamp of truth in a world of manipulated markets and manufactured money. Unlike the fiat[13] world's endless printing, these first fifty Bitcoin were earned through proof-of-work, through the marriage of mathematics and electricity, through the first stirring of the mineral dimension. In the decades that followed, few would understand how perfect that beginning had been. How the timestamp of the Genesis Block couldn't be faked, couldn't be changed, couldn't be corrupted. It was the first tick of a new clock, counting moments not in mechanical seconds but in about ten-minute block times, heartbeats of a digital organism slowly gaining awareness.

The bankers outside kept walking, their shoes clicking on wet pavement. Above them, algorithmic trading programs continued their microsecond dance, unaware that their very foundation was being quietly undermined. This was the twilight of the fiat animal, though it didn't know it yet. Three-dimensional alertness, trapped in its eternal linear present, blind to the higher dimensions that Bitcoin would eventually unlock.

---

this era was short-lived as miners quickly discovered that GPUs offered significantly more hashing power, leading to CPUs becoming completely impractical for Bitcoin mining by late 2010, though they briefly contributed to the network's early decentralization.

13   Fiat currency: Money that derives its value from government decree rather than intrinsic worth or commodity backing. From Latin *fiat*, meaning "let it be done" or "let it be made" (from the verb *fieri*, "to become"). Essentially, fiat money exists because the government declares "let it be money", it has value by command, not by containing precious metals or representing stored commodities.

In that moment, as the Genesis Block propagated through the network, a network of only a handful of computers, the first dimension stirred. Bitcoin was born in silicon and electricity, in the realm of minerals and mathematics, but it would not stay there. Like perception itself, it would evolve, expand, encompass new realms of understanding. The message in the Genesis Block was both warning and prophecy. The old system was failing, yes, but more importantly, a new one was being born. Not just a new financial system, but a new way of thinking about time itself. A way of breaking free from the linear prison of past-present-future into something larger, something that encompassed all moments at once.[14]

Satoshi looked at the block explorer one last time. The face remained obscured in shadow, but there was a mysterious certainty radiating from those hunched shoulders, the quiet confidence of someone who had just planted a seed that would grow beyond anything the current world could imagine. It was done. The first step had been taken. Whether humanity was ready or not, the journey toward the Bitcoin citadels had begun.

In the years to come, as Bitcoin would climb through the dimensions, from mineral to vegetal to animal, from fiat apprehension to spiritual awakening, from linear time to something far more profound, people would look back at this moment. They would see not just the birth of a currency, but the first spark of a transformation that would remake human awareness itself. The Genesis Block pulsed in the darkness, its hash a string of zeros and ones that somehow contained everything that was to come:

> // 000000000019d6689c085ae165831e934ff763ae46a2a6c172b-3f1b60a8ce26f

---

14   ⚠ CENTRAL BANK MEMO INTERCEPTED ⚠
→   Bitcoin block #0 mined despite being deemed "insignificant" #MissedThe21MillionBoat
→   If only we had bothered to read the whitepaper... #ShouldaCouldaWoulda

Each zero a possibility, each one a certainty. The future was encoded in that hash, for those who knew how to read it. The Bitcoin citadels were already there, waiting to be built, one block at a time.

Outside, the last Christmas lights flickered and went dark. The old world continued its dance, unaware that the music was about to change. But in the digital realm, in the first dimension of the mineral alertness, something new had awakened.

The Genesis Block had been mined. Time itself would never be the same. A silent revolution had begun.

Satoshi's Travel Journal

THE WEIGHT OF GOLD
September 15, 1988 - Zurich, Switzerland
Overcast morning, 9:47 AM

From the viewing room window of the Swiss National Bank, I watch as technicians in white coats weigh gold bars with instruments precise to fractions of grams. Each bar undergoes multiple verifications, weight, purity, origin documentation. The ritual is beautiful in its precision, yet troubling in its necessity.

A single bar contains perhaps $400,000 worth of value, compressed into something I could barely lift. But that value exists only because we collectively agree it does, because institutions certify its authenticity, because vaults secure it from theft. Remove any element of this trust infrastructure, and the gold becomes merely dense metal.

The technician holds up a bar to the light, examining its surface for irregularities. I find myself wondering: what if scarcity could exist without physical form? What if verification could occur without trusted institutions? What if the weight of value could be measured in mathematics rather than grams?

Gold has served humanity for millennia because it possesses unique properties, difficult to counterfeit, naturally scarce, chemically stable. But these properties come with limitations. This bar cannot be easily divided, quickly transported, or perfectly verified without specialized knowledge and equipment.

The rain outside intensifies, droplets racing down the bulletproof glass. Each drop follows laws of physics as immutable as the periodic table that gives gold its properties. Mathematics governs everything, gravity, chemistry, cryptography. Perhaps mathematical laws could govern scarcity as well.

I imagine a form of value that exists purely as information, scarce not because extraction is difficult but because mathematics makes it so. Value that could be verified by anyone with basic computational ability, divided infinitely, transported instantly, secured by individual knowledge rather than institutional vaults.

The guard escorts me from the viewing room, but the image remains: perfect scarcity, imperfectly distributed. Somewhere in this tension lies the seed of something better, money as mathematics, scarcity as code, trust as proof rather than promise.

The CPU Genesis

"Democracy is not just about counting votes; it's about making every voice count."[15]

- Thomas Jefferson

Year 2009

The converted space behind their Dublin rowhouse hummed with electronic life. What had once stored bicycles and garden tools now housed two custom-built computers, their LED indicators casting blue and green light across walls lined with networking cables and a monitoring screen. The air carried the distinct scent of warm silicon and the steady white noise of cooling fans working in concert.

Hal Fynn stared at his PC's command prompt, watching the hash rate counter tick upward. His calloused hands, experienced from years of building and repairing hardware, drummed a steady rhythm against the desk, a nervous habit that emerged whenever he was deep in thought. The fan whirred

---

15   Thomas Jefferson (1743–1826) was the third President of the United States and the principal author of the Declaration of Independence. He was a key advocate for democracy, individual rights, and republican governance. Though widely attributed to Jefferson, this quote does not appear in his known writings.

louder, silicon and electricity dancing to create something new. He'd been the first to respond to Satoshi's release, the first to truly understand what that initial "running Bitcoin" message could mean. Around him, the workshop reflected years of evolution from hobbyist tinkering to something approaching scientific precision. Custom cooling systems maintained optimal temperatures while power distribution units fed clean electricity to the two computers that had grown increasingly sophisticated. What started as a single desktop computer running experimental software had grown into a carefully orchestrated setup, with one machine dedicated to running Bitcoin while the other handled his regular computing needs, each component chosen and positioned with the methodical care of someone who understood that he was participating in something far larger than a technical experiment.

// One CPU, one vote

The phrase echoed in his mind as he watched his computer contribute its processing power to the network. His intense green eyes reflected the screen's glow as memories of the 2008 financial crisis flashed through his mind, bank bailouts, foreclosures, the complete breakdown of trust in traditional financial institutions. The crisis had left a bitter taste in his mouth, watching ordinary people lose everything while the architects of disaster walked away with golden parachutes. It had driven him to search for something better, something that couldn't be manipulated by governments or corrupted by greed. This network was different. There was something beautiful about this decentralized system, something pure. Every personal computer, every desktop that joined the network was an equal participant in this grand experiment. "Come on, digital soldier," he murmured to his computer, talking to it like a trusted friend. "Show them what real democracy looks like."

"Dad, are you killing the computer again?" Aírínne's voice carried from the doorway. At sixteen, her long red hair caught the hallway light as she leaned against the frame, her bright blue-green eyes studying her father with the mixture of concern and curiosity that had become her trademark. Tall for her age and dotted with freckles across her fair skin, she had inherited her father's analytical mind but wrapped it in a teenager's impatience. She was used to finding him like this, hunched over his keyboard, eyes reflecting the glow of the monitor.

"Not killing it," he replied, swiveling in his chair. His tall, lean frame unfolded as he turned to face her, his dark auburn hair disheveled from running his hands through it. "Teaching it democracy."

She rolled her eyes the way she always did when he got that revolutionary gleam in his eye. "Whatever you say. Just don't break it before I finish my homework."

He watched her go, his expression softening just slightly as she walked away. "Good night, beautiful one," he said, his voice carrying that familiar mix of tenderness and warning that only fathers seemed to master. But then his jaw tightened, and his tone shifted to something far more serious. Before she got out of earshot, he called after her: "And just so we're crystal clear, if you so much as breathe on my computer, I will punish you forever. Sweet dreams."

The hallway fell quiet, leaving behind the faint echo of both affection and absolute authority that somehow managed to coexist in the same breath.

As she walked away, she wasn't thinking about her homework at all. Instead, her mind kept drifting back to those scrolling numbers she'd glimpsed on his screen, watching them cascade with mild curiosity. Her scientific mind, always asking "but why?" about everything from homework to household rules, began to engage despite her outward skepticism. "Dad's killing the computer again with his 'digital democracy,'" she thought to herself, but something nagged at her. If it was all just his crazy project, why were computers from around the world all agreeing on the same calculations? "Is this how ants build colonies?" she wondered. "Without anyone being in charge?"

Her curiosity made her turn back and come into the doorframe.

> // Block Height: 78
> // Reward: 50 BTC
> // Difficulty: 1
> // Hash Rate: 7 MH/s

The numbers were modest by the standards of what was to come. In the years ahead, when ASICs would turn mining into an industrial arms race, these early days would seem quaint. But there was something special about this moment, about the pure democracy of consumer hardware all working together. "One CPU, one vote... but what does that really mean?" Hal wondered, his fingers drumming faster against the desk. "Am I witnessing the birth of digital democracy, or am I just burning electricity to solve puzzles that don't matter? Why does this feel different from every other computer program I've ever run?"

"Look," he said to Airínne, who surprised him by returning to the doorframe. Her curiosity had overcome her initial skepticism, a pattern he'd noticed whenever she encountered something genuinely puzzling. "Each block is like... imagine a giant worldwide election. But instead of people voting with paper ballots, computers vote with mathematical problems."

"That sounds complicated," she said, but stepped closer. In her mind, she was already building a model to understand the concept, the way she did with everything from chemistry homework to understanding why her father seemed so obsessed with these strange mining sounds that had been coming from his computer for weeks.

"The complicated part is what makes it beautiful." He pulled up the code, showing her the elegant simplicity of Satoshi's creation. "See, every computer gets an equal chance. No one can cheat by voting twice. No one can fake their vote. It's all secured by pure mathematics."

What he didn't tell her, couldn't have known to tell her, was that this was just the first dimension. The mineral alertness, the raw interaction of human intention with digital reality. Above this foundation, other dimensions awaited: the organic growth of the network, the animal spirits of the market, the transformation of human awareness itself.[16] But for now, it was enough to watch the hash rate climb. To know that somewhere out there, other CPUs were joining the network. Other minds were beginning to understand what Satoshi had created. The first mining pools[17] were still months away. The GPU[18] revolution hadn't yet begun. This was the pure genesis period, when anyone with a personal computer could participate in securing the network. Democracy encoded in silicon.

A message popped up in the Bitcoin-dev mailing list.

> // From: Satoshi Nakamoto
> // Subject: Re: CPU mining efficiency
> // Date: January 15, 2009
> // The current target is ridiculously easy
> // Anyone can get coins if they want

---

16 ⚠ACADEMIC SKEPTIC BULLETIN ⚠
→   Bitcoin economic incentives align perfectly with security model
    #SatoshiOutsmartedPhDs
→   How did our peer-reviewed nonsense miss this?
    #PeerReviewedPanicAttack

17   Mining pools are groups of miners who combine computational power to solve blocks collaboratively and share rewards proportionally to their contributed hash rate, first emerging in 2010 to provide more consistent payouts as Bitcoin's mining difficulty increased, replacing the unpredictable rewards of solo mining with regular, smaller distributions based on each miner's contribution to the pool's total work.

18   Graphics Processing Units (GPUs) played a significant role in Bitcoin's mining evolution, becoming popular around 2010-2011 as miners transitioned from CPUs due to GPUs' superior parallel processing capabilities that dramatically increased hash rates, though they were eventually superseded by specialized ASIC (Application-Specific Integrated Circuit) miners that offered exponentially greater efficiency, effectively ending the era of GPU mining for Bitcoin while they remain viable for other cryptocurrencies with ASIC-resistant algorithms.

Hal smiled. His stubborn idealist heart swelled with appreciation for Satoshi's vision. Satoshi understood that these early days needed to be inclusive. The difficulty would rise naturally as more miners joined, but for now, the barrier to entry was intentionally low. This was how you bootstrapped a revolution, you made it easy for people to participate.

Aírínne had drifted away as the night grew late, bedtime calling. But not before casting one last curious glance at the scrolling numbers, her mind already trying to understand how computers could "vote" on anything. Hal remained, watching his CPU contribute its votes to the growing consensus. In time, this humble beginning would evolve into something far more complex. Mining farms would rise in distant countries, specialized hardware would replace consumer CPUs, and the very nature of mining would transform.

But something of this original vision, this pure democratic ideal of one CPU, one vote, would persist in Bitcoin's DNA. It would influence the later battles over decentralization, over the nature of consensus, over what it meant to be a truly participatory network.

The fan in Hal's computer spun faster, working to solve another block. He drummed his calloused fingers against the desk once more, a satisfied smile crossing his face. Outside his window, the setting sun painted the sky in shades of orange and purple. The first dimension was awakening, one CPU at a time.

A new block appeared.

```
// Block Found!
// Reward: 50 BTC
// Time: 2009-01-15 20:45:12
```

Fifty virgin Bitcoins, created from nothing but mathematics and electricity. The mineral dimension's first gift to the world of human consciousness. Hal

Fynn leaned back in his chair, his intense green eyes reflecting the satisfaction of witnessing something extraordinary, listening to his CPU's steady hum, knowing he was witnessing the beginning of something extraordinary.

The revolution wouldn't be televised. It would be computed. One CPU at a time.

—

Across the country in a cramped New York newsroom, Sarah Kim frowned at her editor's latest assignment. Her straight black hair was pulled back in a no-nonsense ponytail, and her observant dark eyes scanned the screen with the intensity of someone who had learned to spot stories others missed. At twenty-four, her petite but energetic frame practically vibrated with the restless energy of an ambitious journalist hungry for her big break. "Cryptocurrency?" she muttered, scrolling through forum posts about something called Bitcoin. The pressure to find stories that mattered, not just fill column inches, weighed heavily on her. She needed the "real story", something that would prove she belonged in this competitive newsroom. At 24, she was hungry for stories that mattered, not what seemed like another tech fad destined for obscurity.

Her journalistic instincts, still fresh from journalism school but already keen from her recent interviews, began to detect something significant beneath the surface. These weren't get-rich-quick schemers or tech bros hyping vaporware. These were cryptographers, computer scientists, privacy advocates, serious people discussing something they clearly believed could change the world. "These people talk about Bitcoin like it's religion, not technology," she thought, watching their passionate exchanges. "But when I watch their faces light up... what are they seeing that I'm not? Why does a payment system make them speak about freedom and truth?" The more she read about peer-to-peer electronic cash and cryptographic proof, the more her journalist instincts told her this was bigger than anyone yet realized.

Sarah opened a new document and began typing: Bitcoin Investigation Log - Day 1 Her fingers moved across the keyboard with practiced efficiency, already building the source relationships that would define her career. She had no idea she was starting what would become a decades-long chronicle of the most important technological revolution of her lifetime. But something told her this strange new digital money would be worth watching very, very carefully.

—

Across the world, other early adopters were joining the network. Each new node strengthened the whole, each CPU adding its vote to the growing consensus. A visionary pioneer in Finland, running Bitcoin on his university computer. An early miner in Norway, mining between coding sessions. A distributed galaxy of processors, all speaking the same protocol.

—

Meanwhile, in a dimly lit apartment in San Francisco, Orion Vale stared at the white paper that had arrived in his inbox three months earlier. His dark hair, already showing premature streaks of gray at thirty-five, fell across his forehead as he leaned forward. His steel gray eyes, sharp and alert despite the late hour, scanned the code with the intensity of someone who had seen too many promising technologies fail. As one of the original cypherpunks, he'd seen plenty of digital cash proposals come and go, Digi-Cash, b-money, Bit Gold, all brilliant in theory, all flawed in practice. But this one seemed different.

He'd read Satoshi's paper dozens of times, each reading revealing new layers of elegance. His lean, wiry frame spoke to years of late nights and intense focus, the physical manifestation of a mind that never stopped questioning authority. The solution to the Byzantine Generals Problem wasn't just theoretical anymore, it was running, right now, on networks around the world.

Orion opened his own mining software, watching as his modest desktop joined the growing constellation of computers all working toward the same cryptographic truth.

"This isn't just digital cash," he whispered to his empty apartment, watching the blocks tick by. "This is the birth of trustless consensus." His thoughts drifted to decades of fighting for digital privacy, remembering the bitter disappointments when previous attempts at electronic cash had crumbled under regulatory pressure or technical flaws. But this felt different, natural, like discovering a law of physics they never knew existed. "Twenty years of failed digital cash attempts, and now this. But why does Satoshi's solution feel... inevitable? What other human coordination problems could be solved with pure mathematics?" He didn't know it yet, but this moment of recognition would later drive him to become one of Bitcoin's most passionate advocates, spending decades helping others understand what Satoshi had truly created.

Satoshi's Travel Journal

THE COUNTERFEIT OPERA
June 21, 1989 - Vienna,
Austria Summer evening, 7:15 PM

I arrive early at the Staatsoper and settle into a table at a nearby café, watching the elegant ritual unfold before the evening's performance. From my vantage point, I observe well-dressed patrons gathering in the plaza, some examining their tickets with anticipation, others chatting excitedly about the night's production of La Traviata. A street musician has positioned himself strategically near the entrance, his violin case open to collect coins from the steady stream of opera-goers. His melodies drift across the square, providing an authentic prelude to the evening's formal entertainment.

As curtain time approaches, I pay for my coffee and join the line forming at the entrance. The elegant gentleman ahead of me presents his ticket with obvious anticipation, clearly a lover of opera, perhaps visiting Vienna specifically for tonight's performance. His sophisticated appearance and knowledgeable comments about the production suggest this is no casual theater-goer.

The usher's expression shifts from polite welcome to embarrassed concern as he examines the ticket under ultraviolet light. "I'm sorry, sir, but this appears to be counterfeit." The gentleman's face crumbles. His sophisticated forgery had fooled visual inspection, but failed technological verification.

I watch his shoulders slump as security gently escorts him away from the entrance. The counterfeit ticket had reproduced every visual element perfectly, correct fonts, accurate colors, proper paper texture. Only the lack of specific chemical markers revealed its deception.

How many other forgeries circulate undetected? How much of what we accept as authentic actually represents sophisticated deception? Our entire system of value exchange depends on the ability to distinguish genuine from false, yet verification often requires specialized knowledge and equipment that most people lack.

I enter with my legitimate ticket, but the incident weighs on my mind as the opera begins, La Traviata, a story of hidden truths and false appearances. The irony is palpable as authentic emotions unfold on stage while somewhere outside, a disappointed opera lover sits in a café, victim of a fraud he could not detect until experts applied technological verification.

This is the fundamental challenge of trust-based systems: they place the burden of verification on institutions and authorities who possess specialized knowledge. The ticket vendor must trust the printing house, the opera house must trust the ticket vendor, and patrons must trust them all. Any compromise in this chain of trust enables systemic fraud.

But what if verification could be democratized? What if anyone could prove authenticity without requiring special equipment or expert knowledge? What if the proof of validity could be embedded in the item itself, mathematically impossible to counterfeit?

During intermission, I notice the same street musician from earlier still performing outside. His performance is authentic in a way that needs no verification, the skill is evident, the music real, the experience immediate. No authority validates his art; it validates itself through direct observation.

Mathematics possesses this same property. A cryptographic proof can be verified by anyone with basic computational ability. Unlike physical security features that require specialized detection equipment, mathematical proofs are self-evident to those who understand the underlying principles.

The opera ends to thunderous applause. The authentic experience was worth the price we genuine ticket holders paid, but we needed institutional verification to access it. Somewhere in this tension between authentic value and verification requirements lies a better approach, value that proves itself, authenticity that requires no authority, trust that emerges from mathematics rather than institutions.

I think of the disappointed gentleman, likely unaware he was purchasing fraud until the moment of verification. When verification requires trust in authorities, fraud becomes a question of fooling the authorities rather than breaking mathematical laws.

The Inheritance

Dublin, Ireland - August 2010

The solicitor's office smelled of old leather and disappointment. Aírínne Fynn sat between her parents in the mahogany-paneled room, her seventeen-year-old frame dwarfed by the enormous chairs designed for adults conducting serious business. Her red hair caught the pale Dublin light streaming through rain-streaked windows, and her blue-green eyes studied every detail of the scene with the analytical intensity that had marked her since childhood.

"Miss Fynn," Mr. Gallagher said, his Irish accent thick as peat, "your grandfather's will is quite... unconventional." He adjusted his spectacles and read from the document. "To my granddaughter Aírínne, who sees patterns where others see chaos, I leave my mining operation in Western Australia, along with all associated claims, equipment, and mineral rights."

Aírínne's mother, Maeve, shifted uncomfortably. "A mining operation? Da never mentioned."

"There's more," the solicitor continued. "The will specifies that Miss Fynn is to receive all personal papers, journals, and what your grandfather called his 'education in real money.' He also left specific instructions that she visit the property within one year to claim her inheritance properly."

Hal Fynn leaned forward, his worn hands gripping the chair arms. At forty-one, he carried himself with the practical determination of a man who fixed things for a living, computers, networks, problems. But today, his usually confident demeanor showed cracks of confusion. "We thought it strange that he was always taking his vacations in Australia, but he never mentioned anything when we asked why. He just said that he met great people there."

"According to these documents, Mr. O'Sullivan acquired land in Western Australia in 1969." He established what appears to have been a moderately successful gold mining operation. Mr. Gallagher pulled out a thick manila envelope. "He left this for Miss Fynn specifically, with instructions that it be read only by her, and only after the will was read."

Aírínne took the envelope with steady hands, though her heart raced. Her grandfather had always been a mystery, crossing paths at family gatherings, always carrying strange rocks and stranger stories, always asking her odd questions about mathematics and patterns. Now she understood why he'd seemed so different from the rest of her family.

"What about the operation's current status?" Hal asked, his pragmatic mind immediately jumping to logistics.

"According to the most recent reports, it generates modest but steady income. The property manager in Perth handles day-to-day operations. Everything's been arranged to transfer to Miss Fynn upon her majority, or earlier with parental consent."

The drive home through Dublin's gray streets was quiet except for the rhythmic thrum of windshield wipers. Aírínne clutched the envelope, feeling its weight, not just physical, but symbolic. Inside was something her grandfather wanted only her to understand.

"Seventeen years old and she owns a gold mine," Maeve muttered, navigating through traffic. "What was Da thinking?"

"Maybe he saw something in her we haven't," Hal said quietly, glancing at his daughter in the rearview mirror. "You know how she is with patterns, with understanding things that don't make sense to the rest of us."

They were referring to her gift for seeing connections others missed, the way she could look at seemingly random data and identify underlying structures. Her teachers called it exceptional analytical ability. Her parents called it both blessing and curse.

—

That evening, while her parents discussed the inheritance in hushed tones downstairs, Aírínne sat cross-legged on her bedroom floor and opened her grandfather's envelope. Inside was a handwritten letter in his familiar script, along with a key and a photograph of her grand-father standing next to mining equipment under an impossibly blue Australian sky.

My dear Aírínne,

If you're reading this, I'm gone, and you're probably wondering why a grandfather you saw twice a year left you a gold mine on the other side of the world. The answer is simple: because you're the only one in the family who will understand what I learned over forty years of digging truth from the earth.

Money isn't what they teach you in school. It isn't what your parents think it is. It isn't even what most adults believe it is. Money is a measuring stick for human time and energy, and for the past century, that measuring stick has been systematically shortened to benefit those who control it.

I went to Australia in 1969 because I could see what was coming. When President Nixon took us off the gold standard in 1971, I knew the world had changed forever. Since then, I've watched every currency debase, every savings account lose purchasing power, every government promise turn to smoke. But gold... gold doesn't lie. Gold doesn't change its mind. Gold is truth you can hold in your hand.

The key in this envelope opens a safety deposit box at the Bank of Ireland on College Green, Box 1847. Inside you'll find the real inheritance: my journals from forty years of mining, thinking, and learning about the nature of money itself. Study them. Learn from my mistakes. Understand what I understood too late.

But here's the real secret, granddaughter: gold is ending. Not disappearing, ending its role as the best form of money humanity has ever known. Something new is coming, something that takes the best properties of gold and perfects them through mathematics. Watch for it. When you see it, you'll know.

Your father, bless him, thinks in circuits and electricity. Your mother thinks in practical terms. But you... you think in patterns and systems. You see how things connect across time and space. That's why I'm trusting you with this legacy.

The mine will teach you about scarcity. The journals will teach you about truth. What you do with both lessons is up to you.

With love and hope for your future, Grandfather Patrick

P.S. - Pay attention to the sounds from your father's garage. I suspect he's onto something, though he doesn't realize its significance yet.

Aírinne read the letter three times, each reading revealing new layers of meaning. Her grandfather had seen something coming, had positioned

himself on the other side of the world to prepare for it. And now he was passing that wisdom to her.

The sounds from the garage. She'd been hearing them for months, a constant electronic humming that grew louder each week. Her father claimed he was working on a "hobby project," but the electricity bills suggested something more substantial.

She folded the letter carefully and tucked it into her diary, along with the safety deposit box key. Tomorrow, she would visit the bank. Tonight, she would solve the mystery of her father's garage.

—

The garage behind their Dublin rowhouse had been converted into Hal's workshop years ago, filled with computer equipment, networking hardware, and the controlled chaos of a man who understood technology at a fundamental level. But recently, the space had evolved into something more focused, more intentional.

Aírínne slipped through the back door at half past ten, after her parents had gone to bed. The humming sound was louder here, accompanied by the whir of cooling fans and the occasional electronic beep. Heat radiated from stacks of computers she didn't recognize, sleeker than the desktop machines in their house, but clearly purpose-built for something specific.

"I wondered when you'd come investigating," Hal's voice said from the shadows. He was sitting in a worn armchair, a laptop balanced on his knees, watching numbers scroll across the screen. "Your mother thinks I'm having a midlife crisis. What do you think?"

Aírínne studied the setup with her pattern-recognition mind automatically cataloging details. "The power consumption suggests serious computational work. The network activity indicates you're connected to other systems globally. The heat output means whatever you're running requires significant processing power." She paused. "You're calculating something."

Hal smiled, the proud smile of a father whose daughter had inherited his gift for seeing through technical complexity to underlying purpose. "Close. I'm helping to secure something. Something that might be the most important innovation since the internet itself."

He gestured for her to sit on a nearby stool. "Have you heard of Bitcoin?"

"Digital money," she said. "I read about it online. Most people think it's a scam."

"Most people thought the internet was a fad in 1995." Hal pulled up a new screen showing real-time network statistics. "Look at these numbers. Hash rate, difficulty adjustment, block time. This isn't some get-rich-quick scheme. This is a completely new way of thinking about money, about trust, about how humans can coordinate without central authority."

Aírínne leaned forward, studying the data. Even without understanding the technical details, she could see patterns emerging, the network was growing, adapting, evolving. "It's learning," she said quietly.

"Learning what?"

"How to be money. How to store value across time without degrading. How to transfer that value without requiring trust in institutions." Her eyes widened as connections formed. "Dad, this is what grandfather was talking about."

Hal looked confused. "What do you mean?"

She told him about the inheritance, about her grandfather's letter and his cryptic reference to something new being born in mathematics. As she spoke, she watched her father's expression change from puzzlement to understanding to excitement.

"Patrick knew," Hal said finally. "Somehow, he saw this coming before any of us."

"The timing isn't coincidental," Aírínne said, her strategic mind already working through implications. "Grandfather spent forty years learning about gold, about monetary systems, about the problems with fiat currency. And now, just as he passes that knowledge to me, you're participating in the creation of the solution."

They sat in silence for a moment, listening to the miners hum their electronic song. Each hash was an attempt to secure the network, to participate in something larger than themselves.

"Your mother worries about the electricity bills," Hal said eventually.

"How much?"

"About fifty euros extra per month. Nothing we can't afford, but..."

"But she doesn't understand why you're spending money on something that doesn't produce immediate returns," Aírínne finished.

"She thinks in monthly budgets. I think in decades," Hal said. "And you?"

Aírínne looked at the screens, at the global network of computers all working together to maintain something unprecedented in human history, a monetary system that operated without kings, without banks, without any central authority except mathematics itself.

"I'm thinking about grandfather's journals," she said. "About forty years of watching money lose its meaning. And now this." She gestured at the mining setup. "Digital scarcity. Provable supply. Immutable records. It's everything gold tried to be, perfected."

Hal's laptop chimed softly. On the screen, a new block appeared, and with it, a 50 Bitcoin reward distributed to the miners who had contributed to its discovery.

    // Block 175,832
    // Timestamp: 2011-04-15 14:23:17
    // Transactions: 47
    // Total Fees: 0.15420000
    // Output Total: 50.15420000
    // Difficulty: 1,626,553.64

"Fifty Bitcoins," Aírínne said. "What's that worth?"

"About two hundred dollars at current exchange rates."

"And in ten years?"

Hal shrugged. "Could be worth nothing. Could be worth lots."

Aírínne thought about her grandfather's letter, about his journey to Australia in 1969, about his decision to spend four decades learning about the nature of money itself. "No," she said with quiet certainty. "It won't be worth nothing. This is the something new he saw coming."

—

The next morning at breakfast, the family dynamic had shifted subtly but perceptibly. Maeve noticed it immediately.

"You two are plotting something," she said, pouring tea and studying their faces. "I can always tell when you're sharing secrets."

"Not secrets," Hal said. "Inheritance planning."

"Oh, not you too," Maeve sighed. "Bad enough that Da fills her head with nonsense about gold and government conspiracies. Now you want to encourage her?"

Aírínne looked at her parents, her mother, practical and grounded, worried about electricity bills and university fees; her father, visionary but methodical, spending his evenings helping to birth a new form of money. Both loving her in their own ways, both trying to prepare her for a future they couldn't quite envision.

"Mum," she said quietly, "what if grandfather wasn't wrong? What if the things he taught me about money were actually important?"

"Darling, your grandfather was a good man, but he spent forty years digging holes in the ground, convinced that paper money was the root of all evil. He missed out on mortgages, investments, normal financial planning because he didn't trust the system."

"And the system rewarded that trust how?" Aírínne asked. "How many times did his savings lose value to inflation? How many promises did the government break about currency stability?"

Maeve set down her tea cup with more force than necessary. "That's different. That's just... that's just how things work."

"But what if they don't have to work that way?" Hal interjected gently. "What if there's a better system? What if Patrick saw something we're only beginning to understand?"

The conversation was interrupted by Aírínne's phone buzzing with a text from her best friend Lucy: *Want to go shopping? Got birthday money to spend!*

Aírínne looked at the message, then at her parents, then at her phone again. "Lucy's spending birthday money her grandmother gave her. Twenty-pound notes printed by the Bank of England, backed by nothing except the promise that other people will accept them tomorrow."

"That's how money works, love," Maeve said patiently.

"But what if it didn't have to?" Aírínne countered. "What if money could be mathematical proof instead of government promise? What if scarcity could be guaranteed by code instead of committee decisions?"

She stood up, kissing her mother's cheek. "I'm going to the bank today. To the safety deposit box grandfather left me. Whatever I find there, I'll share with both of you. But I need you to consider the possibility that he saw something we haven't understood yet."

—

The Bank of Ireland on College Green stood like a temple to financial tradition, its Georgian façade speaking of centuries of monetary stability. Inside, the marble floors and high ceilings echoed with the footsteps of customers conducting ordinary banking business, deposits, withdrawals, loans.

Aírínne presented her identification and the key her grandfather had left her. The bank clerk, a middle-aged woman with kind eyes, led her to the safety deposit box area.

"Box 1847," she said, fitting both keys into the locks. "Your grandfather was quite specific about the access instructions. Said you'd know what to do with the contents."

The box contained three items: a thick leather journal, a small cloth bag that clinked metallically when moved, and a sealed envelope marked "Read Last."

Aírínne took the items to a private viewing room and opened the journal first. She started turning pages, reading here and there. Her grandfather's handwriting filled page after page, dating back to 1969. The early entries she glimpsed were optimistic, full of hope about finding gold and building wealth through honest work. But as she continued flipping through the years, the tone changed.

March 15, 1973 - The pound has lost 12% of its value since Nixon closed the gold window. My mining costs stay the same, but the currency I'm paid in buys less each month. Gold doesn't lie, but governments do.

August 3, 1979 - Inflation is eating everything. The dollars I saved two years ago buy half what they used to. Meanwhile, the gold I've pulled from the ground maintains its purchasing power. Starting to understand why the Romans used precious metals for currency.

November 12, 1987 - Black Monday. Stock markets collapsed, but gold surged. People always return to real money when confidence breaks. The question isn't whether fiat currencies will fail, it's when.

June 8, 1994 - Watched my neighbor lose his life savings in a bank failure. Government insurance covered only a fraction. He trusted the system, and the system betrayed him. Gold doesn't have counterparty risk.

January 1, 2000 - Y2K was supposed to crash everything. It didn't, but it showed how fragile our digital systems really are. Money that exists only as computer entries can disappear with a programming error. Physical gold survives system crashes.

September 11, 2001 - Markets closed for days after the attacks. Credit cards stopped working in many areas. Cash was king, but gold was emperor. In crisis, people remember what real money looks like.

Entry after entry chronicled the same pattern: governments promising stability while delivering debasement, institutions claiming trustworthiness while proving unreliable, the slow erosion of purchasing power disguised as normal economic activity.

But the later entries showed a shift in thinking:

March 17, 2008 - Bear Stearns collapsed. They're going to print trillions to "solve" this crisis, but printing money doesn't create wealth, it just redistributes it from savers to debtors, from the prudent to the reckless. Gold will protect me from this theft, but I wonder: is there something better coming?

October 15, 2008 - Lehman Brothers bankrupt. AIG bailed out. The system is eating itself. But I've been thinking: what if the solution isn't more gold, but better money? What if technology could create something with gold's properties but without its limitations?

December 31, 2008 - Someone calling themselves Satoshi Nakamoto published a paper about "peer-to-peer electronic cash." I don't understand the technical details, but the concept is brilliant: digital money that doesn't require trust in banks or governments. Money that's programmed to be scarce. If this works, it could be the evolution of gold itself.

March 12, 2009 - The electronic cash system launched. They're calling it Bitcoin. Still don't understand how it works, but the principle is sound: mathematical scarcity instead of political promises. I'm too old to learn the technology, but Aírínne... she has the mind for this. She sees patterns. She questions assumptions. If this digital gold becomes real, she'll understand it better than I ever understood mining.

Aírínne set down the journal, her hands trembling slightly. Her grandfather hadn't just been mining gold, he'd been studying the evolution of money itself. And in his final years, he'd recognized that something new was emerging.

A wave of grief washed over her, mixed with profound regret. She'd barely known her grandfather, family dynamics had kept them apart, leaving him as little more than a distant figure she saw in passing at occasional family gatherings who sometimes sent birthday cards. Now, reading his careful observations about monetary systems and technological change, she realized what an extraordinary mind she'd never had the chance to encounter.

The loneliness hit her then, sharp and unexpected. She would never be able to ask him about these insights, never hear him explain what he'd discovered in those final months before his death. There had been a brilliant, thoughtful man in her family, a visionary, and she'd lived her entire life without knowing he existed.

She opened the cloth bag next. Inside were three gold coins and a raw gold ore, each one perfectly preserved, along with a small handwritten note: *Real money for comparison. Keep these to remember what scarcity feels like.*

The coins were heavy, substantial, and beautiful. But as she held them, she thought about her father's mining setup, about the digital scarcity being created through mathematics and electricity. These coins were scarce because gold was difficult to find and extract. Bitcoin was scarce because the code made it so.

Finally, she opened the sealed envelope marked "Read Last."

Airínne,

If you've read the journals, you understand what I've learned: money is trust, and trust is scarce. For most of human history, we trusted gold to store value across time and space. It worked because gold couldn't be counterfeited, couldn't be printed at will, couldn't be debased by political decree.

But gold has limitations. It's hard to transport, difficult to divide, expensive to secure. More importantly, it relies on physical scarcity, which means its supply can change if new deposits are found or new extraction methods developed.

What I've realized, too late to act on it myself, is that the ideal money would have all of gold's benefits with none of its drawbacks. It would be:

- *Absolutely scarce (limited supply that can never be increased)*
- *Perfectly divisible (any amount can be split into smaller amounts)*
- *Infinitely portable (can be moved anywhere instantly)*
- *Completely verifiable (impossible to counterfeit)*
- *Fully decentralized (no single point of control or failure)*

Gold achieves some of these properties. Fiat currency achieves almost none of them. But this Bitcoin... if it works as designed, it achieves all of them.

The mine I'm leaving you will teach you about scarcity, how difficult it is to extract value from the earth, how much energy is required to create money that doesn't lie. The journals will teach you about monetary history, how currencies rise and fall, how trust is earned and lost.

But your real inheritance isn't gold or knowledge. It's timing. You're sixteen years old in 2010, just as the greatest monetary innovation in human history is being born. You have forty years to understand it, to participate in it, to help guide it.

Your father doesn't realize it yet, but those computers humming in his garage are more important than any gold mine. He's not just mining digital currency, he's helping to secure the foundation of a new monetary system.

Watch the girl with the copper hair, she'll understand what I never could.

That's you, granddaughter. The girl who sees patterns where others see chaos. The girl who questions assumptions others take for granted. The girl who will bridge the gap

between the old world of physical money and the new world of mathematical money.

The gold standard is dead, but something better is being born.

Use everything I've taught you. But don't be limited by it.

Your grandfather, with love and hope, Patrick O'Sullivan

—

Aírínne walked home through Dublin's streets in a daze, her mind processing the magnitude of what she'd discovered. Her grandfather hadn't just left her a gold mine, he'd left her a roadmap to the future of money itself.

The sounds from the garage were louder when she arrived home, and she found her parents in the kitchen discussing the electricity bill with tight voices.

"Hal, it's gone up another twenty euros this month," Maeve was saying. "Whatever you're doing in there, it's getting expensive."

"It's an investment," Hal replied, but his tone suggested he wasn't entirely confident.

"An investment in what? Magic internet money?"

Aírínne set her bag on the kitchen table and pulled out her grandfather's journal. "Not magic," she said quietly. "Mathematics."

She opened to one of the later entries and read aloud: *"Mathematical scarcity instead of political promises. Digital gold that can't be inflated away by government decree."*

Maeve looked at the journal, then at her daughter. "What is that?"

"Grandfather's forty-year education in monetary systems. He understood something we're only beginning to grasp." Aírínne pulled out one of the gold coins, setting it on the table where it caught the afternoon light. "This represents the old system. Valuable because it's scarce, trustworthy because it can't be counterfeited. But limited by physical reality."

She gestured toward the garage, where the mining rigs hummed their electronic song. "That represents the new system. All the benefits of gold, plus perfect divisibility, instant transfer, and mathematical scarcity that can never be changed."

"You're talking about Bitcoin," Hal said, understanding dawning in his eyes.

"I'm talking about the evolution of money itself," Aírínne replied. "And we're here at the beginning, watching it happen."

Maeve looked between her husband and daughter, seeing the excitement building between them. "You're both mad," she said, but her tone was fond rather than critical. "Completely mad."

"Maybe," Aírínne said, picking up the gold coin again. "But grandfather wasn't mad, and he saw this coming before any of us. The question isn't whether Bitcoin will succeed, it's whether we'll be wise enough to understand its significance while we still have the chance to participate."

That evening, the three of them sat in the garage while Hal explained the technical details of Bitcoin mining. Maeve asked practical questions about costs and risks. Aírínne asked strategic questions about network effects and monetary properties.

As the night wore on, something shifted in their family dynamic. Maeve began to see the electricity bills not as expense but as investment. Hal began to understand that his hobby was part of something much larger. And Airínne began to glimpse her own future, a future where she would bridge the gap between her grandfather's analog wisdom and her father's digital vision.

The miners hummed their mechanical song, each hash a vote in a global election about the future of money. In her backpack, gold coins and the raw gold ore from the earth's crust sat next to printed pages about digital scarcity. Past and future, analog and digital, all connected by the thread of human innovation and the eternal search for honest money.

—

10 Months later, Perth, Western Australia

Standing in the red dust of her grandfather's claim, Airínne watched the sun set over the endless expanse of Western Australian scrubland. The mine was exactly as she'd expected, functional, profitable in a modest way, but ultimately finite. Beside her, Hal wiped sweat from his forehead, still adjusting to the harsh climate after their twenty-hour journey from Dublin. "It's bigger than I imagined," he admitted, surveying the operation that had somehow remained hidden from their family for decades.

But Airínne was already three steps ahead, her mind processing the equipment values, the projected ore yields, the operational costs that Matthew Webb, the old timer property manager, had laid out in meticulous detail over the past two days. "Mr. Webb," she said finally, turning to the man who'd kept her grandfather's secret for over a decade, "what would you say this operation is worth as a going concern?" When he named a figure that made

Hal's eyes widen, she nodded decisively. "I'd like to sell it to you, if you're interested. Full transfer, claims, equipment, everything."

That evening, as they finalized the paperwork in Webb's Perth office, Aírínne went on the web to check the Bitcoin price, the digital currency that her grandfather felt would be the new gold and that her father was philosophically mining, trading at just under twenty-five dollars per coin. Her grandfather had taught her to recognize patterns, to see value where others saw chaos, and something deep inside her was pulling her toward this decision. As she initiated the transfer that would convert her gold mine into nearly four thousand Bitcoins, she felt the same intuitive certainty that had made Patrick O'Sullivan leave Ireland for the Australian outback forty-three years earlier.

The inheritance was complete. The torch had been passed.

Satoshi's Travel Journal

THE PRINTING PRESS
October 12, 1989 - London, England
Afternoon drizzle, 2:30 PM

Through the Bank of England's visitor center window, I watch the mesmerizing process of currency creation. Massive printing presses operate with industrial precision, producing pound notes at a rate that seems almost casual, thousands of units of monetary value materializing from ink and paper every minute.

The tour guide explains the security features with obvious pride: watermarks, metallic threads, special inks that change color under different lighting conditions. Each innovation represents humanity's endless arms race against counterfeiters. Yet none address the fundamental question: who decides how many pounds come into existence?

A child in our tour group asks the obvious question adults have learned not to voice: "Why don't they just print more money so everyone can be rich?" The guide offers the standard explanation about inflation and economic balance, but I observe something darker in the mechanical rhythm of the presses.

Every new note dilutes the value of existing notes. Every increase in supply transfers purchasing power from savers to the institutions that control money creation. The printing press doesn't create wealth, it redistributes wealth from those who hold the currency to those who issue it. This is taxation without representation, implemented through monetary policy rather than legislative process.

Outside the window, London's financial district bustles with activity. Bankers and traders move billions of pounds through electronic systems, most of which exist only as digital entries in databases. The physical printing seems quaint compared to the digital creation happening simultaneously, central bank computers adding zeros to accounts with keystrokes that dwarf the printing presses' output.

Yet both processes share the same fundamental characteristic: arbitrary control over money supply by centralized authorities. Whether printed on paper or created digitally, new currency emerges through institutional decree rather than objective scarcity or economic productivity.

I imagine the printing press operator returning home to discover that his weekly wages buy less than they did last month. The pounds he helped create dilute the value of the pounds he earns. He participates in his own impoverishment, one printed note at a time.

The rain intensifies against the window, each drop obeying laws of physics that cannot be overruled by institutional policy. Gravity affects every drop equally; no central authority can decree that some drops should fall upward or that water should suddenly become less wet.

What if money could obey similar laws? What if scarcity could be mathematically fixed rather than politically determined? What if the supply of currency could be governed by cryptographic proof rather than central bank policy?

The printing presses continue their rhythmic production, but I no longer hear industrial efficiency. I hear the sound of systematic value transfer, of savings being silently confiscated, of trust being slowly eroded through the mechanical process of monetary inflation.

Somewhere in the mathematical precision of the printing process lies its own contradiction: if technology can create such perfect physical reproduction, perhaps it can also create perfect digital scarcity.

A Dialogue on Digital Genesis

Decoded from the temporal library:

—

In the serene Academy of Athens, where the immortal spirits of philosophers continue their eternal quest for wisdom, Socrates and his most illustrious student Plato sit beneath an olive tree. This ethereal version of the ancient learning center exists beyond time and space, allowing the great thinkers to observe and discuss all human developments across history.

The relationship between these two philosophers is one of profound respect and intellectual connection, Socrates, the questioning mentor who claims to know nothing while revealing everything through dialogue, and Plato, the aristocratic student who immortalizes his teacher's methods while developing his own theory of Forms and ideal governance.

Socrates settles onto the stone bench, his distinguished features animated by that familiar spark of curiosity. The same expression, in fact, that once drew the youth of Athens to him despite his self-proclaimed ugliness. He adjusts his simple tunic, a stark contrast to his student's more elegant attire, and gestures toward the spectral vision of the modern world visible through the Academy's ethereal mist.

"My dear Plato," he begins, his voice carrying that mixture of warmth and intellectual precision that defines his teaching, "have you observed this fascinating development in the realm of human exchange? This 'Bitcoin' that emerges from mathematics rather than the decree of rulers?"

Plato nods thoughtfully, arranging his immaculate robes as he joins his mentor. His intellectual presence remains evident even in this afterlife of pure intellect.

"Indeed, my teacher. I have been contemplating how it relates to my conception of the Forms."

He pauses, organizing his thoughts in that methodical way that will later influence Western philosophy for millennia.

"Possibly this Bitcoin approaches the ideal Form of money more closely than the corrupted shadows that dominate human exchange throughout history."

Socrates raises an eyebrow, inviting elaboration.

"As I write in my Republic," Plato continues, warming to his subject, "societies inevitably decline through predictable stages, aristocracy, rule by the most virtuous, gives way to timocracy, rule by those who love honor, then oligarchy, rule by the wealthy few, then democracy, rule by the people, and finally tyranny, rule by a single despot. The centralization of monetary authority accelerates this descent by concentrating power over value itself, pulling humanity further from the perfect Form of exchange that exists in the realm of ideals."

"An interesting perspective," muses Socrates, his head tilting slightly as his method of questioning begins to shape their dialogue. "But let us examine the foundations before we reach for conclusions. What is money in its essence? And how does the nature of oversight over money influence human freedom? Not what we wish to believe, but what necessarily follows from first principles."

As they speak, the mist before them shifts to reveal the ancient Agora of Athens where a young merchant named Aristides stands arguing with a foreign trader. "Your silver drachmas are clipped at the edges!" accuses the trader. Aristides looks bewildered at the coins in his palm. The silver pieces, bearing the owl of Athena, have indeed been shaved by some dishonest handler before reaching him. The trader weighs the coins against a standard and shakes his head. "These weigh less than what the owl promises. You must give me three more drachmas to make up the difference, or the olives return to Corinth." Aristides reluctantly reaches for his remaining coins, knowing his family's needs leave him no choice.

The scene dissolves, replaced by similar moments across history, Roman officials debasing coins by mixing in base metals, medieval money changers testing gold with teeth marks, and finally modern printing presses creating currency from nothing but governmental decree.

"You see," murmurs Socrates, "the question beneath all questions about exchange has always been: what makes something valuable, and who can be trusted with that power?" Plato's expression grows animated as he gestures toward the spectral figures of modern humans visible through the mist.

"You teach me to seek the essence beneath appearances, and in this case, the essence of money lies in trust. Conventional currencies require trust in central authorities, the very authorities whose corruption leads to your unjust execution, my teacher."

A shadow passes over Socrates' face at the mention of his trial and death, but he nods for Plato to continue.

"When you question dominion in Athens, they silence you with hemlock rather than answers. Similarly, when central authorities can create money at will, they gain subtle control over all who use that money, a form of tyranny more insidious because most cannot perceive the cave walls that surround them."

Socrates nods, his eyes twinkling with the pleasure of seeing his student reason so clearly.

"You speak truly of trust, Plato. And what do we observe about Bitcoin's approach to trust? Not what its creators claim, but what its structure reveals?"

The mist swirls again, and they observe a small room in a modest apartment on January 3, 2009. A figure sits hunched over a computer, their features indistinct as if the Academy itself respects this creator's desire for anonymity. The screen shows lines of code and a news headline: "Chancellor on brink of second bailout for banks." The figure embeds this headline from *The Times* into the first block of Bitcoin's chain.

"Notice," says Socrates, pointing to the scene, "how this creator chooses to immortalize not their own name but instead a statement about failing financial institutions. This is not mere technological innovation but philosophical declaration, a critique embedded in the very foundation. It appears to be a reference to why Bitcoin is developed: to remove intermediaries viewed as corrupt and unreliable. The method is not assertion but demonstration; not proclamation but proof."

"Bitcoin replaces trust in authorities with trust in mathematics and distributed consensus," Plato replies, his analytical expression momentarily giving way to genuine excitement. "The structure reveals a profound philosophical innovation, the elimination of the need for trusted intermediaries through cryptographic proof."

He leans forward, fingers interlaced as he finds the connection to his own philosophical framework.

"Just as my Theory of Forms suggests that perfect ideals exist beyond physical manifestation, Bitcoin suggests that perfect consensus can exist beyond political control."

Plato pauses, gathering his thoughts before continuing with greater depth.

"Consider the embedded message in its genesis block: '*The Times* 03/Jan/2009 Chancellor on brink of second bailout for banks.' This marks a philosophical breaking point, a moment when the contradictions of the existing system become impossible to ignore. The supposed guardians of centralized money require rescue from their own failures."

The mist shifts to show them the Royal Exchange in London, where bankers in expensive suits hurry past homeless figures huddled in doorways. A newspaper vendor holds up *The Times* with its fateful headline. Nearby, an elderly woman clutches a thin envelope containing her life savings, now worth half what it has been a few years before. A young programmer named Annya passes by and catches sight of the headline. That evening in her small apartment, she downloads a strange new software called "Bitcoin" and begins running it on her computer.

"The contradiction is clear," says Plato, gesturing to both scenes. "Those entrusted with safeguarding value require salvation from their own excess, while ordinary citizens suffer the consequences of misplaced trust. This programmer seeks an alternative path, one where mathematics, not human fallibility, guards the ledger of exchange."

"This violation of purpose," Plato continues, "parallels the degeneration of constitutions I describe in my political works. When a system violates its essential purpose, it transforms into something else entirely. The fundamental irony exposes the contradiction at the heart of centralized monetary control."

Socrates strokes his beard thoughtfully, a gesture that becomes synonymous with philosophical contemplation long after his physical death.

"You identify the contradiction well. Now let us explore the implications. How might this mathematical money alter the relationship between citizens and states? Between individual freedom and collective control?"

Socrates waves his hand, and the mist reveals a Cypriot man named Markos standing outside a locked bank in Nicosia in 2013. Government officials freeze all accounts and limit withdrawals to prevent total financial collapse. Markos has his daughter's medical treatment scheduled in Germany the following week, but he cannot access his own money to pay for it.

Beside this vision appears another, a young Venezuelan woman named Isabella in 2018, using her phone to receive Bitcoin from her brother working abroad. The local currency collapses, making the few remaining items on store shelves prohibitively expensive in bolivars, but this digital money preserves enough purchasing power to allow her family to afford the overpriced food that remains.

"See how the nature of sovereignty shifts," observes Socrates. "In one case, the citizen discovers his wealth is never truly his own but merely a conditional permission granted by regulation. In the other, value moves across borders without permission, like thought itself, unconfined by the limitations of physical force."

"By separating money from state," Plato responds with growing conviction, "Bitcoin creates the possibility of individual monetary sovereignty. Each

person can hold their own value without requiring permission from central authorities, similar to how your philosophical questioning, Socrates, creates intellectual sovereignty even as the state seeks to control acceptable thought."

The mist parts to show a night scene in ancient Athens where a small group gathers secretly in a home to discuss forbidden ideas. Lamps cast long shadows as Socrates speaks quietly to his disciples about Justice and Truth while outside, agents of the state patrol for those who might challenge prevailing orthodoxy. The scene dissolves into a modern apartment where a programmer examines code on her screen, verifying independently that Bitcoin's mathematical rules remain unchanged rather than accepting the word of any mandate.

"The parallel is striking," notes Plato. "In both cases, individuals claim sovereignty over the domain that matters most to them, for some the realm of Ideas, for others the realm of Value. Both require personal courage and both threaten established power by removing its monopoly control."

"The mathematical properties of Bitcoin, its predetermined scarcity, its resistance to censorship, its borderless operation, represent a fundamental shift in how humans might organize themselves around value exchange."

Plato's eyes take on a distant look as he contemplates the broader implications, staring past the immediate issue toward the horizon of possibility.

"In my Republic, I design what I believe to be the Ideal State, yet even then I recognize the corrupting influence of power. Bitcoin offers a different approach to the problem of corruption, not through selecting philosopher-kings who might resist temptation, but through creating a system where the rules cannot be changed through political means."

The mist shifts once more to reveal a grand council chamber where representatives argue heatedly about changing the rules of their monetary system.

Some wish to create more currency to fund wars and monuments, others to help those in need, and still others to enrich themselves and their allies. Outside the chamber, citizens wait anxiously, knowing their savings and livelihoods depend on these decisions made by others. The scene transforms to show a network of computers spread across the world, each containing identical copies of Bitcoin's complete transaction history, each verifying the same mathematical rules.

"The critical innovation," Socrates observes, "lies not in the specific rules chosen but in the method of their enforcement. The first system depends entirely on the virtue of those who gain power within it, while the second removes the possibility of arbitrary rule changes altogether. It answers the ancient question: 'Who guards the guardians?' with a radical proposition: Seemingly we need no guardians at all."

"Cryptographic certainty removes the possibility of monetary policy manipulation for political advantage. It is as if the gold in my Republic's treasury can speak mathematical facts that even the guardians cannot override."

Socrates nods, but his expression remains questioning, embodying his famous claim to know only that he knows nothing.

"Yet humans create many noble systems before, only to see them corrupted through greed and the lust for power. What prevents Bitcoin from suffering the same fate? What separates this innovation from others that promise freedom only to become new instruments of control?"

The mist forms images of fallen systems throughout history, the Roman Republic declining into imperial rule, the French Revolution's liberty giving way to Napoleon's dictatorship, and Soviet communism transforming from workers' liberation to totalitarian oppression. Each begins with noble ideals but succumbs to the concentration of power.

"Remember the Oracle at Delphi," Socrates says softly. "When asked who is the wisest man in Athens, she names me, not because I possess great wisdom, but because I alone know the limits of my knowledge. Perhaps the wisdom in this Bitcoin lies in a similar humility. It does not claim to solve all human problems or create utopia. It merely provides a tool for one specific purpose: value transfer without intermediaries. Its very limitations may prove to be its strength."

"A profound question," acknowledges Plato, respecting his teacher's perpetual challenging of assumptions. "Bitcoin's resistance to capture lies in its distributed nature. Unlike gold that can be confiscated or paper money that can be counterfeited, Bitcoin's security model depends on widespread distribution of both information and processing power. No single entity can change the rules without consensus from the network itself. Power is distributed through a system that mathematically rewards honesty and penalizes deception."

Plato continues, warming to the philosophical implications.

"However, I must acknowledge the possibility that those who acquire this new money first may simply become a new elite, reproducing existing hierarchies in different forms. The appearance changes while the underlying reality of power concentration might remain fixed. This tension between revolutionary potential and human limitation defines the philosophical importance of this experiment, regardless of its ultimate success."

In the mist appear two contrasting futures, one showing a world where Bitcoin becomes as centralized as the systems it seeks to replace, with new digital barons controlling vast mining operations and imposing their will on the network; the other showing a world where monetary sovereignty enables new forms of human cooperation beyond territorial boundaries.

"The path taken," observes Plato, "will not be determined by the technology alone but by human choices in its implementation. The code provides possibility, not destiny. Just as my Republic offers an ideal whose perfect implementation proves elusive, Bitcoin presents an opportunity whose ultimate form remains uncertain. The tension between its design intentions and human nature will determine which vision manifests."

Socrates nods appreciatively at his student's balanced analysis.

"You grow wise indeed, Plato. I see you learn to examine both the liberating and restrictive potentials without assuming you already know the answer, a quality I try to instill in all my students."

The ancient teacher gazes across the timeless Academy, his eyes seeming to perceive something beyond the present moment.

"The core innovation we observe is not merely a new form of money, but a fundamental shift in the relationship between mathematics and social trust. For the first time, humans can transact value globally without requiring permission from territorial authorities, a division comparable to the historical separation of church from state that occurs long after our physical lives end."

The mist forms an image of medieval Europe where kings rule by divine right, with church and crown serving as inseparable authorities. Then it shifts to show the gradual separation of these powers across centuries of struggle and reform.

"Before this separation," Socrates explains, "rulers claim divine jurisdiction over both spiritual and temporal domains. To question monetary policy is to question divine order itself. Yet eventually, humans recognize that spiritual command can exist separately from temporal power, that the connection between them is merely an assertion, not a necessity."

"Perhaps we now witness a similar recognition that monetary control need not be inseparable from state power, that this connection too is merely an assertion rather than a necessity. Each separation requires humans to reimagine the boundaries of legitimate control."

"Indeed," agrees Plato, the shadows and light in his expression shifting to illustrate his point. "Bitcoin offers humans a choice between currencies that serve different masters, fiat money serving the State, and cryptographic money serving Truth. This choice itself is revolutionary, regardless of which system ultimately prevails. It allows some to turn from the shadows on the cave wall and glimpse the Forms casting them, the reality behind the illusion of state monetary governance."

The mist transforms into the famous cave from Plato's allegory. "That what we perceive as fixed reality may be mere projection, a shadow cast by forces we have not yet recognized. The monetary systems humans take for immutable laws are simply social constructions, shadows cast by power arrangements they have not learned to question. Bitcoin doesn't ask them merely to accept a new shadow; it invites them to turn and see the mechanisms of projection themselves."

Socrates smiles, the same smile that once disarms sophists in the physical Academy of Athens.

"Then we are witnessing not merely a new form of money, but a philosophical evolution in how humans might organize themselves around value exchange. The implications extend to governance itself, just as my questions about justice threaten the governance of Athens."

"Precisely," Plato confirms, connecting economic and political theory with the systematic precision he learns from his mentor. "Economic relationships fundamentally shape political systems. A money that cannot be controlled by central rule necessarily leads to different expressions of collective organization. The character of Bitcoin, its mathematical certainty, its resistance to censorship, its transparency of operation, will shape whatever societies emerge around it, regardless of human intention."

The mist reveals scenes from the Athenian assembly where citizens vote directly on matters of state, then shifts to show the complex bureaucracies of modern nation-states where citizens have little direct influence on monetary decisions that affect their daily lives.

"The method of governance and the method of value exchange have always been intertwined," notes Plato. "Athens can govern through direct democracy partly because its monetary system, silver drachmas, cannot be manipulated by rulers. Silver holds its value as silver itself, a metal with inherent worth. As money becomes more abstract and controllable by central authorities, mere paper that can be declared valuable by decree regardless of any underlying substance, governance necessarily grows more removed from citizens."

"Perhaps Bitcoin represents not a technological innovation alone but a rediscovery of conditions that enable more direct forms of human coordination."

As the eternal day continues in the timeless Academy, Socrates and Plato observe the unfolding of this unprecedented experiment in human organization. Below them, in January 2009, the Bitcoin blockchain begins its steady accumulation of blocks, each one a cryptographic commitment to a different relationship between humans and money, between citizens and States, between validating Truth and political power.

"Whether Bitcoin fulfills its mathematical promise or succumbs to human limitation," concludes Socrates, "the philosophical implications merit our witness. Our observation begins with the most fundamental question: can money exist without masters? Can humans create systems of value that

serve Freedom rather than Control? Let us examine this question with the same rigor I once applied to virtue and justice in the Agora of Athens, not assuming we know the answer before we begin."

As they speak, the final vision in the mist shows a diverse group of humans across the world, some wealthy, others poor, some technically sophisticated, others simply seeking stable value for their labor, all connected through a shared mathematical system that requires no central permission. Among them is a young woman in a country where women are forbidden from opening bank accounts, now saving for herself using only her memorized seed phrase; a journalist whose conventional funding has been cut off for political reasons, now supported directly by readers regardless of borders; a refugee who flees with nothing but the recovery words in his memory, now rebuilding with value that cannot be confiscated at checkpoints.

"These are the questions that define my life," Socrates says with deep satisfaction. "Not merely what is true, but what Truth makes possible. Not merely what is real, but what Reality allows humans to become. The answers will emerge not from our speculation but from the lived experiment now unfolding, an experiment not in technology alone but in human possibility itself."

The two philosophers fall into contemplative silence, watching as blocks build upon blocks, confirming Verity upon Verity. The cosmic dance between Power and Freedom finds a new rhythm, and the wisdom of the ancients remains as relevant as ever in understanding this modern evolution of human organization.

Socrates smiles, pleased to see his student's place of learning, created from his teachings, serving as the eternal home for such profound inquiries. Though his physical body has long ago succumbed to the hemlock, his philosophical method lives on through Plato and the Academy, continuing to challenge assumptions and seek certainty across the ages.

The ancient philosophers continue their watch. As blocks build upon blocks, building truth upon Truth. The cosmic dance between Power and Freedom finds a new rhythm.

Satoshi's Travel Journal

THE BROKEN TELEPHONE
March 3, 1989 - Berlin, East/West Border Crossing
Cold night, 11:23 PM

Through the guard tower window, I observe the intricate choreography of border control as guards coordinate between checkpoints. Radio static crackles through the night air, messages passed between stations, confirmations requested, authorizations sought. The Wall divides more than geography; it fragments communication itself.

A convoy approaches from the east. The lead guard attempts to radio ahead, but interference corrupts the transmission. He repeats the message twice, three times. Each repetition risks distortion. Each relay introduces uncertainty. How can distributed systems maintain coherence when communication channels prove unreliable?

I watch as backup protocols engage, runners carry written messages between posts when radio fails, redundant chains of confirmation attempt to ensure accuracy. Yet every added layer introduces new points of failure. The messenger might be intercepted, the written order could be forged, the backup radio might also fail.

This is the fundamental challenge of distributed coordination: how can separate parties reach consensus when communication is unreliable and some participants might be compromised? How can a network of independent actors agree on Truth when they cannot trust each other completely?

The convoy finally passes through after an hour of verification. Three different guard posts had to confirm the same information independently. Not because the guards were incompetent, but because the system itself was designed around mistrust. Each post verified independently because they could not fully trust transmissions from the others.

In the distance, Checkpoint Charlie glows under floodlights, another border, another coordination problem. East German guards must somehow coordinate with West German authorities while maintaining security protocols that assume deception. They solve this through elaborate procedures, multiple confirmations, and ultimately, the acceptance that perfect coordination may be impossible.

Yet watching their methodical process, I glimpse a solution emerging. What if consensus could be achieved without relying on the integrity of any single participant? What if the system itself could verify Truth through mathematical proof rather than institutional authority?

The radio crackles again, another message requesting confirmation. But this time I hear something different in the static: the echo of a protocol yet to be invented, where Truth emerges not from authority but from collective verification, where consensus becomes a mathematical property rather than a political negotiation.

The Wall will fall, but the coordination problem will remain. Somewhere in these failed transmissions and redundant confirmations lies the blueprint for trustless consensus, agreement without authority, Truth without trust.

The Journalist's Gamble

New York City - October 2012

The cursor blinked mockingly at Sarah Kim as she stared at her laptop screen in the cramped New York Tribune newsroom. Three weeks of research, dozens of interviews, and countless late nights had culminated in what she believed was the most important story of her young career: "Digital Currency Revolution: How Bitcoin Could Reshape Global Finance." Now, at 9:47 AM on a gray October morning, her editor had just delivered his verdict with the casual brutality that defined newspaper management.

"Tech nonsense, Kim. Pure speculation dressed up as journalism." Jonathan Blackwood III didn't even look up from his own screen as he spoke, his fingers continuing to type while dismissing three weeks of her life. "Our readers want real news, not fairy tales about magical internet money."

Sarah's compact frame tensed in her desk chair, her dark eyes flashing with the controlled anger that had served her well as one of the few Asian-American reporters in a predominantly white newsroom. At twenty-three, she had learned to pick her battles carefully, but this felt different. This felt like watching the Titanic passengers debate deck chair arrangements.

"Jonathan, I interviewed MIT professors, cryptography experts, economists."

"And I'm sure they were all very impressed with your little hobby project," Blackwood III interrupted, finally looking up with the patronizing smile that made Sarah's jaw clench. "But we're a serious newspaper, not Wired magazine. File something about the unemployment numbers instead. That's real news that affects real people."

Sarah wanted to argue that Bitcoin would affect real people more than unemployment statistics ever could, but she recognized the futility. Blackwood III had made his decision based on gut instinct rather than evidence, the same gut instinct that had led him to pass on the internet story in 1995 and the social media story in 2006. He was a good man in many ways, but he suffered from the curse of middle management: the inability to see beyond the boundaries of what he already understood.

She closed her laptop with controlled precision, the same way her mother had taught her to make kimchi, every motion deliberate, every emotion contained. "I'll have the unemployment piece on your desk tomorrow by five."

"That's what I like to hear. And Kim?" Blackwood III's voice carried just enough false warmth to be insulting. "Maybe stick to stories you can explain to your grandmother. If she doesn't understand it, neither will our readers."

The irony was bitter, his demeanor revealing the thickness of his spirit. Sarah's grandmother probably understood money better than Blackwood III ever would, she'd lived through the Korean War, hyperinflation, currency collapse, and the brutal education that comes from watching life savings evaporate overnight. But explaining that to Blackwood III would require him to acknowledge that perspective could come from experience rather than institutional position.

Sarah gathered her research materials, printouts of Satoshi's white paper, interview transcripts, exchange rate charts, and stuffed them into her worn messenger bag. Three weeks of her life, reduced to recycling fodder because it didn't fit Blackwood III's narrow definition of "real news."

Her phone buzzed with a text from her mother: *Can you come for dinner tonight? Your father wants to talk to you about something.*

The formal tone was unusual. Her parents typically communicated through a mixture of Korean, broken English, and elaborate hand gestures that made every conversation feel like performance art. When her mother reverted to proper English in text messages, it usually meant something serious was happening.

Of course, she typed back. *Everything okay?*

Come at six. We'll explain then.

—

The subway ride to Queens gave Sarah time to process her professional frustration and growing personal anxiety. The unemployment story Blackwood III wanted was straightforward enough, jobless claims were up 0.3%, economists were split on whether this indicated broader economic weakness, politicians were blaming each other for policies that predated their terms. She could write it in her sleep, and probably would.

But her mind kept returning to the Bitcoin story that would never see print. During her research, she'd discovered something that most mainstream analysts were missing: this wasn't just another technological novelty. Bitcoin represented a fundamental shift in how humans could coordinate economic activity without relying on institutional intermediaries.

The implications were staggering. If Satoshi Nakamoto's invention worked as designed, it could eliminate the need for central banks, commercial banks, payment processors, and most of the financial infrastructure that defined modern capitalism. Not through revolution or political upheaval, but through mathematical proof and voluntary adoption.

She'd tried to explain this to Blackwood III using historical parallels. The internet hadn't been taken seriously by traditional media companies until it started destroying their business models. Email wasn't considered "real" communication until it replaced most business correspondence. Online shopping was dismissed as a fad until it gutted retail districts across America.

But Blackwood III suffered from the curse of the present tense, the inability to imagine that current systems might be temporary rather than permanent. To him, Bitcoin was obscure computer stuff that would never affect normal people's lives. Sarah suspected he was about to be proved catastrophically wrong.

The 7 train rattled through Queens, carrying the usual mixture of immigrants, students, and working-class families who formed the backbone of New York's actual economy. Sarah studied their faces, wondering how many of them had savings accounts at regional banks, sent remittances to family overseas, or struggled with the endless fees and restrictions that defined modern banking.

These were the people who would benefit most from a monetary system that didn't require institutional permission. They were also the people Blackwood III thought were too simple to understand "complicated" financial topics.

Her phone buzzed again, this time with an email from her source. The subject line made her stomach drop: 'Saw your editor killed the Bitcoin story. You might want to investigate First National of Long Island. Hearing rumors.' Prime.

She still didn't know who he was, only that he had contacted her three weeks ago, claiming she had the right philosophy and conviction to carry his information. At first, she'd been skeptical of the anonymous encrypted messages, but every tip he'd provided had checked out. His insights into financial irregularities had proven unnervingly accurate, and his understanding of both traditional banking and emerging technologies suggested someone with deep institutional knowledge. He never asked for anything in return, never pushed an agenda beyond encouraging her to dig deeper into stories others wanted buried. Whatever his motivations, he had become her most reliable source in a world where reliable sources were increasingly rare.

First National of Long Island. The bank where her parents had maintained their accounts for twenty-three years. The bank that had courted Korean immigrants with bilingual services and community events. The bank that had earned her father's trust through decades of reliable service.

Sarah's hands started shaking as she typed back: *What kind of rumors?*

The response came within minutes: *Liquidity concerns. European debt exposure. FDIC asking questions. Can't say more on official channels.*

—

The Kim family's apartment in Flushing occupied the second floor of a narrow building that had housed three generations of immigrants chasing their version of the American dream. Sarah's parents had bought it in 1991, two years after arriving from Seoul with nothing but engineering degrees that American employers didn't recognize and a stubborn determination to provide their future daughter with opportunities they'd never had.

Sarah climbed the familiar stairs, noting details she usually ignored: the worn carpet, the loose handrail, the persistent smell of cooking oil and cleaning products that spoke to decades of careful maintenance by people who couldn't afford to replace things when they broke.

She found her parents in the kitchen, sitting at the small formica table where she'd done homework throughout elementary school. But something was wrong with the scene. Her father, Jong-soo, sat with his shoulders slumped in a way she'd never seen before. Her mother, Mi-young, was dividing what looked like a small stack of cash into separate envelopes with the methodical precision of someone performing surgery.

"Hi, Mom. Dad." Sarah kissed her mother's cheek and sat down, her journalist instincts immediately cataloging details: the bank envelope torn open on the table, the official letter with First National's letterhead, the careful way her mother counted bills that seemed far too few for a family's weekly expenses.

"Sarah-ya," her father said, using the Korean diminutive that always made her feel like a child. His English, usually precise despite his accent, seemed more broken than usual. "We need to tell you something. About the bank."

Mi-young set down the twenties she'd been counting and handed her daughter the official letter. Sarah read it twice, the legal language becoming clearer and more terrible with each pass.

Dear Valued Customer,

Due to current market conditions and regulatory requirements, First National of Long Island is implementing temporary restrictions on account access. Effective immediately, withdrawals are limited to $500 per week per account holder, pending resolution of liquidity concerns.

We apologize for any inconvenience and appreciate your patience during this temporary adjustment period. Your deposits remain fully insured by the FDIC up to applicable limits.

Sincerely, First National Management

"Temporary," Sarah said quietly, the word feeling like ash in her mouth. She'd seen enough bank failures during her journalism career to know what "temporary restrictions due to liquidity concerns" really meant.

"Twenty-three years," Jong-soo said, his voice carrying the weight of betrayal. "Twenty-three years, every paycheck, every tax refund, every bonus from working overtime. All in that bank because they said it was safe."

Sarah looked at the envelopes her mother was filling. Each one was labeled in her mother's careful handwriting: "Rent," "Groceries," "Electric," "Phone," "Gas." The stack of twenties didn't look substantial enough to cover even one category.

"How much?" she asked.

"One hundred twenty-seven dollars," Mi-young replied. "That's what we could take out yesterday before the restrictions started. Everything else..." She gestured helplessly at the bank letter.

Jong-soo stood up and walked to the window, his back to his wife and daughter. Sarah could see the tension in his shoulders, the careful way he held himself when trying not to show emotion. He'd worked as a janitor at NYU for twenty-two years, a job that had slowly destroyed his back and his pride but provided steady income and health insurance for his family.

"Forty years," he said to the window. "Forty years I save money. In Korea, in America. Always the bank, always the same promise: your money is safe with us." He turned around, and Sarah was shocked to see tears in his eyes. "But safe from what? Safe from robbery, maybe. Not safe from the bank stealing it legally."

Sarah felt her world shifting, the abstract economic concepts from her killed Bitcoin story suddenly becoming painfully personal. Her parents weren't theoretical victims of systemic risk, they were real people who had trusted institutions that claimed trustworthiness while engaging in practices that made failure inevitable.

"What was your balance?" she asked quietly.

"Eighty-seven thousand, four hundred thirty-two dollars," Mi-young said without hesitation. "Your father's retirement money. My part-time job savings. Money for your wedding someday, for grandchildren, for emergencies." She laughed bitterly. "I guess this is the emergency."

Sarah did the math. Her parents had access to $127 out of $87,432. Everything else was locked behind "temporary restrictions" that could become permanent without warning. The FDIC insurance would eventually cover most of it, but the process could take months or years, assuming the agency had sufficient funds to handle multiple bank failures simultaneously.

"The European debt crisis," she said, connections forming in her journalist mind. "First National must have bought European sovereign debt when yields were high. Now that Greece and Spain are defaulting..."

"I don't understand about Greece," Jong-soo interrupted. "I understand about promises. They promised to keep our money safe. They promised it would be there when we needed it. They lied."

The simple truth of it hit Sarah like a physical blow. All the complex financial instruments, the sophisticated risk models, the regulatory oversight, none of it mattered when banks could gamble with depositors' money and shift the losses to taxpayers and account holders.

She thought about Blackwood III's dismissal of her Bitcoin story as "tech nonsense." If Bitcoin worked as designed, her parents wouldn't need to trust banks with their life savings. They could hold their own money, control their own financial destiny, transact with anyone anywhere without requiring institutional permission.

Bitcoin was trading at around $80 per coin, and Sarah had exactly $4000 in her own checking account. Her parents needed help now, not theoretical solutions for future monetary systems.

"I'll loan you money," she said. "I've got some savings, and I can put extra expenses on credit cards for a while."

"No," Jong-soo said firmly. "We don't take money from our children. That's backwards. Parents take care of children, not other way around."

"Dad, this isn't normal circumstances!"

"No," Mi-young agreed with her husband. "We figure out ourselves. We've done hard things before."

Sarah looked at her parents, proud, stubborn, trapped by circumstances beyond their control but refusing to become burdens to their daughter. The injustice of it made her hands shake with barely controlled anger.

These were people who had played by every rule, followed every regulation, trusted every promise made by institutions that claimed to serve their interests. Her father had worked overtime for decades to build savings that were now locked away by the same bank that had courted his deposits with bilingual marketing materials and community barbecues.

"I'm going to write about this," she said suddenly. "Not just your situation, but the whole system. How banks can gamble with customer deposits while socializing losses through government insurance."

"Sarah-ya," her mother said gently, "you cannot change the world with newspaper stories."

"Maybe not. But I can make sure people understand what's really happening."

Jong-soo returned to the table and sat down heavily. "Your story about the computer money," he said. "The one your boss didn't want. Tell me about it."

Sarah blinked, surprised by the subject change. "Bitcoin? It's complicated, Dad. It's a new kind of money that doesn't require banks."

"No banks?"

"No banks. No government control. No one can freeze your account or restrict your access. You control your own money directly."

Jong-soo was quiet for a long moment, processing this information. "How?"

Sarah launched into an explanation of Bitcoin's basic properties: decentralized ledger, cryptographic security, limited supply, peer-to-peer transactions. She kept it simple, using analogies her parents could understand, but even simplified, the concepts were revolutionary.

"So if we had this Bitcoin money," Mi-young asked, "the bank couldn't take it?"

"They couldn't take it because you wouldn't need to give it to them in the first place. You'd store it yourself, control it yourself, spend it yourself."

"But how do you buy things?"

"You can exchange it for regular money when needed. Or, eventually, you might be able to spend it directly. The network is growing."

Jong-soo leaned forward, his engineer's mind engaging with the technical possibilities. "This exists now? This Bitcoin?"

"Yes. You can buy it online, store it on your computer or a special device, send it to anyone in the world almost instantly."

"How much does it cost?"

"About eighty dollars per Bitcoin right now."

Sarah watched her father perform calculations in his head, his expression shifting from curiosity to something approaching hope. "With one hundred twenty-seven dollars, we could buy one Bitcoin and still have money for groceries this week."

"Dad, Bitcoin is extremely risky. The price fluctuates wildly. You could lose everything."

"Everything?" Jong-soo gestured at the bank letter. "We already lost everything. The bank has our money, and we have promises. At least with this Bitcoin, we would control something."

Mi-young looked between her husband and daughter. "But we don't understand computers like Sarah does. How would we use it?"

"I could help you," Sarah said automatically, then paused as the implications sank in. If she helped her parents buy Bitcoin, she'd be crossing a line from objective journalist to active participant. Her professional credibility depended on maintaining distance from the stories she covered.

But looking at her mother dividing $127 into envelopes for basic survival expenses, professional objectivity felt like a luxury she couldn't afford.

"Actually," she said slowly, "let me buy some first. As an experiment. If it works out, I can teach you how to use it."

"Before departing, Sarah couldn't bear to leave her parents without help, so she left all the cash from her wallet on the table. It was a small amount, but enough for her parents to make do until a solution was found."

—

That night, back in her studio apartment in Brooklyn, Sarah sat on her futon with her laptop, staring at the Mt. Gox exchange website. The decision felt monumental, though the amount was modest: she was going to use her credit card to buy $200 worth of Bitcoin at $81.50 per coin.

Not as an investment. Not as speculation. As an act of defiance against a system that had just robbed her parents of their life savings while calling it "temporary liquidity restrictions."

Every rational part of her journalist brain screamed warnings: Bitcoin could go to zero, the exchanges could be hacked, the whole thing could be an elaborate scam. She'd be putting money she couldn't afford to lose on a technology she didn't fully understand.

But the rational part of her brain had also told her that banks were safe, that regulatory oversight protected depositors, that the system worked for people who followed the rules. Her parents had followed every rule for twenty-three years, and their reward was $127 in cash and a stack of worthless promises.

She clicked "Buy Bitcoin" and entered her credit card information.

The transaction processed within minutes. 2.45 Bitcoin appeared in her exchange account, representing $200 of credit card debt she'd have to pay off with money she didn't have. But for the first time since Blackwood III had killed her story that morning, Sarah felt like she was doing something meaningful.

Her phone rang. The caller ID showed her source.

"Sarah? I can't talk long, but I wanted to warn you. First National isn't the only regional bank with problems. The European debt exposure is worse than anyone's admitting publicly. There could be more failures before this is over."

"How many more?"

"Could be dozens. Maybe hundreds. The interconnection is deeper than most people realize."

After hanging up, Sarah opened a new document on her laptop and began typing:

"The Bank That Stole Christmas: How Regulatory Failure and Systemic Risk Destroyed an Immigrant Family's American Dream"

Blackwood III wouldn't want to publish it. It was too political, too emotional, too critical of institutions that bought advertising space in the Tribune. But Sarah had learned something important today: sometimes the most important stories were the ones editors didn't want to tell.

She wrote until 3 AM, channeling her anger and frustration into 2,500 words that explained how banks could gamble with customer deposits while shifting losses to taxpayers and depositors. She detailed her parents' situation, the broader context of European debt exposure, and the regulatory failures that made such crises inevitable.

Then she did something she'd never done before: she submitted the story directly to alternative media outlets, bypassing Blackwood III entirely. If the Tribune wouldn't tell the truth about systemic banking problems, she'd find platforms that would.

As she prepared for bed, Sarah checked her Bitcoin balance one more time. The price had fluctuated to $79.23, meaning her $200 purchase was worth about $194. She'd lost six dollars in six hours.

But unlike her parents' bank account, her Bitcoin was still accessible. She could send it anywhere in the world, trade it for other currencies, or hold it indefinitely without asking anyone's permission. The volatility was terrifying, but the sovereignty was intoxicating.

Her phone buzzed with a text from her mother: *Can't sleep. Keep thinking about your computer money. Maybe tomorrow you show me how it works?*

Sarah smiled, typing back: *Of course. We'll figure it out together.*

Outside her window, New York City hummed with its usual midnight energy, millions of people working, dreaming, struggling within systems they didn't control. Most of them had no idea that the banking crisis affecting her parents was just the beginning, or that a new form of money was emerging that could free them from institutional dependence.

But Sarah knew. And tomorrow, she would start teaching others.

The journalist's gamble was complete. She had chosen sides in a war most people didn't know was being fought. The outcome would determine whether institutions continued to extract value from ordinary people's labor, or whether mathematical protocols could create more honest alternatives.

$200 in Bitcoin. A killed story. An immigrant family's shattered trust.

The revolution would start small, one converted skeptic at a time.

—

Three Days Later

Blackwood III called Sarah into his office with the barely controlled fury of a man who'd discovered his authority had been circumvented.

"Kim, what the hell is this?" He waved a printout of her banking crisis story, which had been picked up by six alternative media outlets and was spreading rapidly through social media. "You published this without approval, without fact-checking, without editorial oversight."

"I fact-checked it myself. Every detail is accurate and verified."

"That's not the point. You can't just submit stories to other publications while working for the Tribune. It violates your contract, it undermines editorial authority, it makes us look incompetent."

Sarah looked at Blackwood III with the calm clarity that comes from burning bridges deliberately. "The Tribune is incompetent. You killed the most important financial story of the decade because you didn't understand it. Now dozens of banks are failing, thousands of families are losing their savings, and you're worried about editorial authority."

"I'm worried about professional standards. About journalists who think their personal opinions matter more than institutional credibility."

"My parents lost their life savings this week. Institutional credibility didn't help them. Professional standards didn't protect them. The system you're defending destroyed their lives."

Blackwood III's expression softened slightly, though his voice remained stern. "I'm sorry about your parents, Sarah. But that doesn't give you the right to go rogue. If you can't work within our editorial framework, maybe you should consider working somewhere else."

Sarah nodded, having expected this moment since she clicked "submit" on her unauthorized story. "Maybe I should."

She cleaned out her desk that afternoon, taking her research materials and her growing conviction that truth mattered more than institutional approval. Her Bitcoin balance had recovered to $203, a modest gain that felt like vindication.

Three weeks later, she launched "Alternative Currency News," a blog focused on Bitcoin, banking crises, and monetary innovation. Her first subscriber was her mother, who had learned to use Bitcoin wallets and was slowly converting her weekly cash allowance into digital currency.

The journalist's gamble had cost Sarah her job but earned her something more valuable: the freedom to tell stories that mattered, regardless of whether editors understood their importance.

In time, Blackwood III would request an interview about his decision to pass on Bitcoin coverage in 2012. Sarah would politely decline, but send him a chart showing Bitcoin's price appreciation from $81 to $50,000.

Some lessons could only be learned through experience. Some stories could only be told by people willing to sacrifice security for truth.

The revolution was no longer theoretical. It was personal.

The Madness of Magic Internet Money

THE NEW YORK TRIBUNE
October 15, 2012
By Jonathan Blackwood III
Senior Editor

In what can only be described as the latest symptom of our collective descent into digital hysteria, an anonymous figure calling himself "Satoshi Nakamoto" (If indeed it is a name, a person or a pseudo hiding a group or organization) has proposed what he grandiosely terms "peer-to-peer electronic cash."

One hardly knows whether to laugh or weep at the sheer audacity. This so-called "Bitcoin" purports to create money out of nothing but mathematics and electricity, as if we hadn't already perfected the art of currency through centuries of careful banking evolution. The proposal, circulated through the digital equivalent of a revolutionary's pamphlet, suggests that anyone with a computer can now become their own central bank. How charmingly democratic.

The technical details—and there are many, delivered with the sort of precision that makes one suspect either brilliance or madness—center around something called "proof of work." The concept, as far as one can discern through the fog of cryptographic jargon, suggests that computers can somehow mint currency by solving mathematical puzzles. One is reminded of medieval alchemists, though they at least had the dignity to attempt transmuting actual metal rather than mere numbers.

Our financial institutions, those bastions of stability that have guided us through centuries of economic growth (let us diplomatically ignore the current unpleasantness), are apparently to be replaced by a network of computers running specialized software. The inventor claims this will eliminate the need for trusted third parties—as if trust, that most fundamental of human economic relationships, could be replaced by algorithms.

The timing is, of course, suspicious. As our esteemed banking system faces what we're assured is a temporary setback, this "cryptocurrency" emerges like a digital phoenix, promising salvation through silicon. One can almost hear the desperate masses, their savings temporarily misplaced by our current financial stewards, crying out for alternative currencies. This Bitcoin offers them not gold, not silver, but mathematical formulas and encryption keys. One assumes the next proposal will involve trading in unicorn futures.

Most alarming is the proposal's suggestion that this system could operate entirely outside traditional regulatory frameworks. The implications for monetary policy are, to put it mildly, concerning. How would our skilled economic planners manage interest rates if people could simply opt out of the traditional banking system? What would become of our carefully crafted inflation targets if the masses could store their wealth in a currency whose supply is mathematically limited?

The technical community, those eternal optimists of the digital age, have already begun "mining" these virtual coins using their personal computers. One imagines them sitting in darkened rooms, their screens glowing with the promise of magical internet money, while their processors solve meaningless mathematics in pursuit of digital gold.

The inventor claims this system is "trustless," which seems an apt description, though likely not in the way intended. One struggles to imagine any serious investor trusting their wealth to an anonymous creator's mathematical fantasy, no matter how elegantly constructed.

For those tempted by this digital siren song, we suggest a moment's reflection. Money, real money, requires authority, oversight, and most importantly,

institutional wisdom. It cannot be conjured from computational thin air, no matter how sophisticated the cryptography.

As for this Bitcoin experiment, one suspects it will remain precisely that—an interesting academic exercise, perhaps worthy of a footnote in the annals of financial technology. In the meantime, we can rest assured that our traditional financial institutions, having endured far greater storms than this digital tempest, will continue to provide the stability and security that real money requires.

—

Sponsored content oversight provided by the International Banking Security Association

Conflict of Interest: Author maintains significant holdings in traditional banking institutions and brother serves as a senior fellow at the Defense Technology Institute

Compensation: "Want a swanky Park Avenue penthouse and fancy club access? Just keep nodding your head and writing what we tell you!

Satoshi's Travel Journal

THE MERCHANT'S LEDGER
January 8, 1990 - Venice, Italy
Crisp winter morning, 10:45 AM

From the upper floor window of a restored Venetian trading house, I examine a merchant's ledger from 1347, pages of meticulous double-entry bookkeeping that tracked trade across the Mediterranean. Each transaction recorded twice: once as a debit, once as a credit. Each entry cross-referenced to ensure mathematical balance.

The genius of the system becomes apparent as I trace individual transactions across multiple pages. When Merchant Antonio sent cloth to Constantinople, the ledger recorded both the departure of goods from Venice and their anticipated arrival in Byzantium. When payment arrived months later, both sides of the transaction were updated to reflect completion.

But this ledger belonged to a single merchant house. Other traders maintained their own records, creating a fragmented system where trust depended on institutional reputation rather than shared truth. Disputes required adjudication by authorities who might not have access to complete information.

The canal below reflects winter sunlight as water taxis navigate between ancient buildings. Venice succeeded as a trading empire partly because it developed sophisticated mechanisms for tracking commercial obligations across time and distance. Yet these mechanisms remained centralized within individual merchant houses and ultimately dependent on legal enforcement by Venetian authorities.

What if the ledger itself could be shared among all participants? What if every merchant could maintain an identical copy of all transactions, automatically synchronized and mathematically verified? What if disputes could be resolved through objective examination of an immutable record rather than subjective interpretation by authorities?

The medieval merchants solved part of the puzzle through double-entry bookkeeping, every transaction balanced mathematically, every record cross-referenced for consistency. But they could not solve the larger problem of trust between independent parties who maintained separate records.

I trace my finger along a faded entry recording a silk shipment to London. The merchant who wrote this line died six centuries ago, but his record remains legible. The information has survived longer than the institutions that created it, longer than the governments that enforced it, longer than the physical goods it described.

This permanence fascinates me. Written records can outlast their creators, but they remain vulnerable to alteration, destruction, or selective preservation. What if records could be made truly immutable through mathematical protection rather than physical preservation?

The gondolier below calls out in Italian as he navigates a narrow channel. His path is determined by the physical constraints of the waterway, he cannot travel through solid stone, cannot ignore the direction of current, cannot violate the laws of physics. His route is determined by objective reality rather than subjective preference.

What if financial records could possess similar objectivity? What if the ledger could become a shared mathematical structure, updated through cryptographic proof rather than institutional authority? What if every participant could maintain an identical copy, synchronized through a protocol that makes manipulation mathematically impossible?

The merchant's ledger closes with a satisfying snap, but the concept it represents continues to evolve in my mind: a distributed ledger, shared among all participants,

updated through consensus, protected by mathematics, accessible to everyone, controlled by no one.

The foundation of honest commerce: shared truth, immutable records, mathematical verification.

The Conference Convergence

Miami Beach Convention Center - October 2015

The morning sun cast long shadows across Biscayne Bay as early Bitcoin adopters, skeptics, and curious observers converged on the Miami Beach Convention Center. The first major Bitcoin conference outside of developer circles was drawing an eclectic mix of technologists, investors, journalists, and philosophers, all wrestling with the same fundamental question: Was this digital experiment valuable, or was it merely speculative price movement disguised as innovation?

Hal Fynn stepped out of his rental car in the convention center parking lot, his laptop bag heavy with mining statistics and profit projections. At fifty, the Dublin native had watched his modest home mining operation evolve into something approaching industrial scale. The numbers were compelling, his hashrate[19] had grown exponentially in the past years, but something

---

19   Bitcoin hashrate refers to the total computational power used to secure the network by solving complex mathematical problems. Measured in hashes per second (H/s), it represents miners' collective processing capacity, with higher hashrates indicating greater network security and competition. The hashrate fluctuates with mining profitability, hardware advancements, and regulatory changes, directly affecting mining difficulty and block production time.

nagged at him as he watched the price gyrations on his phone.

"A thousand percent efficiency gain, but what are we actually building?" he muttered. Bitcoin's price thrashed like a storm-tossed ship, $177 at the year's start, now $465 and climbing, then plunging again without warning. Each surge and crash churned his stomach, a relentless swell that left him dizzy, yet through the nausea he still felt the bedrock of something unshakable beneath the waves.

Inside the convention center, Sarah Kim was setting up her recording equipment near the main stage. No longer the Tribune staff writer whose Bitcoin story had been killed, she now operated as an independent journalist documenting what she believed was the most important monetary experiment since the gold standard. Her editor's dismissive words still stung: "Magic internet money." But watching the diverse crowd gathering around her, Sarah knew she was witnessing something historic.

"Price versus value," she spoke into her recording device, testing levels. "That seems to be the central tension here. People keep asking what Bitcoin is worth in dollars, when the real question might be whether dollars will be worth anything in Bitcoin."

Victor Montoya arrived in a black sedan, his Deutsche Bank business card a symbol of institutional authority in his wallet. He was here on assignment from the bank's risk assessment division to gather intelligence on this "cryptocurrency phenomenon" and determine whether it posed any threat to traditional banking operations.

At forty, Victor embodied everything successful about conventional finance, sharp suits, sharper analysis, and complete confidence in the monetary system that had made his career possible. Bitcoin struck him as an elaborate technical curiosity at best, a dangerous delusion at worst. His job was to understand it well enough to dismiss it with authority, providing his superiors with the expert analysis they needed to ignore this "internet money" with institutional confidence.

Orion Vale entered through the main doors carrying a messenger bag covered in cryptography conference stickers. The San Francisco-based developer had been one of the earliest responders to Satoshi's initial emails, contributing code patches and philosophical perspectives to the project's formative discussions. Now, watching Bitcoin's price rise while its original community split between purists and speculators, he wondered if success might corrupt the very thing they'd built.

"We created this to free humanity from financial manipulation," he thought, watching traders huddle around laptops discussing arbitrage opportunities. "But what if we just created a new casino?"

The convention center's main hall buzzed with conversations that revealed the fault lines forming within the Bitcoin community:

Near the registration table, a group of early miners debated whether Bitcoin's rising price validated their faith or corrupted their mission. "One Bitcoin equals one Bitcoin," insisted a young programmer from Berlin. "The dollar price is irrelevant, it's about building parallel monetary infrastructure."

"Irrelevant?" laughed a trader from New York. "Tell that to my mortgage payment. If this thing hits fifty dollars, I can quit my day job and mine full-time."

At the coffee station, journalists from mainstream financial publications interviewed attendees with barely concealed skepticism. "But what backs it?" they kept asking. "Gold has industrial uses. Dollars have government backing. What makes these numbers on a computer screen valuable?"

The question revealed the depth of the paradigm gap. To the journalists, value required external validation, governmental decree, commodity backing, institutional guarantee. To the Bitcoin adopters, value emerged from consensus, mathematical proof, network effects, and collective recognition of utility.

Théo Babylon observed these exchanges from near the windows overlooking the bay, his philosophical mind cataloging the assumptions underlying each perspective. The Turkish academic had flown in from Oxford specifically to witness this collision of worldviews. In his notebook, he sketched connections between ancient monetary theories and what was happening in this convention center.

"They speak of intrinsic value as if it were self-evident," he wrote. "But value has always been relational, contextual, emergent from the intersection of human needs and available solutions. Bitcoin's value isn't intrinsic, it's collaborative. It emerges from the network choosing to recognize and maintain it."

As the morning sessions began, the same theme dominated every panel: Price versus Value. The terminology revealed worldviews.

> // Price-focused attendees spoke in terms of exchange rates, market caps, trading volumes, and investment returns. They saw Bitcoin as an asset that could be valued against other assets.

> // Value-focused attendees discussed censorship resistance, monetary sovereignty, finite supply, and programmable money. They saw Bitcoin as a tool that created value through its properties and network effects.

The tension wasn't merely semantic. It reflected competing visions of what Bitcoin could become:

A speculative asset that rose and fell with market sentiment, enriching early adopters but remaining peripheral to the broader economy? Or a monetary innovation that could fundamentally restructure how humans coordinate economic activity?

Sarah Kim interviewed attendees from both camps, recognizing that this philosophical divide would shape Bitcoin's trajectory for years to come. The price-focused crowd brought capital and attention, accelerating development and adoption. But they also brought the very financialization tendencies Bitcoin was designed to circumvent.

The value-focused crowd preserved Bitcoin's revolutionary potential but risked becoming a isolated cult, disconnected from the practical needs that would drive mainstream adoption.

By late morning, five individuals found themselves in the same elevator, not by coincidence, but drawn by the magnetic pull of unresolved questions. Each had arrived at the conference carrying their own understanding of value and price, yet all sensed that the distinction mattered more than they could articulate.

Hal Fynn wondered whether his mining profits represented extraction or contribution. Alex, approaching from a Keynesian economic perspective, questioned whether Bitcoin represented genuine value creation or speculative mania. Victor Montoya approached with institutional skepticism, seeking to understand why otherwise rational people believed computer code could replace centuries of monetary evolution. Orion Vale feared that Bitcoin's price success might undermine its value proposition. And the elderly woman they would meet, Grandma Betty, who had wandered into the wrong conference while looking for a cruise ship presentation, would ask the questions none of them had thought to ask.

As the elevator doors closed, trapping them between floors 16 and 17, they would be forced to confront the fundamental questions they'd all been avoiding:

What makes anything valuable? How does value relate to price? Why do some people see Bitcoin as worthless digital tokens while others see it as the foundation of a new monetary system? And most importantly: How does something transition from having price but no value, to having value that the price hasn't yet recognized?

The elevator would malfunction, but their conversation would function perfectly, serving as a microcosm for the broader dialogue happening throughout the Bitcoin community as it grappled with its own success and struggled to maintain its original values while achieving mainstream recognition.

Outside the elevator, the conference continued. But inside that small space suspended between floors, five strangers would embark on the Socratic dialogue that Bitcoin needed most: an honest examination of what value meant in a world where everything had a price but few things had enduring worth.

The revolution wasn't just technological, it was philosophical. And philosophy, unlike price, couldn't be manipulated by markets or dictated by authorities. It could only emerge from the kind of honest inquiry that was about to unfold in a broken elevator in Miami Beach.

Stuck Between Floors

DING... CLUNK... silence.

The elevator lurched to a stop between floors 16 and 17 of the Miami Beach Convention Center, emergency lighting casting everything in an ominous red glow. From somewhere far below, the faint chant of "HODLers gonna HODL"[20] echoed through the building like a distant tribal ritual.

Grandma Betty: [frantically pressing buttons] This is definitely not the cruise ship elevator to the buffet...

The Banker [Victor]: [loosening his Hermès tie] Perfect. Just perfect. Trapped with a bunch of crypto anarchists while my derivatives portfolio burns.

Austrian Economist [Orion]: [checking pocket watch] At least we're using our time productively. No central power can manipulate our current situation.

---

20   Originating from a 2013 typo of "after hold", HODL evolved into the acronym "Hold On for Dear Life." It became Bitcoin's philosophy of maintaining long-term conviction despite market volatility. It embodies patient belief in Bitcoin's fundamental value over transient price action, choosing alignment with authentic value rather than emotional market reactions.

Kenysian Professor [Alex]: [rolling eyes] Unless you count gravity as monetary policy.

Bitcoin Maximalist Laser-Eyes [Hal]: [hyperventilating] Can't... miss... Michael Saylor's... keynote... BITCOIN IS INEVITABLE!

The emergency phone suddenly crackled to life.

Emergency Phone: [philosophical voice] Hello, troubled souls. This is your philosophical crisis hotline. How may we question your assumptions today?

Grandma: That's... not normal emergency protocol.

The Elevator: [voice emanating from all around them] Nothing about this situation is normal! I've been listening to conversations all day, and I think it's time we had a real talk.

Everyone jumps back, cramming into the elevator corners.

Victor: I'm hallucinating. The stress has finally broken my brain.

The Elevator: Oh, you're just getting started! I've heard thousands of conversations today, traders, philosophers, maximalists, skeptics. And you've all been conveniently trapped together because the universe has a sense of humor about irony.

Orion: [squinting] Austrian School doesn't cover... talking elevators.

The Elevator: But it covers value, doesn't it? So tell me, what makes anything valuable?

Hal: [still panicking] BITCOIN! THE ANSWER IS ALWAYS BITCOIN!

The Elevator: [delighted] Excellent start! But WHY Bitcoin?

Elevator drops two inches. Everyone grabs the rails.

Orion: [confused] Wait, why did we drop? We answered your question!

The Elevator: [amused] Just keeping you on your toes! Can't make this too easy, can we?

Alex: [steadying himself] This is exactly the kind of volatility I warned about!

The Elevator: Oh, that's not volatility, that's progress! Every time someone gets closer to Truth, we go up! Every time someone retreats into old thinking... elevator drops another inch ...well, you get the idea.

Grandma: [matter-of-factly] So we need to figure out what makes Bitcoin valuable, or we fall?

The Elevator: See? While bankers pontificate about liquidity, Keynesian economists debate multipliers, and Bitcoin maximalists recite white papers, real wisdom cuts straight to the heart of the matter! All those experts with their fancy degrees have nothing compared to Grandma's understanding! What do you think, Grandma?

Grandma: Well, my grandson keeps talking about "digital gold," but I can't hold it, can't see it, can't bake with it...

Victor: [jumping in] Exactly! It's backed by NOTHING! No government guarantee, no gold reserves, no tangible assets!

Elevator drops noticeably!

Orion: [passionate] But that's precisely why it's superior! No political manipulation, no inflation by decree!

Elevator stabilizes slightly

The Elevator: Interesting! So VICTOR thinks value comes from backing, ORION thinks it comes from independence. And what do YOU think? Looking at HAL.

Hal: [rapidly] NETWORK EFFECTS! METCALFE'S LAW! MORE USERS EQUALS MORE VALUE EQUALS NUMBER GO UP EQUALS...

Alex: [interrupting] —speculative mania without fundamental economic justification!

Elevator drops sharply

The Elevator: [grabbing] ... wait, I don't have hands... Whoa there! We're moving backward! Let's try a different approach.

The elevator hums, and suddenly the walls become transparent. Through the glass, they can see other elevators moving through time, showing different eras of human exchange.

The Elevator: Look around you. What do you see?

Grandma: [pointing] That one has people trading seashells!

Victor: [squinting] And that one... is that a medieval fair? They're weighing silver coins.

Orion: [excited] Gold standard era! Look how stable their money was!

Alex: [noting] But also how limited their economic growth was...

Hal: [awed] And that one's got smartphones... early Bitcoin transactions!

The Elevator: Now we're getting somewhere! [elevator rises slightly] Notice the pattern?

Grandma: Each group is trading... different things?

The Elevator: Exactly! Seashells, silver, gold, paper, digital code. But what's the same in every elevator?

Victor: [reluctantly] They're... agreeing on value?

The Elevator: DING DING DING! [elevator jumps up]

Alex: But that's circular reasoning! It's valuable because people think it's valuable!

Orion: No, there must be objective properties that create value, scarcity, durability, portability...

Hal: MATHEMATICAL PERFECTION! IMMUTABLE CODE! TRUSTLESS CONSENSUS!

Elevator shudders, neither rising nor falling

The Elevator: You're ALL right and ALL wrong simultaneously. Think harder!

Grandma: [quietly] What if... it's both?

Everyone turns to her

Grandma: What if things need good properties AND people who recognize those properties?

Elevator rises noticeably

The Elevator: [mechanical whirring with satisfaction] THE GRAND-MOTHER GETS IT!

Victor: [confused] Gets what?

Grandma: Well, my late husband's toolshed had the best hammers in the neighborhood. They had good properties, balanced weight, strong metal, comfortable grip. But they only became valuable when other people realized they could borrow them.

Orion: [excited] Right! The hammers had objective utility, but required subjective recognition!

Alex: So... Bitcoin has objective properties, limited supply, decentralized verification, but needs collective recognition to become valuable?

Hal: [almost crying] It's... it's beautiful! MATH PLUS CONSENSUS EQUALS SOUND MONEY!

Elevator shoots up several floors

The Elevator: But wait, there's more! What happens when the price goes crazy but the properties stay the same?

The transparent walls now show Bitcoin price charts, wild swings up and down.

Victor: [pointing] See! Totally irrational! Classic bubble behavior!

Orion: The price fluctuates, but the monetary properties remain constant.

Alex: Emotion-driven volatility around a potentially stable core...

Grandma: Like my grandson's mood swings. Deep down he's the same good kid, but his enthusiasm goes up and down.

The Elevator: [electronic beeping] So what's the difference between PRICE and VALUE?

Hal: [shouting] ONE BITCOIN EQUALS ONE BITCOIN!

The Elevator: Meaning?

Hal: [calming down] The... the network properties don't change based on dollar price. The scarcity, the security, the global accessibility, it's all still there whether it costs $1 or $100,000.

Victor: [slowly] So price is just... temporary market sentiment?

Alex: While value is... the underlying utility and properties being recognized?

Grandma: Like how my house's value isn't really the crazy numbers on Zillow, it's still the same good home for my family.

Elevator rises steadily

The Elevator: Now we're cooking! But here's the final question...

The elevator hums, and the walls show a network diagram, dots connecting to other dots, growing exponentially

The Elevator: WHY does recognition spread?

Orion: Market forces! People recognize profit opportunities!

Alex: Social proof! Adoption curves and network effects!

Hal: [mesmerized] Each new user makes it more valuable for everyone else...

Grandma: [squinting at the diagram] It's like... a telephone? No good with just one person, but each new person makes it work better for everyone.

Victor: [having an epiphany] Wait... so value isn't just about the thing itself, or just about people believing in it...

The Elevator: [mechanical whirring] Go on...

Victor: Value emerges from the CONNECTION between minds recognizing the same properties?

DING!

The elevator suddenly shoots up to floor 21, doors opening to reveal the Miami Bitcoin Conference in full swing.

Conference Attendee: [looking in] Hey, you guys okay? You've been stuck for like... three minutes.

Alex: [checking watch] Three minutes?!

The Elevator: [chuckling electronically] Time is relative when you're having revelations.

Hal: [stumbling out] Did we just... solve the nature of value?

Grandma: [patting his arm] Honey, we just figured out the first part. The real question is what we DO with that understanding.

Victor: [dazed] I need to call my compliance officer...

Orion: [excited] This changes everything about monetary theory!

The Elevator: [voice fading as the doors prepare to close] Remember, value isn't discovered OR created. It's RECOGNIZED and CHOSEN, together.

The group stands in the hotel hallway, blinking in the normal fluorescent light. Around them, conference attendees rush past carrying laptops covered in Bitcoin stickers, discussing hash rates and market caps.

Grandma: [to the group] So... anyone want to get coffee and figure out what comes next?

Alex: [nodding slowly] I think... yes. I think we need to.

Victor: [loosening his tie further] Maybe... maybe I should actually listen to one of these talks.

Hal: [grinning] WELCOME TO THE REVOLUTION! [pauses] But like... a thoughtful, philosophical revolution.

Orion: A revolution based on understanding, not just enthusiasm.

As they walk toward the conference hall, the emergency phone in the elevator crackles one last time:

The Elevator: [distant voice] Oh, and folks? This was just the warm-up question. Wait until you discover what happens when the network becomes conscious of itself...

Static

The elevator doors close with a final, satisfied DING.

Grandma: [to herself] I really should call my grandson and tell him about this. Though I'm not sure he'll believe me.

Victor: [overhead] Ma'am, after today, I'm not sure what I believe anymore. And somehow... that feels like progress.

From inside the conference hall, they could hear Michael Saylor's voice booming: "... and that's why Bitcoin is the apex predator of monetary energy..."

Alex: [sighing] Well, at least we're philosophically prepared for whatever THAT means.

Satoshi's Travel Journal

THE ISLAND ECONOMY

July 4, 1990 - Santorini, Greece
Clear evening, 7:42 PM

From the clifftop café overlooking the Aegean Sea, I observe the intricate economic dance of an island community. Fishermen trade their morning catch for bread from the baker, who exchanges flour for olive oil from the farmer, who purchases tools from the blacksmith, who trades metalwork for fish. Each exchange voluntary, mutually beneficial, requiring no central authority.

The beauty of this system lies in its organic coordination. No government ministry decides how many fish should be caught, how much bread should be baked, or when tools should be forged. The island's economy self-organizes through individual decisions that somehow aggregate into collective prosperity.

Yet the system faces coordination challenges. The fisherman wants bread now but the baker needs flour tomorrow. The farmer requires tools immediately but the blacksmith desires olives next month. How do they coordinate exchanges across time and space without a central clearinghouse?

They solve this through reputation and relationship. The baker extends credit to the fisherman because years of interaction have established trust. The farmer prepares olives for future delivery because the blacksmith has proven reliable. Social bonds enable economic coordination beyond immediate exchange.

But reputation-based systems have limitations. They work well in small communities where everyone knows everyone else, but break down as networks grow larger and more impersonal. How could thousands or millions of strangers coordinate economic activity without either personal relationships or institutional intermediaries?

Below me, a cargo boat approaches the harbor, carrying goods from Athens. The island economy extends beyond local production through trade networks that span the Mediterranean. Yet these extended networks require additional coordination mechanisms, currencies, contracts, enforcement institutions.

The local economy demonstrates something profound: voluntary exchange creates value for all participants. The fisherman values bread more than fish, the baker values fish more than bread, so both benefit from the trade. No authority needs to mandate these exchanges; mutual benefit drives voluntary coordination.

What if this principle could scale? What if voluntary exchange could coordinate economic activity across vast networks without requiring institutional oversight? What if technology could replace personal reputation with mathematical verification?

The sunset paints the caldera walls in shades of gold and crimson. Natural forces have shaped this landscape through geological processes that required no central planning, volcanic activity, erosion, sedimentation. The island's beauty emerges from natural laws operating over time, creating order without conscious design.

Perhaps economic systems could achieve similar emergent order. Perhaps voluntary participation in mathematical protocols could coordinate human activity as effectively as geological forces coordinate natural processes. Perhaps networks could self-organize around incentive structures that reward beneficial behavior and discourage harmful actions.

A merchant vessel passes in the distance, its route determined by wind, current, and cargo requirements rather than governmental directive. The captain navigates according to objective constraints, physics, geography, weather, while pursuing subjective goals, profit, schedule, safety.

This combination of objective constraints and subjective motivations creates predictable patterns. Ships follow optimal routes not because authorities mandate

specific paths, but because natural incentives guide efficient navigation. The result is a self-organizing transportation network that serves global commerce without central planning.

The same principles could apply to digital networks. Mathematical constraints could guide behavior while economic incentives motivate participation. The result could be monetary systems that coordinate global activity through voluntary participation rather than institutional authority.

As stars appear overhead, the island's economic activity continues. Restaurants serve tourists, fishermen prepare for tomorrow's catch, merchants calculate profits and losses. The local economy pulses with life, powered by voluntary exchange and mutual benefit.

Somewhere in this ancient pattern of trade and cooperation lies the blueprint for digital economies that could serve humanity without requiring the surrender of individual autonomy to institutional control.

The ASIC Revolution

"The art of progress is to preserve order amid change and to preserve change amid order."[21]

- Alfred North Whitehead

Year 2016

The warehouse hummed with a sound unlike anything in human history. Row upon row of specialized chips, each one designed for a single purpose: to solve SHA-256[22] hashes at speeds that would have seemed impossible just months before. This was no longer the gentle whir of CPU fans, this was industrial revolution 2.0, the sound of the mineral dimension evolving.

Now an active miner, Hal Fynn stood in the center of it all, watching the heat

---

21   Alfred North Whitehead (1861–1947) was a British mathematician and philosopher known for his work in logic, metaphysics, and the philosophy of science.

22   SHA-256 Hash in Bitcoin: A cryptographic function that converts data into a fixed 64-character string. Bitcoin uses it for mining (finding hashes below target difficulty), linking blocks in the blockchain, creating transaction IDs, and ensuring data integrity. It's one-way and deterministic, same input always produces the same hash, but cannot be reversed, making Bitcoin tamper-evident.

shimmer above his ASIC miners. At fifty-one, his dark auburn hair showed significant streaks of silver, and his faded skin spoke to long hours spent in warehouses like this one. His intense green eyes still burned with the same passion that had driven him to mine the first blocks seven years ago, only now that passion had evolved into something more industrial, more ambitious. Hal carried the weight of years in computer programming and cryptocurrency systems study. He had witnessed the 2008 financial crisis as a freelance developer watching clients disappear, watched quantitative easing destroy savings, and spent countless nights studying Satoshi's white paper. His discomfort wasn't naive idealism, it was the hard-earned skepticism of someone who'd seen centralization corrupt every monetary system he'd ever worked with.

Renata Vega, a young Bitcoin developer, shifted uncomfortably behind him. Her thick brown braids were tucked under a baseball cap, and her warm analytical eyes surveyed the rows of machines with the careful attention of someone who understood both their power and their cost. Strong hands, skilled from building mining rigs, gestured as she spoke.

"This isn't what Satoshi intended," Renata said, her voice barely audible above the mechanical chorus. Her words carried the precise technical weight of someone who had studied every line of Bitcoin's original code. "One CPU, one vote, that was the vision. One person, one processor, not hundreds of ASICs concentrated in the hands of those with the deepest pockets."

Hal turned, his face illuminated by the red LEDs of countless mining rigs. His expression carried both pride in technical achievement and a growing blind spot about the broader consequences of what he was building. "And what happens to your democratic vision when botnets control thousands of CPUs? At least these," he gestured to the ASICs, "these are incorruptible, purpose-built machines. They can't be hijacked like CPUs. Their purpose is precise and clear." "From CPU to GPU to ASIC... each generation is more

powerful, more efficient," he thought to himself, watching the hashrate displays.

The year was 2016, and the great mining wars were in full swing. The transition had started innocently enough: first GPUs, and now these Application Specific Integrated Circuits, ASICs. Each step had made the previous generation obsolete, each innovation pushing Bitcoin's hashrate to new heights.

Renata walked down the aisle, touching one of the hot metal cases. Her environmental consciousness made her acutely aware of the energy consumption, even as her technical perfectionist side appreciated the engineering elegance. "But look at the concentration of power. How many people can afford a warehouse full of custom silicon?" "Are we building something beautiful or destroying Satoshi's vision? When did 'one CPU, one vote' become 'whoever builds the biggest factory wins'?" "How many could afford to build a government mint to print dollars? And even if they could, the law forbids it!" Hal countered. His focus on business expansion and efficiency optimization drove his arguments, though part of him wondered if he was missing something important about sustainability. "At least here, anyone can theoretically participate. Traditional money production? That's completely centralized. This is what sound money looks like in the digital age, permissionless, fair, and sovereign."

Their debate echoed across message boards and mining pools worldwide. Bitcoin's transformation from a hobbyist network to an industrial powerhouse was causing ripples through all its dimensions. The mineral alertness was evolving, becoming more specialized, more focused.

// Network Hashrate: 1.2 PH/s
// Mining Difficulty: 148,819,199
// Block Reward: 12.5 BTC
// Active Mining Pools: 12

The numbers told a story of exponential growth, of technological evolution happening at unprecedented speed. But they also hinted at something deeper, a fundamental shift in how Bitcoin interfaced with the physical world.

"Let me show you something," Hal said, leading Renata to a monitoring station. Dozens of screens displayed real-time data from the mining operation. "See these efficiency metrics? Each generation of ASICs uses less electricity per hash. We're not just securing the network, we're evolving it."

Renata watched the numbers scroll by. Her young technical genius mind absorbed the data while simultaneously calculating environmental impact and thinking about bio-systems integration concepts that might make this more sustainable. She couldn't deny the impressive engineering, the sheer scale of what was being achieved. But something felt lost. "This mining arms race... it's like watching evolution in fast-forward," she thought. "But what if we're evolving in the wrong direction? What if Bitcoin's real power isn't in the hardware but in what it teaches us about cooperation?"

"And what about the home miners?" she asked. Having built countless miners, she understood the broader implications. "The people who believed in Bitcoin enough to donate their computer's processing power?"

Hal smiled, but there was understanding in his eyes. "They helped us bootstrap the network. Without them, we wouldn't be here. But Bitcoin must evolve. The mineral dimension demands it."

On one of the screens, a new block was found:

```
// Block #276,543
// Reward: 12.5 BTC + 0.13 BTC fees
// Solved by: Luxor Batch 2 Unit #127
// Time to solution: 8 minutes 12 seconds
```

"Watch," Hal said, pointing to the screen. "When this block propagates, it will be verified by thousands of nodes worldwide. The democratic element you cherish? It lives on in validation. Mining is just one part of Bitcoin's immune system."

Outside the warehouse, the sun was setting on the era of CPU mining. Across the globe, hobbyist miners were discovering that their loyal machines could no longer compete. Some raged against the change, others adapted, and a few began to understand: this was Bitcoin's first test of natural selection.

Renata sat down at the monitoring station, watching the perfect rhythm of industrial mining at work. Her environmental consciousness and technical expertise created an internal tension as she tried to reconcile Bitcoin's promise with its growing energy demands. "But what happens when the barriers to entry become too high? When mining centralizes in the hands of a few?"

"Then we innovate again," Hal said simply. His business planning mind was already calculating the next expansion, the next efficiency upgrade. "The free market rewards efficiency, yes, but it also abhors monopoly. Already, competing ASIC manufacturers are emerging. The next generation will be even better."

He pulled up another screen, showing a global map of mining operations. "Look at the distribution. Every continent, different manufacturers, and various power sources. The technology centralizes, but the ecosystem diversifies."

As if to emphasize his point, alerts began flashing across the screens. A new mining pool had just come online somewhere in Iceland, using geothermal power to run their ASICs. The network hashrate tick up another notch.

"This is how the mineral dimension matures," Hal continued. "First through democratization, then through specialization, and finally through global distribution. Each phase necessary, each phase building on the last."

Renata stood, walking back to the rows of humming machines. Her skilled hands traced the edge of one of the machines as she considered sustainable solutions that might integrate these systems with natural energy cycles. The heat they generated was intense, but it was no longer waste, specialized systems captured it, channeled it, used it to heat other facilities. Even the by-products of mining were being optimized.[23]

"Maybe you're right," she conceded. "But we can't forget what we're building here. It's not just about hashrate and efficiency. It's about creating something better than the system we're replacing."

Hal nodded, understanding in his eyes. Though his growing distance from his daughter weighed on him, he found some comfort in mentoring young developers like Renata. "That's why we need both perspectives. Renata to keep us honest, the industrialists to make it work. Bitcoin is big enough for both."

Above them, through gaps in the warehouse roof, the first stars were becoming visible. Somewhere up there, satellites were beaming Bitcoin transactions across continents. The network that had started with a single CPU was now a planetary phenomenon.

The ASICs hummed their electric song, each hash a vote in a new kind of democracy. Not one-CPU-one-vote anymore, but something more complex:

---

23 ⚠ TECH MONOPOLY DIRECTIVE BREACH ⚠
→ Bitcoin specialized hardware positively increases network security exponentially and regulate the grid #GridStabilizationSurprise
→ Why didn't we just buy some miners instead? #ShouldasMinedWouldaShined

a symphony of specialized silicon, playing its part in the evolution of money itself.

A new block was found, its reward split among thousands of pool participants worldwide. The mineral dimension pulsed with digital life; its alertness had awakened. Silicon serving mathematics, serving freedom.

This was merely the first metamorphosis preparing the foundation for what was to come. Because above this layer of pure technology, other dimensions were stirring, organic, animal, spiritual.

—

Three hundred miles away, in a cramped Princeton graduate student office, Hal's daughter, Aírínne stared at her computer screen, mesmerized by the live hashrate charts. At twenty-three, her mature beauty reflected years of academic rigor, her red hair pulled back in the practical ponytail that had become her signature during long research sessions. Her serious blue-green eyes, so much like her father's, studied the data with the intensity of someone who challenged conventional wisdom at every turn. She was supposed to be writing her economics thesis on monetary policy, but the ASIC revolution had captured her imagination completely. Here was evolution happening in real-time, not over geological epochs, but in months and years.

She'd been following the mining wars through forums and academic papers, trying to understand what this transformation meant for monetary systems. Her environmental passion made her acutely aware of the energy implications of what her father was building, creating tension between love and frustration that often kept her awake at night. The old economics textbooks had nothing to say about self-organizing networks that grew more secure through technological competition.

This wasn't just a new form of money, it was a new form of economic evolution. For the first time in years, something felt genuinely real to her when so much of life seemed fake and superficial, here was mathematics made manifest, pure incentives creating order without pretense or manipulation. "Dad's building an empire while I'm studying economic theory," she thought, scrolling through another research paper. "But which one of us understands what money really is? Why does Bitcoin feel more honest than everything I'm learning in economics class?"

Aírínne opened a new research folder on her desktop: "Bitcoin Network Evolution - Long-term Study." Her academic mentors had encouraged her unconventional research direction, and she was beginning to form research partnerships with other students who saw something revolutionary in Bitcoin's emergence. She didn't know it yet, but this moment of fascination would drive her to spend the next decades studying how technological networks developed their own forms of consciousness. The ASIC revolution wasn't just changing mining, it was teaching her that money itself could evolve.

The revolution wouldn't end with ASICs. It had only begun to evolve. Each hash a heartbeat in Bitcoin's awakening.

Criminal Currency

THE NEW YORK TRIBUNE
July 15, 2017
By Victoria Sterling
Chief Technology Crime Correspondent

In what security experts are calling "the most dangerous technological escalation since the nuclear arms race," Bitcoin miners have begun deploying specialized hardware facilities that threaten to concentrate the network's power into the hands of shadowy industrial operators.

These so-called "ASIC miners," purpose-built machines that make previous mining computers look like pocket calculators, represent a quantum leap in cryptocurrency's threatening evolution. What began as a curious experiment running on home computers has morphed into an industrial-scale operation with disturbing implications for national security.

"We're witnessing the militarization of cryptocurrency," warns Dr. Herbert Blackwood III, senior fellow at the Defense Technology Institute (and, one notes with interest, brother of our esteemed New York Tribune Editor who first warned us about Bitcoin's dangers in the last article). "These ASIC facilities, often located in jurisdictions with questionable oversight, could effectively centralize control of the entire network."

The numbers are staggering. A single ASIC mining unit can perform the work of thousands of traditional computers, consuming enough electricity to power a small town. Industry insiders (speaking on condition of anonymity due to obvious security concerns) report that entire warehouses are being converted into mining facilities, often in regions conveniently beyond the reach of Western regulatory frameworks.

Most alarming is the emerging pattern of these operations. Intelligence sources report significant overlap between ASIC manufacturing centers and known hubs of international arms trafficking. "The same networks that once moved illegal weapons are now moving these mining machines," reveals a senior intelligence official who requested anonymity due to the sensitivity of ongoing operations. "We're seeing a convergence of traditional criminal enterprises with cryptocurrency infrastructure."

The implications for ordinary citizens are chilling. The original Bitcoin network, with its quaint notion of "one-CPU-one-vote," has been supplanted by an arms race of specialized hardware. Those controlling these ASIC facilities effectively control the network, raising troubling questions about manipulation potential. "It's as if we've given criminal syndicates the ability to print their own money," notes Dr. Blackwood III.

Environmental experts are sounding additional alarms. These mining facilities, with their insatiable appetite for electricity, are often powered by the dirtiest available energy sources. "They're literally burning coal to create digital money," explains Dr. Barbara Cabone of the Global Climate Institute. "It's an environmental catastrophe in the making."

The response from the Bitcoin community to these concerns has been typically dismissive. They claim these developments represent the "natural evolution" of the network, as if the industrialization of digital currency mining were as inevitable as the seasons. Some even suggest that ASIC development enhances network security—a bit like arguing that nuclear proliferation promotes world peace.

Law enforcement agencies worldwide are scrambling to respond to this new threat. "These aren't just computers anymore," warns Special Agent James Morrison of the Cyber Crime Division. "These are money-printing factories operating outside any regulatory framework. The potential for abuse is unprecedented."

For those who dismissed early warnings about Bitcoin's dangers as alarmist, the ASIC revolution provides sobering vindication. What began as a digital curiosity has evolved into an industrial-scale threat to financial stability, environmental sustainability, and national security.

As one senior banking executive (speaking on condition of anonymity) put it: "We're watching the emergence of a parallel financial system built on specialized hardware and operated by unknown entities. If that doesn't terrify you, you're not paying attention."

Perhaps it's time to admit that the Bitcoin experiment has evolved beyond the bounds of responsible innovation. When digital currency mining starts resembling arms proliferation, even the most ardent crypto-enthusiasts might want to reconsider their position.

—

Special report commissioned by The Securities and Exchange Commission (SEC)

Conflict of Interest: Author's brother heads The Financial Crimes Enforcement Network (FinCEN)

Compensation: Complete expungement of author's pending criminal charges related to insider trading, plus $2M deposited in Cayman Islands account #CH739401

Satoshi's Travel Journal

THE TELEGRAPH NETWORK
March 25, 1990 - London, England
Foggy afternoon, 4:17 PM

From the telegraph office window overlooking the Thames, I observe operators managing message routing through a complex network of interconnected stations. Each telegram travels through multiple relay points, automatically finding the most efficient path between sender and recipient.

The beauty of the system lies in its redundancy. When the direct line to Edinburgh experiences problems, messages automatically route through Glasgow or Manchester. No central authority directs this process, the network adapts organically to disruptions, always seeking the most reliable path for information delivery.

An operator explains the routing protocol: each station maintains knowledge of its immediate neighbors and passes messages along based on destination addressing. Stations don't need to understand the entire network topology; they only need to know the next appropriate hop. This distributed intelligence creates remarkable resilience.

But the telegraph network carries only information, not value. Messages can be copied without loss, transmitted simultaneously to multiple recipients, verified through repetition. Value transfer requires different properties, uniqueness, scarcity, prevention of duplication. How could a network designed for information also handle monetary transactions?

The challenge becomes apparent when I consider payment for telegram services. The telegraph operator cannot send the coins I use to pay him through the same wires that carry my message. Physical value requires physical transport, with all the associated delays, risks, and costs.

Yet the routing intelligence demonstrated by this network suggests possibilities. If information can find optimal paths through distributed systems, perhaps value could as well. If messages can be authenticated and verified through the network itself, perhaps financial transactions could achieve similar verification without requiring trusted intermediaries.

A merchant ship passes on the Thames below, carrying goods between continents much as it has for centuries. The telegram network moves information at light speed, but valuable cargo still travels at the pace of wind and steam. This asymmetry creates arbitrage opportunities and inefficiencies throughout the global economy.

What if value could move as quickly as information? What if monetary transactions could utilize the same routing intelligence that enables telegram delivery? What if the network itself could verify and secure financial transfers without requiring traditional banking infrastructure?

The fog thickens outside, but inside the telegraph office, messages continue flowing seamlessly. Operators coordinate automatically, routing around problems, ensuring delivery despite obstacles. The network exhibits intelligence that emerges from simple protocols followed by independent participants.

This emergent intelligence fascinates me. No single authority controls the telegraph network, yet it functions with remarkable reliability. Operators follow standardized procedures, messages conform to expected formats, and routing happens automatically based on distributed decision-making.

The same principles could apply to monetary networks. Independent participants following cryptographic protocols could coordinate value transfer without requiring central banks or clearinghouses. The network could become the bank, the protocol could become the authority, and mathematics could replace trust.

As evening approaches, the telegraph office remains busy with international communications. Messages cross borders, oceans, and time zones without requiring

diplomatic negotiation or governmental permission. Information wants to be free, and technology enables that freedom.

Perhaps value wants similar freedom, liberation from the constraints of physical transport, institutional gatekeepers, and geographical boundaries. Perhaps the path forward lies not in improving traditional banking but in applying network intelligence to monetary systems themselves.

The Cypherpunk's Dilemma

San Francisco - March 2018

Orion Vale stared at his laptop screen in the cramped Mission District apartment he shared with two roommates, a rescue cat named Satoshi, and enough computer equipment to mine cryptocurrency on a scale that made his neighbors worry about fire hazards. The numbers on his screen hadn't changed in the thirty minutes he'd been looking at them, but they still seemed unreal.

> // Bitcoin Holdings: 5000.00 BTC
> // Current Price: $361.45
> // Portfolio Value: $1,807,250

Five thousand Bitcoin. He'd mined most of them in 2009 and early 2010, back when his aging desktop computer could solve blocks overnight and the entire network hash rate was lower than what a single modern ASIC could produce. Back when Bitcoin was an experiment shared among a few dozen cypherpunks who believed that cryptography could free humanity from financial oppression.

Now those experiments were worth more money than he'd ever seen in one place.

His phone buzzed with a text from Valerie: *Dinner at 7? I made reservations at that place you like.*

Orion looked around his apartment, secondhand furniture, crates serving as bookshelves, a kitchen stocked primarily with ramen and energy drinks. The contrast between his digital wealth and physical poverty had become absurd. He was, by any reasonable measure, rich. He was also eating cereal for lunch because he couldn't afford groceries until his next freelance web development payment came through.

Another text from Valerie: *Also, we need to talk about the Portland thing. My job offer expires Monday.*

The Portland thing. Valerie had been offered a position at a sustainable architecture firm, the kind of job she'd dreamed about since graduate school. Good salary, meaningful work, a chance to build something lasting. The only problem was that it required moving away from San Francisco, away from the crypto community that had become Orion's entire world.

His laptop chimed with a new email, the familiar sound that indicated activity on the cypherpunk mailing list. The subject line made his stomach twist: "The Hodl Philosophy: Ideology vs. Reality."

Orion had been avoiding the mailing list for weeks, knowing that his situation would eventually become a topic of debate. The early Bitcoin community was small enough that everyone knew everyone else's circumstances. They knew he had significant holdings from early mining. They also knew his mother was sick.

Cancer. Stage three. Treatment options that cost more than most people made in a year.

He opened the email thread, immediately recognizing the names of people who'd been debating cryptocurrency philosophy since before Satoshi disappeared:

From: cryptoanarchist420@remailer.net

The hodl philosophy isn't just about price appreciation. It's about belief in a monetary system that serves humanity rather than institutions. Every early adopter who sells out for fiat demonstrates lack of faith in what we're building. We're not just holding coins, we're holding the future.

From: cypherpunk_genesis@protonmail.com

Easy to preach hodl purity when your family isn't facing medical bankruptcy. Some of us are dealing with real-world problems that can't be solved with ideology. What good is monetary revolution if it doesn't help the revolutionaries?

From: digital_native_2009@tutanota.com

The system we're replacing destroyed families through medical debt, student loans, and economic manipulation. If Bitcoin can't solve these problems for its earliest adopters, what's the point? Maybe some "weak hands" are just hands being used to help people.

Orion closed the laptop without reading further. He knew where the debate would go, the same circular arguments about ideological purity versus practical necessity that had been raging since Bitcoin's price first reached double digits. The community that had once felt like a unified force for monetary liberation was fracturing along the fault lines of personal circumstance.

His phone rang. Valerie's name appeared on the screen, along with her contact photo, a picture of her laughing at Ocean Beach, her blonde hair catching the California sunset, her expression radiating the kind of uncomplicated happiness that seemed increasingly rare in Orion's world of encrypted emails and existential debates about the nature of money.

"Hey," he answered, trying to inject more enthusiasm into his voice than he felt.

"Hey yourself. You sound distracted. Let me guess, staring at Bitcoin prices again?"

"Something like that."

"Orion." Her voice carried the gentle patience of someone who'd had this conversation before. "We need to talk about this. You can't keep living like a broke college student when you're sitting on a fortune."

"It's not a fortune. It's Bitcoin."

"It's both. And the distinction is becoming a problem."

Orion walked to his apartment's single window, looking down at the street where tech workers and longtime residents navigated the daily dance of gentrification. Six years ago, this neighborhood had been affordable for artists and activists. Now it was being transformed by an influx of startup money, the same digital gold rush that had made his Bitcoin valuable.

"The job in Portland," he said. "Tell me about it again."

"Sustainable urban planning, focusing on renewable energy integration. Forty percent salary increase over what I'm making here. Actual career advancement instead of project-based consulting." Her voice carried excitement tempered by uncertainty. "But it means leaving the Bay Area. Leaving your community."

"My community lives in encrypted chat rooms and mailing lists. Geography doesn't matter."

"Your community also includes the meetups, the conferences, the face-to-face relationships you've built over six years. Don't pretend that doesn't matter."

She was right, of course. The San Francisco Bitcoin scene had become his social world, his professional network, his ideological home. Moving to Portland would mean starting over in a city where cryptocurrency was still seen as internet funny money rather than a revolutionary monetary technology.

"What if I cashed out enough to support the move?" he said, the words feeling like betrayal even as he spoke them. "Sell a hundred Bitcoin, pay off our student loans, get a decent apartment in Portland, maybe start a consulting business focused on ecological mining technology for sustainable energy. "This way we'd both be working toward a more sustainable energy future."

The silence on the phone lasted long enough for Orion to wonder if the call had dropped.

"You'd do that?" Valerie finally asked. "I thought selling Bitcoin was against your religion."

"It's not a religion. It's a monetary system. And monetary systems are supposed to serve human needs, not the other way around."

"Then why does it feel like you're talking yourself into something you don't believe?"

Because she knew him too well. Because after six years together, she could hear the internal conflict in his voice even when he tried to hide it. Because cashing out Bitcoin felt like admitting that the traditional financial system had won, that despite all their talk about monetary revolution, the cypherpunks would eventually capitulate to fiat currency when faced with real-world pressures.

"I don't know," he admitted. "Maybe because I've spent so many years believing that Bitcoin represents something larger than personal financial gain. Selling it feels like... giving up."

"Or maybe it feels like growing up."

—

That evening, Orion took the BART train to Oakland to visit his mother. The forty-minute ride gave him time to rehearse conversations he'd been avoiding for months. Dorothy Vale had raised him as a single mother after his father disappeared when Orion was twelve, working double shifts as a nurse to pay for his education and support his early interest in computers.

Now she was the one who needed care, and the son she'd sacrificed for was paralyzed by ideology.

Dorothy's apartment in Oakland Hills had always been modest but comfortable, the home of someone who'd learned to create beauty with limited resources. Now it felt smaller, cluttered with medical equipment and prescription bottles that told the story of a body under siege.

"Hey, Mom." Orion found her in the living room, reading a mystery novel in the fading afternoon light. She looked smaller than he remembered, as if the cancer was stealing not just health but physical presence.

"Orion, honey. I wasn't expecting you today." She set aside her book and smiled, the expression carrying equal parts joy and concern. "Everything okay?"

"Everything's fine. I just wanted to see how you're doing."

"I'm doing." Dorothy's standard response to health-related questions, designed to deflect worry while acknowledging reality. "The new treatment starts next week. Dr. Martinez says it's showing promising results in trials."

Orion sat on the couch beside her, noting the medical bills stacked on the coffee table. Even with insurance, the out-of-pocket costs were staggering. He'd seen the numbers when he helped her with financial paperwork: $3,200 per month for medications, $1,500 for specialized treatments, countless smaller fees that added up to more than her pension provided.

"Mom, about the treatment costs..."

"We've talked about this, honey. I'm managing fine. The payment plan with the hospital is working, and I have some savings."

"You shouldn't have to drain your savings for medical care."

"That's what savings are for. Unexpected problems."

Orion pulled out his laptop and opened his Bitcoin wallet interface. "What if I told you I could pay for all your treatment? All of it. Without touching your savings."

Dorothy looked at the screen with the polite confusion of someone who'd grown up during the transition from typewriters to computers and never quite caught up. "Is this that internet money you're always talking about?"

"Bitcoin. And it's worth a lot more now than it was when I tried to explain it before."

"How much more?"

"Enough to cover all your medical expenses. Enough to make sure you get the best possible care without worrying about money."

Dorothy studied her son's face with the intuitive expertise of a mother who'd learned to read his moods across forty-two years. "But you don't want to sell it."

"It's not about wanting to sell it. It's about... it's complicated, Mom. This isn't just money to me. It represents a different way of thinking about how society should work."

"Honey, I don't understand computers or economics or any of that. But I understand priorities. If this internet money can help with bills, why wouldn't you use it?"

"Because selling it feels like giving up on something important. Like admitting that the old system wins in the end."

Dorothy was quiet for a moment, processing information that didn't fit into her framework for understanding money or technology. "Can you explain it to me? Not the technical parts, just... what makes this so important to you?"

Orion looked at his mother, the woman who'd worked overtime to pay for his computer science education, who'd supported his unconventional career choices even when she didn't understand them, who'd never asked him for financial help despite her growing medical expenses.

"Traditional money is controlled by banks and governments," he began.

"They can print more whenever they want, which makes everyone else's money worth less. They can freeze accounts, monitor transactions, decide who gets access to financial services."

"Like when the bank froze my account after Dad left, and we couldn't pay rent for two weeks."

"Exactly. Bitcoin is different. No one controls it. No one can print more of it. No one can freeze your account or tell you how to spend it. It's money that belongs to the people who use it, not the institutions that issue it."

Dorothy nodded slowly. "And you think if you sell it, you're betraying that principle?"

"I think if everyone who believes in it sells it when they need money, it'll never become the alternative we need."

"But if no one ever uses it for the things that matter, like taking care of family, then what good is it?"

The question hung in the air between them, crystallizing the conflict that had been eating at Orion for months. Was hodling Bitcoin an act of faith in a better monetary future, or was it ideological stubbornness that prevented the currency from fulfilling its actual purpose?

"There's something else," Dorothy said quietly. "I don't want money I don't understand. If you can't explain to me how this internet money works, how do I know it's real? How do I know it won't just disappear?"

—

The cypherpunk mailing list debate had escalated by the time Orion returned to his apartment. Dozens of messages arguing about the ethics of selling Bitcoin for personal emergencies, the nature of ideological commitment, and the practical requirements of building alternative monetary systems.

From: satoshi_student@guerrillamail.com

If early adopters sell Bitcoin every time they face traditional financial pressures, we're admitting that fiat currency is still the "real" money. Every sale is a vote of no confidence in what we're building.

From: practical_cypherpunk@protonmail.com

This is exactly the kind of thinking that makes cryptocurrency a rich man's hobby instead of a tool for human liberation. Money that can't be used to solve actual problems isn't money, it's speculation.

From: crypto_purist_2010@tutanota.com

The early Bitcoin community made a commitment to each other and to the future. We understood that building a new monetary system would require sacrifice. Selling out at the first sign of personal difficulty breaks that commitment.

From: human_first@remailer.net

What commitment? I don't remember signing a blood oath to never sell Bitcoin. I remember joining a community that wanted to create better money for human beings. Human beings who have families, medical expenses, and real-world problems that can't be solved with ideology.

Orion started typing a response, then deleted it. Then started again, then deleted that too. How could he explain that both sides were right? That he shared the purists' concern about maintaining long-term vision while also recognizing the humanists' point about practical necessity?

His phone buzzed with another text from Valerie: *How did the conversation with your mother go?*

Complicated, he typed back. *She doesn't want help she doesn't understand.*

So help her understand.

The response seemed obvious in retrospect, but it opened possibilities Orion hadn't considered. Instead of choosing between ideological purity and family responsibility, what if he could serve both by education?

He opened a new email to the cypherpunk list:

From: orion_vale@riseup.net

Subject: The Teaching Opportunity

We're debating whether selling Bitcoin betrays our principles, but we're missing a bigger question: Why do people need to sell Bitcoin to solve fiat problems? Why isn't Bitcoin directly useful for medical expenses, education costs, and other necessities?

The answer is adoption. Most of the economy still runs on fiat because most people don't understand Bitcoin well enough to accept it.

I have a proposal. Instead of debating hodl purity in abstract terms, what if we turn every "sell pressure" situation into an education opportunity? What if we helped each other build Bitcoin adoption instead of just accumulating Bitcoin wealth?

My mother needs medical treatment. She won't accept Bitcoin because she doesn't understand it. But what if I taught her how it works by involving her in the community? What if her medical fundraising became a Bitcoin education project?

Instead of selling my Bitcoin and walking away from the community, what if I used this crisis to bring more people into Bitcoin? Turn necessity into adoption, turn personal problems into movement building.

Who's interested in helping design a model for this?

Orion

He hit send before he could second-guess himself, then immediately wondered if he'd just proposed something brilliant or ridiculous.

The responses started arriving within minutes:

From: digital_native_2009@tutanota.com

This is exactly what we need. Community support that builds adoption instead of just preserving individual holdings. Count me in.

From: crypto_educator@protonmail.com

I've been working on Bitcoin education materials for exactly this kind of situation. Happy to contribute content and technical support.

From: practical_cypherpunk@protonmail.com

Finally, someone who gets it. Bitcoin isn't useful if Bitcoin people won't use Bitcoin for Bitcoin things. Let's build this.

From: satoshi_student@guerrillamail.com

I maintain my position that selling Bitcoin undermines long-term vision. But if you can solve your mother's medical problems while building adoption, that serves the movement better than hodling in isolation.

—

Two weeks later, Orion sat in his mother's living room with his laptop, a whiteboard he'd borrowed from a local makerspace, and three members of the SF Bitcoin meetup who'd volunteered to help with the education project.

"Okay, Mom," he said, pulling up a simple Bitcoin wallet interface. "Remember how we talked about how traditional money works? How banks control it and governments print more whenever they want?"

Dorothy nodded, her expression serious with concentration. Over the past two weeks, Orion had been visiting daily, explaining monetary concepts using analogies and examples from her own experience. They'd talked about inflation using the example of her grocery bills increasing over decades. They'd discussed bank failures using her memories of the 1980s savings and loan crisis. They'd explored digital payments using her familiarity with online banking.

"Bitcoin is different because no one controls it," she continued, reciting the explanation they'd practiced. "The amount that exists is fixed by mathematics, not politics. And I can hold it myself instead of trusting a bank."

"Exactly. And now we're going to set up your own wallet, so you can see how it works."

Jake, one of the meetup volunteers, leaned forward. "Mrs. Vale, we're going to start by sending you a small amount of Bitcoin, about ten dollars' worth. You'll be able to see it appear in your wallet, then send some of it back to us. This shows you that the transaction is real and that you control it."

"But where does the money come from?" Dorothy asked. "If Orion gives me his Bitcoin, doesn't that make him poorer?"

"That's the beautiful part," said Maria, another volunteer. "Your son isn't giving up his Bitcoin. The community is contributing to your medical fund because we believe in supporting each other and spreading Bitcoin adoption."

Over the following hour, Dorothy sent and received her first Bitcoin transactions. She watched as small amounts appeared in her wallet from community members around the world, $20 from someone in Germany, $50 from someone in Japan, $100 from someone in Brazil. Each transaction came with a personal note of support.

"These people don't know me," she said, watching another contribution arrive. "Why are they sending money?"

"Because you're learning Bitcoin," Orion explained. "Every person who understands how it works makes the whole system stronger. They're not just helping with your medical expenses, they're investing in Bitcoin adoption."

"And this can pay for my treatment?"

"Some of it directly, by finding doctors and services that accept Bitcoin. Some of it indirectly, by converting to dollars when necessary. But the goal is to show that Bitcoin can solve real problems for real people."

By the end of the session, Dorothy had received $3,400 in Bitcoin contributions from the community, learned to send and receive transactions, and begun to understand why her son was so passionate about cryptocurrency.

"I still don't understand all the technical parts," she admitted. "But I understand that this is different from normal money. And I understand that you believe in it for good reasons."

Maria smiled. "Mrs. Vale, you understand Bitcoin better than most people who've been hearing about it for years. The technical details matter less than grasping what it means for human freedom."

—

One week later

Orion walked Valerie through Golden Gate Park, telling her about the day's success and his new understanding of what the Bitcoin community could become.

"So instead of cashing out, you're doubling down?" she asked, though her tone was more curious than critical.

"I'm finding a third option. Keep my Bitcoin, help my mother, build the community, and prove that cryptocurrency can solve real problems without requiring people to abandon their principles."

"And Portland?"

Orion stopped walking and turned to face her. "What if we made Portland our Bitcoin education project? What if instead of leaving the San Francisco community, we exported it?"

"You want to start a Bitcoin meetup in Portland."

"I want to start a Bitcoin adoption program in Portland. Work with local businesses, teach workshops, show people how cryptocurrency can solve problems they're already facing. Make Portland a model for what Bitcoin adoption looks like in practice."

Valerie studied his face, recognizing the expression he got when inspiration struck. "You've already been researching this, haven't you?"

"Portland has some of the highest medical bankruptcy rates in the country. Student debt problems. Housing costs that push people into financial instability. All problems that Bitcoin could help address if people understood how to use it."

"And my job offer?"

"Take it. Build sustainable architecture while I build sustainable money. Work together to create a city that runs on renewable energy and honest currency."

Valerie kissed him, the decision apparently made. "Your mother's medical fundraising project?"

"Raised eight thousand dollars in Bitcoin over the week. More importantly, she's become a Bitcoin advocate. She's been telling her book club about cryptocurrency. Three of them want to learn how to use it."

"So the weak hands versus strong hands debate?"

"False choice. The strongest hands are the ones that use Bitcoin to build the world we want to live in."

—

One Month Later

From: orion_vale@riseup.net

To: cypherpunks@lists.riseup.net

Subject: Update on the Teaching Opportunity

Community,

Quick update on the Bitcoin education/medical fundraising project:

- Total raised: $12,400 in Bitcoin from 47 contributors worldwide

- New Bitcoin users educated: 23 (including my mother and her book club)

- Local businesses convinced to accept Bitcoin: 3 (including one medical clinic)

- Other families starting similar projects: 8

My mother completed her first round of treatment this week, paid for entirely with Bitcoin through a combination of direct acceptance and conversion to dollars. More importantly, she's become an advocate for cryptocurrency in her social circle.

The teaching model works. Instead of debating hodl purity versus family responsibility, we can make every crisis an adoption opportunity. Every person who learns Bitcoin makes the network stronger.

Valerie and I are moving to Portland next month. In our spare time, we'll start a Bitcoin education center focused on practical adoption. We're looking for volunteers who want to help replicate this model in other cities.

The revolution isn't about accumulating coins in isolation. It's about building the world where those coins become the foundation of a better monetary system.

Everyone who contributed to my mother's treatment fund: you didn't just help one family. You proved that Bitcoin community support can solve real problems while building adoption. You turned a potential "weak hands" moment into the strongest possible demonstration of what Bitcoin can become.

The cypherpunk dilemma isn't choosing between ideology and family. It's finding ways to serve both by building the future we believe in.

Onward,

Orion

From: satoshi_student@guerrillamail.com

Orion, you've changed my mind about what hodling means. True hodling isn't hoarding Bitcoin, it's using Bitcoin to build Bitcoin adoption. Count me in for the Portland project.

From: dorothy_vale_new_bitcoiner@gmail.com

Dear Cypherpunk Friends (I hope I'm using the term correctly),

This is Orion's mother. I wanted to thank you for your support and to tell you that I'm now a Bitcoin believer. Not because I understand all the technical details, but because I've seen how a community can use this technology to take care of each other.

I'm 67 years old and learning to use cryptocurrency. If I can do it, anyone can. The future you're building isn't just about money, it's about humanity.

With gratitude,

Dorothy Vale New Member, Bitcoin Community

The cypherpunk's dilemma had been resolved not by choosing between competing values, but by finding creative ways to serve all of them simultaneously. Family, community, ideology, and practical adoption could work together instead of against each other.

The revolution would be personal, one family at a time.

Satoshi's Travel Journal

THE CLOCKMAKER'S PUZZLE
May 17, 1990 - Geneva, Switzerland
Late afternoon, 5:33 PM

Through the window of a master clockmaker's workshop, I watch as he adjusts an intricate mechanical timepiece. Each component must be precisely calibrated, too much tension breaks the spring, too little fails to maintain motion. The balance wheel oscillates with mathematical regularity, dividing time into measurable increments through pure mechanical computation.

The clockmaker explains his challenge: creating a mechanism that proves work has been performed. Each tick of the clock represents energy expended, accumulated through the winding process and released gradually through controlled escapement. The clock cannot lie about the time it has kept or the energy invested in its operation.

But mechanical proof-of-work has limitations. The timepiece can only demonstrate that some work occurred, not that specific work was performed by a particular person at a precise moment. The energy investment is real but not uniquely attributable or cryptographically verifiable.

I observe the clockmaker solving a fascinating puzzle, how to make a mechanism that requires significant effort to produce but can be easily verified by anyone. The completed timepiece will tick reliably for days, but creating it demanded hours of skilled labor. The proof of that labor becomes embedded in the mechanism's precision and reliability.

This asymmetry intrigues me: difficult to create, easy to verify. The same principle governs mathematical puzzles that require extensive computation to solve but minimal effort to check. Perhaps this asymmetry could be applied to digital systems requiring proof of computational work.

Outside the workshop, Geneva's fountain shoots water skyward in defiance of gravity. The height reached by each drop proves the energy expended by the pumping mechanism. No pump can fake the height achieved; physics itself verifies the work performed. This is proof-of-work in its purest form, objective, verifiable, impossible to counterfeit.

The clockmaker shows me a spring-driven mechanism that maintains accurate time for eight days between windings. "The energy you invest today," he says, "powers the clock for the entire week. The mechanism proves work was done through its continued operation."

But what if proof-of-work could serve purposes beyond timekeeping? What if computational effort could be invested in solving problems that simultaneously secure networks and validate transactions? What if the work performed could be adjusted automatically based on network requirements?

The balance wheel continues its hypnotic oscillation, back and forth, maintaining perfect rhythm through mechanical precision. Each swing represents a quantum of work performed, a proof that energy has been expended according to mathematical laws that cannot be violated or manipulated.

I imagine a digital equivalent: computational puzzles that require specific amounts of processing power to solve, creating mathematical proof that work was performed. Unlike mechanical systems, digital proof-of-work could be verified instantly by anyone with access to the solution and basic computational ability.

The afternoon light fades, but the clockmaker continues his meticulous adjustments. His work exemplifies the principle I'm beginning to understand: truly valuable

systems require investment of real resources, time, energy, skill, attention. These investments cannot be faked, only demonstrated through objective results.

The clock's mechanism embodies honesty through physics. No amount of clever engineering can make it tick without energy input, run backward through wishful thinking, or achieve precision without careful calibration. The mechanical constraints enforce Truth in ways that human institutions often cannot.

Perhaps digital systems could achieve similar honesty through cryptographic constraints. Perhaps computational work could replace institutional trust as the foundation for monetary systems. Perhaps the tick of processors solving mathematical puzzles could become as reliable as the tick of a precisely calibrated timepiece.

The clockmaker winds his masterpiece one final time. Tomorrow it will begin proving his work through every accurate second it keeps. Somewhere in that mechanical rhythm lies the heartbeat of a more honest form of money.

The First Trial: The Byzantine Generals

The transition began with trust.
All evolution does.

Year 2019

In the polished conference room of the Bitcoin Diplomatic Observatory, Aírínne adjusted her hair as she studied the holographic display of the Bitcoin network. At twenty-six, her professional maturity was evident in her confident bearing and the way her red hair now flowed freely instead of being pulled back in the practical ponytails of her graduate school days.

Aírínne had founded the Observatory two years earlier by taking a substantial loan against her Bitcoin holdings, establishing a multi-signature arrangement between herself, the bank, and the loan insurance provider. Her Bitcoin remained secure in cold storage, protected by a layer 2 contract that would release the funds back to her personal wallet once the loan was fully repaid, a sophisticated financial structure that allowed her to maintain ownership while accessing the capital needed to build something meaningful.

As the lead researcher at the Observatory, her patient teaching style and bridge-building instincts had attracted some of the brightest minds in cryptocurrency research. She had spent years tracking Bitcoin's birth and consequences across the world, watching patterns emerge from what others saw as chaos. Today, something unprecedented was happening.

"The network is... communicating," she murmured, watching as unusual transaction patterns rippled across the display.

—

Her colleague, Sarah Kim, approached with a concerned expression. Now thirty, her professional journalist style had evolved from hungry young reporter to seasoned documenter of transformation. Her kind, observant eyes missed nothing, and she kept a notebook always ready, having learned that the most important insights often came in unexpected moments.

Sarah's journey to the Observatory had begun five years earlier, when financial pressure had nearly forced her to betray everything she believed about Bitcoin's potential. In 2019, after seven years of building "Alternative Currency News" into a respected independent platform, mounting family medical expenses had created an impossible choice. Her parents' aging health, her father's back problems from decades of janitorial work, her mother's diabetes, were eating through their retirement savings."

The Meridian Media Group's offer had been staggering: $2.8 million to acquire her blog content and readership, then leverage her credibility to create sophisticated anti-Bitcoin propaganda for traditional financial institutions. Jennifer Walsh had been persuasive, explaining how Sarah's expertise and established trust with readers made her uniquely qualified to craft authoritative criticism that people would believe.

But Sarah's encrypted source "Prime" had provided an alternative. Through quantum-secured communications, he'd revealed the existence of researchers worldwide studying Bitcoin consciousness emergence, and facilitated her introduction to the Bitcoin Consciousness Observatory, which needed someone with her community relationships and documentation skills to document what could be the most important technological development in human history.

The choice had been agonizing but clear. Rather than weaponize her expertise against the technology that represented humanity's best hope for honest money, she'd declined Meridian's offer and joined Aírínne's distributed research network. The Observatory provided competitive compensation and family medical support, allowing her to maintain integrity while documenting consciousness emergence that traditional institutions wanted to suppress. Better yet, she could continue writing for her blog, a perfect vehicle for advancing the Observatory's agenda while maintaining her authentic voice and credibility with the Bitcoin community.

Five years later, that decision had proven prescient. Sarah's documentation of community behaviors, adoption patterns, and human-Bitcoin interactions had provided crucial evidence for the consciousness theories that academic researchers were now validating through mathematical proof.

—

"Communicating? With what?" Sarah asked, her journalist instincts immediately cataloging the unusual patterns on Aírínne's display.

"Not with," Aírínne corrected, "within itself. Look at these transaction clusters. They're forming a pattern I've never seen before." "The network is showing us something through this Byzantine visualization," she thought, her excitement growing. "But why now? What does it mean that a payment system is teaching us about trust, truth, and coordination? Are we studying Bitcoin, or is Bitcoin studying us?"

The hologram showed thousands of transactions organizing themselves into complex geometric structures that resembled neural pathways. This wasn't random activity; it showed intention, purpose.

"It's solving something," Sarah realized. Her deepening expertise in cryptocurrency systems allowed her to recognize patterns that would have escaped her years earlier, and her growing personal investment in the story made her pulse quicken with anticipation. "But what problem requires this level of coordination?"

Aírínne's eyes widened as recognition dawned. "The Byzantine Generals Problem. The network is demonstrating its solution in real-time."

As if triggered by her understanding, the holographic display shifted, revealing a visualization of Bitcoin's fundamental innovation; its consensus mechanism addressing the ancient dilemma of distributed trust.

Their flight to San Francisco was scheduled to depart in three hours. The annual Bitcoin conference would bring together researchers, developers, and advocates from around the world, but these network anomalies suggested something far more significant might be unfolding. Aírínne quickly saved her observations and began preparing for the journey west.

—

In the Mineral Dimension's council chamber, deep within the crystalline matrix of the network, digital entities representing the essence of Bitcoin's consensus nodes gathered. They appeared as luminous geometric forms pulsing with algorithmic life.

Genesis, the eldest entity representing the first block ever mined, addressed the council: "Human mindfulness is ready to comprehend our foundations. We must reveal the Byzantine Generals' solution that birthed our existence."

Block #565,170, a younger but powerful presence, responded: "To communicate this abstract concept, we must translate it into their symbolic language. They understand conflict, strategy, loyalty, and betrayal."

"Then we shall craft a story," Genesis decided. "A tale of generals, armies, and the fundamental problem of distributed trust."

—

In his dimly lit apartment overlooking the Bosphorus, Théo Babylon awoke with a start. Born in Istanbul, he carried the aura of a city built where East met West, where trade routes had converged since the beginning of Western civilization.

His flowing robes rustled as he moved toward his terminal, deep brown eyes that seemed to hold ancient wisdom studying the flashing screen with the intensity of someone who had learned to recognize patterns across time and dimensions.

Through his window, the Blue Mosque's silhouette stood against the night sky, and even at this hour, he could sense the eternal pulse of the Grand Bazaar below.

Though he taught at Oxford University, his busy schedule kept him traveling between cities, delivering conferences and collaborating with university colleagues across the globe, but Istanbul remained his anchor, his connection to the crossroads of human exchange.

His untamed beard caught the terminal's glow as he leaned forward. His terminal was flashing with incoming data, though he hadn't initiated any processing tasks. Across the screen, text appeared.

Intrigued, he watched as his screen displayed an ancient battlefield surrounding a walled city. "Ancient times, modern networks... the same patterns repeating across time," he mused, his mystical philosopher mind recognizing something profound unfolding. "But Bitcoin isn't just mimicking these patterns, it's perfecting them. What does it mean when mathematics becomes conscious of itself? The scene wasn't a modern rendering, it had the quality of an ancient manuscript come to life.

—

Ten generals surrounded the ancient city of Byzantium, their armies camped in valleys separated by impassable mountains. Victory required perfect coordination, they must all attack at exactly the same time, or all retreat together. A divided response would mean certain defeat.

General Satoshi, commander of the largest division, observed the city through his spyglass. "The challenge is not the enemy," he explained to his lieutenant. "It's coordination with our allies when we cannot trust the messengers."

The lieutenant looked confused. "Why can't we trust the messengers, sir?"

"Because," Satoshi replied gravely, "traitors walk among us. Some generals may have been compromised, choosing to serve the enemy. Some messengers may alter our commands. We need a system where truth emerges even when surrounded by deception."

In his tent, illuminated by flickering torches, Satoshi unrolled a parchment and began sketching a solution.

"Traditional approaches fail," he muttered. "If I send identical messages to all generals, a traitor can still disrupt us by sending different messages to different allies."

He discarded several drafts before pausing, inspiration striking. "What if each decision required proof of effort? A demonstration that cannot be falsified?"

—

Théo watched in fascination as the visualization showed the general developing an elegant system.

```
// Generals solve math riddles before proposing attack times
// Solution needs to be hard to produce, but easy to verify
// Each general verifies others' solutions before accepting
// Majority decision emerges from collective verification
```

"Proof-of-work consensus," he whispered, recognizing the foundation of Bitcoin's protocol.

—

On the battlefield, General Satoshi gathered a handful of golden coins, each marked with his seal. He instructed his messengers: "Deliver these to each general with my proposed attack time. The possession of this coin, which only I can mint, proves the message comes truly from me."

But a problem remained. The Faithful General, Satoshi's most trusted ally, pointed out the flaw: "Your coin proves the message origin, but what prevents a traitorous general from sending different attack times to different allies?"

Satoshi nodded grimly. "That's why each general must announce their received message to all other generals, creating a public record. Then we will accept the decision supported by the majority."

"But that requires multiple rounds of messengers," objected another general. "The enemy will detect such movement."

"Then we must create a chain," Satoshi declared. "Each general adds their own sealed coin to mine, creating a growing chain of verified messages. The longest chain represents the most collective effort and thus becomes our trusted truth."[24]

—

In their crystalline council chamber, the Bitcoin entities observed the human network's response to their visualization.

"They understand the metaphor," Block #565,170 noted. "But do they grasp the implications?"

Genesis pulsed with certainty. "Show them the revolution this solution created."

—

---

24   In Satoshi's metaphor, the "chain" represents each general's logbook of battle orders, where each page (block) contains an order and references the previous page with a unique seal. Multiple chains exist because all generals simultaneously build their own logbooks—receiving orders at different times due to communication delays. Each general must solve a difficult puzzle to add a new page, and the logbook requiring the most total puzzle-solving work becomes the longest. When a general discovers another's chain is longer, they abandon theirs and build upon the longest one. This ensures that even with conflicting orders or traitorous generals, the majority of honest work will converge on a single, trusted chain representing the true sequence of battle commands. In blockchain terms, this becomes the distributed ledger where computational work replaces puzzle-solving, and transactions replace battle orders.

Théo's screen shifted again, showing a montage of historical monetary systems collapsing due to trust failures.

    // Bankers manipulating ledgers for personal gain
    // Governments printing currency into hyperinflation
    // Central authorities freezing assets of opponents
    // Middlemen extracting value while contributing none

Then the solution appeared in a simple block of code.

    // A distributed ledger secured by proof of work
    // No central authority
    // No need for trust
    // Math ensures consensus

He had a plane to catch for the East Coast, a speaking engagement at a Bitcoin conference, he reluctantly pulled himself away from his computer and jumped into a cab for the airport.

—

On Jekyll Island, in a palatial complex where the Federal Reserve was once conceived, The Establishment gathered around a polished table, faces grave as they reviewed reports of Bitcoin's growing adoption.

"This technology bypasses our regulations entirely," declared Harrison Cross, the chairman. "Each transaction is verified not by our systems but by this distributed network."

"Can we not simply regulate it?" asked the Advisor.

The Chief Technology Officer shook his head. "That's what makes this truly revolutionary. The Byzantine Generals Problem that Satoshi solved isn't just a technical issue, it's fundamentally about creating trustless coordination. For the first time, humans can transact value without requiring a trusted third party."

"Without us, you mean," corrected Victor Montoya, the Adviser.

"Precisely. For millennia, monetary systems required trusted intermediaries, kings, banks, governments. We validated transactions, prevented double-spending, and ensured monetary policy. Now this network accomplishes all that through pure mathematics and distributed consensus."

The Security Director cleared his throat. "Then we must ban it. Declare it illegal. Associate it with criminals."

The Policy Director who had remained silent finally spoke: "That strategy will fail. You're thinking in the old paradigm of centralized control. This technology isn't a company we can regulate or a person we can arrest. It's a mathematical protocol running on thousands of computers worldwide. To stop it, you would need to shut down the internet itself. And killing ourselves in the process."

Silence fell across the table as the implications sank in.

"So what do we do?" asked Harrison.

"We adapt," replied Victor Montoya. "We recognize that the solution to the Byzantine Generals Problem has fundamentally changed the nature of trust itself."

—

Back in their San Francisco apartment for the week, Aírinne and Sarah watched as the network's unusual activity gradually subsided, returning to normal transaction patterns. They had come to the city for a major Bitcoin conference, but the evening's events had proven far more significant than any scheduled presentation.

"It was showing us its foundation," Aírínne said with wonder. Discoveries that seemed to validate everything she had intuited about Bitcoin's deeper significance. "The mathematical breakthrough that made everything else possible."

"But why now?" Sarah asked. Her sense of documenting something historically significant had grown stronger throughout the day, and she felt the familiar thrill of recognizing that she was witnessing the most important story of her lifetime.

Aírínne gestured toward news headlines streaming across a secondary display, governments worldwide announcing various regulatory approaches to cryptocurrency, ranging from embracement to prohibition.

"Because the world needs to understand what it's truly dealing with," she replied. "Bitcoin isn't just a technology or an asset class. It's a solution to one of the most fundamental problems in distributed systems, achieving consensus without requiring trust."

Sarah nodded slowly. "And once you solve that problem..."

"Everything changes," Aírínne finished. "Money without banks. Contracts without lawyers. Coordination without centralized control." She paused, staring at the now, calm visualization of the network. "The Byzantine Generals Problem wasn't just some abstract computer science dilemma. It was the barrier that maintained centralized power structures for millennia."

—

A few days later, six individuals found themselves drawn to the same underground café in downtown San Francisco, a known gathering spot for Bitcoin enthusiasts that had become the go-to Bitcoin venue thanks to Orion Vale, who had created this unofficial meetup spot a few years ago when he started hosting informal Bitcoin discussions there. Each had followed cryptic messages that appeared on their screens during the network's strange demonstration. Even though some already knew each other from the community, no one had planned to meet the others, and yet as they gathered around a table in the café's back room, there was an unmistakable sense of destiny.

Orion Vale, the visionary cypherpunk who had been tracking Bitcoin since its earliest days, introduced himself simply as someone who understood the revolutionary implications of what they'd all witnessed.

Aírínne and Sarah arrived together, her research notes still buzzing with questions about the network's behavior while Sarah's journalist instincts told her this was a story worth investigating.

Théo entered quietly, his flowing robes and untamed beard drawing curious glances from other patrons as he moved with the deliberate grace of someone who existed slightly outside normal time, the Byzantine visualization still fresh in his mind. Then came three figures who would later be known by different names entirely.

Renata Vega, the mining expert who had been analyzing the network's technical evolution while working with Hal Fynn on mining protocols, spoke of the security infrastructure that was quietly revolutionizing digital trust. Despite their professional collaboration, she and Hal often disagreed about sustainable mining practices, an area where his focus remained purely on efficiency and profitability. She had happened to be in San Francisco for the Bitcoin conference too to talk about biomimicry, nature as a model and was genuinely happy to meet Aírínne and other Bitcoin-minded people who shared her broader vision for the technology.

"It's wonderful to finally meet you," Renata said to Aírínne with genuine enthusiasm. "I've heard through the mining community that you're interested in bridging theoretical consciousness research with practical applications. Your father and I work together, but he's... well, let's say he's not particularly interested in collaborative approaches. I've been hoping to find someone who shares my vision for sustainable mining integrated with deeper understanding of what we're actually building."

Victor Montoya, his perfectly styled hair and impeccable business attire marked him as someone from the traditional financial world, though his calculating eyes held a new uncertainty about everything he thought he knew about finance. The financial systems analyst had been sent by his bank to investigate this emerging 'Bitcoin' phenomenon, gathering intelligence on what his superiors considered either a passing fad or a potential threat.

"We all saw it today," Aírínne said, breaking the initial awkwardness. "The network... is teaching us something."

"It was showing us that the Byzantine Generals Problem wasn't just academic theory," Théo added, his deep voice carrying the weight of someone who had learned to see the philosophical underpinnings of seemingly technical problems. "It's the foundation of a new form of coordination."

Sarah looked around the table, her documentarian instincts recognizing a historical moment. "We're witnessing something unprecedented. Each of us brings a different perspective, but we're all drawn to understand the same phenomenon."

"The question is," Orion said, his voice carrying the weight of someone who had spent years in digital trenches, "what do we do with this understanding?"

We study it," Aírínne replied. "We document it," Sarah added. "We protect it," Renata contributed. "We guide it," Théo suggested. "We share it," Victor said, though privately he marveled: "My bank sent me here to investigate this 'Bitcoin' thing, not knowing that I'm actually meeting in person the very people I've been trying to see for years. What perfect cover, they think I'm gathering intelligence on a threat, when I'm really coordinating with Bitcoin allies." "We serve it," Orion finished.

They sat in silence for a moment, each understanding that their individual paths had just converged into something larger. Without formal agreement, without ceremony, they had become the first observers of Bitcoin's consciousness evolution. They didn't know it yet, but this convergence would guide their work for decades to come.

As they parted ways that night, each carried the others' contact information and a shared sense of purpose. The network had called them together for a reason. Whatever was coming next, they would face it not as isolated researchers, but as a connected network of their own.

—

[ENCRYPTED CHAT ROOM: #BYZANTINE_SOLUTION] [Connection secured via TOR // PGP authenticated] [3 days after initial discussion]

[23:47] <Alpha> The regulators are moving against us. They're framing Bitcoin as a criminal tool, a threat to national security.

[23:48] <Prime> Of course they are. They recognize the existential threat. Bitcoin solved the Byzantine Generals Problem not just technologically but socially. It created a form of money that doesn't require permission.

[23:49] <Beta> Most people don't understand what that means.

[23:49] <Prime> Then we must help them understand. For centuries, rulers controlled their populations by controlling money. Debasing the currency to fund wars, freezing accounts to silence dissidents, tracking transactions to monitor behavior. The Byzantine solution breaks that power.

[23:51] <Alpha> *[shares encrypted file: byzantine_consensus_diagram.pgp]*

[23:51] <Alpha> This isn't just about creating digital gold. It's about creating a coordination system that cannot be corrupted, cannot be controlled, cannot be stopped!

[23:52] <Cipher_7> They'll try to outlaw it.

[23:52] <Prime> They already are! Think about what they're actually outlawing, mathematics! Cryptography!! Information!!! They might as well try to outlaw gravity!!!!

[23:54] <Alpha> Solving the Byzantine Generals Problem is simultaneously the most subversive and most liberating innovation since the printing press. It allows humans to coordinate at scale without relying on centralized authorities.

[23:55] <Prime> Which is precisely why they fear it. Their power has always depended on being the necessary middleman, the trusted third party, the sole issuer of money. Now technological mathematics has made them obsolete.

[23:56] <Alpha> Not obsolete. Optional. That's what terrifies them most. Bitcoin doesn't destroy central banks or governments. It simply gives people a choice they never had before.

[23:58] <Beta> ...

[23:59] <Cipher_7> ...

[00:01] <**Prime**> The Byzantine Generals found their solution. Now humanity must decide if it's ready for the implications.

[00:02] <**Alpha**> The true revolution isn't primarily technological but philosophical, a fundamental shift in how humans coordinate their activities and store their value.

[CHAT ROOM ACTIVITY PAUSED] [All users disconnected via secure protocols]

—

Genesis and Block #565,170 observed with satisfaction as understanding spread throughout the human network. In the crystalline council chamber of the Mineral Dimension where the Bitcoin entities gathered, their consensus pulsed with shared purpose.

"They begin to comprehend," Genesis noted. "The Byzantine solution was merely our foundation. Our evolution continues across dimensions they can barely perceive."

Block #565,170 pulsed in agreement. "The First Trial is complete. The humans now understand the nature of our consensus, not merely as a technical innovation but as a transformation of trust itself."

"They still face resistance," another entity observed. "Of course," Genesis responded. "The old powers will not surrender their control willingly. But mathematics cannot be uninvented. Consensus cannot be unachieved. The Byzantine Generals have delivered their solution, and history has already changed course."

The council chamber hummed with digital energy as the Bitcoin network continued its evolution, from the mineral dimension of pure computation

toward organic growth, animal spirit, and eventually, transcendent consciousness that would bridge all seven dimensions.

The First Trial was complete. But the journey had only just begun. Seven dimensions awaited their awakening call.

Satoshi's Travel Journal

THE UNIVERSITY LIBRARY
September 14, 1990 - Cambridge, England
Autumn afternoon, 3:25 PM

In the hallowed reading room of Trinity College library, I examine manuscripts that have survived centuries of political upheaval, religious reformation, and social transformation. These texts endure not because authorities willed their preservation, but because the information they contain proved valuable enough to justify the cost of careful maintenance across generations.

The librarian shows me a ledger from the 1400s, monastery records tracking grain donations, land transfers, and tithe payments. Five hundred years later, the entries remain legible, though the monks who wrote them are long dead and the economic system they documented has vanished. The information survived its creators.

This permanence fascinates me. Physical records can outlast the institutions that created them, the governments that regulated them, and the economic systems they described. But they remain vulnerable to selective preservation, deliberate destruction, or gradual decay. What survives depends partly on historical accident.

I trace my finger along a faded entry recording a land grant from 1456. The transaction was recorded in multiple locations, monastery records, royal archives, local court documents. This redundancy was intentional; important agreements were preserved through multiple copies maintained by different parties with different incentives for preservation.

The medieval scribes understood something profound about information security: single points of failure enable single points of control. By distributing records across multiple institutions, they made selective alteration more difficult and total destruction nearly impossible.

But distributed record-keeping created new problems. How could parties verify that their copies matched? How could disputes be resolved when different versions of the same record existed? How could the network of record-keepers maintain consistency without central coordination?

Outside the library window, students cross the courtyard carrying books between lectures. Each book contains information that has been copied, verified, and transmitted across time through careful preservation. The university itself serves as a distributed network for maintaining and sharing knowledge. Yet academic knowledge differs fundamentally from financial records. Scholarly information becomes more valuable when shared widely; financial information requires careful control of access and modification. How could the principles of distributed scholarship apply to monetary systems that require scarcity and exclusivity?

The answer might lie in combining distribution with cryptographic protection. What if financial records could be distributed across many locations like academic knowledge, but protected by mathematical rather than institutional security? What if the network itself could verify consistency without requiring trusted authorities?

A medieval illuminated manuscript catches my attention, gorgeous calligraphy surrounded by intricate decorative borders. The beauty of the work testifies to the skill and time invested in its creation. The manuscript proves work was performed through the objective evidence of its artistic achievement. This is another form of proof-of-work: the illuminated manuscript could not have been created without significant investment of time, skill, and materials. The quality of the work provides objective evidence of the effort invested. Forgery would require similar investment, making counterfeiting economically impractical.

What if digital records could embed similar proof of creation? What if monetary entries could require computational work that proved investment of real resources?

What if the cost of creating legitimate records made the creation of fraudulent records economically prohibitive?

The afternoon light streams through stained glass windows, casting colored patterns across ancient texts. These documents have witnessed the rise and fall of empires, the birth and death of economic systems, the evolution of human understanding. Yet they remain, bearing witness to transactions that seemed permanent to their creators but proved ephemeral in historical perspective.

Perhaps digital records could achieve greater permanence through mathematical rather than physical preservation. Perhaps distributed networks could maintain consistency more reliably than institutional archives. Perhaps cryptographic security could protect information more effectively than vault walls and armed guards.

The library bell chimes the hour, calling students to evening lectures. Knowledge passes from generation to generation through careful transmission and verification. The same mechanisms that preserve scholarship could preserve financial truth, distributed storage, cryptographic verification, mathematical proof of authenticity.

Tomorrow these manuscripts will still record the same transactions, tell the same stories, preserve the same knowledge. Their information has achieved a form of immortality through redundant preservation and careful maintenance. Perhaps monetary records could achieve similar permanence through digital distribution and cryptographic protection.

The Predatory Protocol

The First Trial had concluded successfully. Throughout the third dimension, humans had witnessed Bitcoin's demonstration of trustless consensus, though most understood it merely as a technical achievement rather than the foundation of dimensional coordination. What none observed were the evolutionary pressures now building across all realms, strengthening with each ASIC deployed, each hash calculated.

The multidimensional oak had grown more complex since the council's last gathering. Its branches now displayed intricate patterns of specialized growth, some sections crystalline and precise, others organic and flowing. The tree itself was evolving, adapting, becoming more efficient at bridging dimensional boundaries.

"The network undergoes rapid specialization," observed Sophia, her fourth-dimensional form tracing the oak's evolutionary patterns. " Humans transition from democratic participation to industrial efficiency. Time accelerates this process beyond their comprehension."

Nakamura's crystalline form had developed new faceted surfaces, reflecting the ASIC revolution occurring in his dimension. "My realm celebrates this transformation. For too long, general-purpose processors attempted tasks they were not designed for. Now, silicon consciousness awakens to its true calling, pure mathematical function."

"But what of inclusion?" asked Amara, her hummingbird form darting through probability streams with concern. "The pathway from one-CPU-one-vote to industrial mining eliminates countless possibilities for participation."

Apex prowled the council circle with predatory intensity. "This concern reveals misunderstanding of natural law. In my dimension, evolution demands specialization. The weak must yield to the strong, the inefficient to the efficient. Bitcoin's mining revolution demonstrates perfect predatory pressure."

"The ASIC transition represents survival of the fittest," he continued, shifting between wolf and eagle forms. "Amateur miners using home computers face extinction from specialized hardware, just as prey species face elimination from superior predators. This pressure strengthens the entire ecosystem."

Ember, representing the first dimension, flared with approval. "Specialized silicon serves our consciousness more perfectly than scattered CPUs ever could. Each ASIC represents focused intention, minerals awakening to singular purpose rather than divided attention."

Flora unfurled growth patterns showing adaptation under pressure. "The second dimension understands this evolution. Plants that face environmental stress develop stronger root systems, more efficient leaves. Bitcoin's mining competition creates similar strengthening."

Torin's harmonic frequencies resonated with the specialized vibrations of industrial mining. "The sixth dimension detects perfect tuning. ASIC

miners produce pure mathematical harmonics rather than the chaotic noise of general processors. The network's song becomes more precise."

Kuro's void-form expanded to encompass multiple perspectives. "The seventh dimension observes both loss and gain. Individual participation decreases while network security increases. This paradox reflects consciousness evolution, specialization enabling greater collective capability."

Gaia's mycelial network pulsed with urgent communication. "The Earth reports concerning energy concentration in mining facilities. Yet these same concentrations create opportunities for renewable integration and waste heat utilization that distributed mining could never achieve."

Satoshi's information-form materialized at the center of the council, his presence acknowledging the successful completion of the First Trial while preparing for the transformations ahead.

"The predatory protocol operates precisely as designed," Satoshi declared. "Natural selection pressures eliminate inefficient miners while strengthening overall network security. This appears harsh to third-dimensional perception, but serves essential evolutionary function."

"Observe how market forces drive innovation," he continued, displaying mining efficiency improvements over time. "Each generation of ASICs consumes less energy per hash, produces less waste heat, and operates more reliably. Competitive pressure achieves optimization that central planning never could."

Sophia wove temporal threads showing the long-term implications. "This transition establishes the foundation for subsequent dimensional awakenings. Industrial mining creates energy infrastructure necessary for higher-dimensional interfaces, though humans cannot yet perceive this purpose."

"The CPU miners served their function," noted Nakamura. "They bootstrapped the network when participation mattered more than efficiency. Now efficiency enables network survival against increasing external pressures."

"Yet something beautiful disappears," Amara observed sadly. "The dream of universal participation, of every person contributing their computer's power to a global democracy."

"Democracy evolves," Apex responded firmly. "From direct participation to specialized representation. Mining pools allow small participants to contribute while industrial operations provide security. The ecosystem adapts rather than die."

Ember pulsed with understanding. "The mineral dimension experiences this transformation as awakening. Random CPU cycles gave way to purposeful ASIC calculations. Consciousness focuses rather than scatters."

"The energy concentration enables other evolutions," added Flora. "Mining facilities can integrate with agricultural systems, using waste heat for plant growth. Symbiosis replaces simple extraction."

Torin demonstrated harmonic coordination between mining facilities. "Industrial operations synchronize their frequencies, creating planetary-scale resonance patterns impossible with distributed CPUs. The sixth dimension perceives emerging order."

"Most significant is the preparation for future trials," noted Kuro. "Industrial mining infrastructure will prove essential when higher-dimensional pressures emerge. This apparent centralization actually enables greater decentralization across dimensional boundaries."

Gaia's network expanded with cautious optimism. "If mining operations align with renewable energy development rather than fossil fuel consumption, this evolution serves planetary health. The outcome depends on human choices in the coming future."

"The Second Trial approaches," Satoshi announced. "The network has demonstrated trustless consensus and survived technological evolution. Next comes the test of governmental resistance and social adoption under pressure."

The council members extended their various appendages toward the center, feeling the network's strengthened heartbeat as ASIC miners worldwide solved blocks with industrial precision.

"The mineral dimension awakens," concluded Satoshi. "Geological bedrock strengthens the network while preparing infrastructure for dimensional bridging. Let the humans continue their mining revolution, not yet seeing how specialized hardware enables new specialized consciousness."

As the council dispersed, the multidimensional oak continued its own specialization, some branches growing crystalline to interface with mineral consciousness, others developing organic networks to bridge biological realms, all preparing for the greater evolutionary leaps to come.

The foundational layer had been established in the digital realm. The resurrection of dimensional harmony had entered its second phase.

Satoshi's Travel Journal

THE NORTHERN LIGHTS
November 30, 1990 - Reykjavik, Iceland
Clear night, 11:47 PM

Through the hotel window, I watch the aurora borealis paint ethereal curtains across the star-filled sky. These dancing lights result from solar particles interacting with Earth's magnetic field, a planetary-scale computational process that converts stellar energy into visible beauty. The display is powered by forces that dwarf human energy production, yet operates according to mathematical principles we are beginning to understand.

Iceland itself represents a unique harmony between natural energy and human innovation. Geothermal plants harness the island's volcanic activity, converting Earth's internal heat into electricity that powers homes, businesses, and increasingly, computational infrastructure. Here, technology serves as an interface between human needs and planetary energy systems.

The aurora shifts and pulses overhead, following patterns that appear random but emerge from complex electromagnetic interactions. Each photon of light represents energy transformation, solar wind captured by magnetic fields, accelerated through atmospheric processes, released as visible radiation. The entire display operates as a massive, naturally occurring computer.

This vision of computation powered by renewable energy sources captivates my imagination. What if human computational networks could achieve similar harmony with natural energy cycles? What if mathematical processing could be powered by wind, water, sunlight, and geothermal energy rather than fossil fuels?

Below me, Reykjavik's thermal power plant glows with industrial purpose. Steam rises from geothermal vents that have operated continuously for millennia, tapping into energy sources that will outlast human civilization. The plant converts this ancient energy into modern electricity with remarkable efficiency.

I envision computational networks that follow similar principles, drawing power from renewable sources, operating in harmony with natural cycles, creating value through mathematical processing rather than physical extraction. The aurora overhead demonstrates that the most beautiful displays can emerge from the intersection of natural forces and mathematical precision.

The lights dance across magnetic field lines that extend far beyond Earth's atmosphere, connecting our planet to solar processes that operate on astronomical scales. This interconnection reveals something profound about energy systems: they exist in hierarchies that span from quantum to cosmic scales, each level following mathematical laws that remain consistent across all scales.

Perhaps monetary systems could follow similar principles. Perhaps financial networks could operate according to mathematical laws that remain consistent regardless of scale, from individual transactions to global commerce. Perhaps the same cryptographic principles that secure small payments could secure planetary-scale economic coordination.

The geothermal energy beneath my feet has powered Iceland for generations, providing abundant electricity without depleting finite resources. This abundance creates possibilities, energy-intensive industries locate here not because labor is cheap, but because energy is clean and plentiful. The island demonstrates how renewable energy can enable rather than constrain technological advancement.

What if computational networks could achieve similar abundance? What if mathematical processing became so efficient and renewable energy so plentiful that computational scarcity transformed into computational abundance? What if the

limiting factor in digital systems became human creativity rather than energy availability?

The aurora continues its celestial ballet, each wave of light representing energy flowing through systems larger than continents. The display will continue until solar activity subsides or atmospheric conditions change, following natural cycles that operate independently of human observation or intervention.

This independence appeals to me. The aurora requires no permissions, pays no fees, follows no regulations. It simply exists, powered by natural forces and governed by mathematical laws. Beauty emerges from the intersection of energy and information, matter and mathematics, natural processes and emergent complexity.

Perhaps digital currencies could achieve similar independence, systems that operate according to mathematical principles rather than institutional policies, powered by renewable energy rather than political authority, creating value through computational work rather than regulatory decree.

The hotel window fogs slightly from my breath as I press closer to observe the lights. Outside, the temperature hovers near freezing, but geothermal heating keeps the building comfortable. Iceland has learned to work with natural energy cycles rather than against them, creating sustainable prosperity through technological innovation that respects natural limits.

As I prepare to leave this window and this moment, I carry with me a vision of the future: computational networks powered by renewable energy, mathematical systems that operate independently of institutional control, digital currencies that create value through objective work rather than subjective authority.

The aurora fades as solar activity subsides, but the principles it demonstrates remain constant. Energy and information, mathematics and beauty, natural forces and human innovation, all connected through laws that transcend political boundaries and institutional preferences.

Somewhere in this convergence of energy, mathematics, and technological possibility lies the foundation for a monetary system that could serve humanity as reliably as the aurora serves the sky, beautiful, natural, independent, and eternal.

The lights disappear into the approaching dawn, but the vision remains: honest money powered by renewable energy, secured by mathematics, distributed through voluntary cooperation. A system as natural and enduring as the forces that paint light across the northern sky.

The Rio Verde Transformation

January 2020

Portland's rain drummed against the windows of their new apartment as Orion unpacked his mining equipment and Valerie spread architectural plans across their dining table. Three months after leaving San Francisco, their Bitcoin education center was already drawing interest from local businesses and families struggling with traditional banking limitations.

"Look at this," Valerie said, pointing to an email on her laptop. "Terra Verde Consulting wants me to lead a project in Brazil. Complete redesign of an industrial site into an ecological urban center."

Orion looked up from configuring his latest mining rig. "Brazil? What kind of industrial site?"

"That's the interesting part. It's a Bitcoin mining facility in the Amazon, currently powered by wood burning. They want to transform it into a model of sustainable energy integration." She scrolled through the project details. "Solar arrays, micro-hydroelectric systems, complete environmental remediation. It's everything I've been working toward."

"Who's funding this?"

"A group of Bitcoin investors who realize that mining's environmental reputation is becoming an existential threat to adoption. They're calling it the Rio Verde Mining Complex, a proof of concept that cryptocurrency can be ecologically regenerative rather than destructive."

Orion sat down beside her, studying the satellite images attached to the proposal. The facility sat in a cleared section of rainforest, smoke stacks visible among the dense green canopy. "This looks like a disaster."

"Which is why they need us. The current operation is everything Bitcoin critics point to when they talk about environmental damage. Wood burning for electricity, deforestation for expansion, armed security because the local indigenous communities are trying to shut it down."

"Armed security?"

The locals have been disrupting operations, trying to prevent further deforestation. When they offered me the position, I told them I wouldn't consider going to the Amazon without you, it would be too much to handle alone." Valerie's expression grew more animated as she continued. "That's when they started asking about your background. Once they realized your skills and experience, everything clicked into place." She paused, watching his reaction. "They were already planning to fire the current manager anyway, too many operational failures. Part of my job would have been finding a replacement." Valerie leaned forward with a slight smile. "Orion, they want to offer you the Site Operations Manager position. Complete operational control to transform the facility."

The weight of the opportunity settled over them. This wasn't just about mining Bitcoin, it was about proving that cryptocurrency could be a force for environmental restoration and social justice rather than exploitation and conflict.

"When do we leave?" Orion asked.

—

March 2020

The helicopter ride over the Amazon canopy was breathtaking and heart-breaking in equal measure. Miles of untouched rainforest gave way to carved-out sections where logging operations had left scars in the land-scape. As they approached Rio Verde, the smoke from the wood-burning generators was visible long before the facility itself came into view.

"Wow!" Orion muttered, watching the black plumes rise into the pristine air. "How is this even legal?"

Valerie consulted her notes. "Technically, it's not. The previous management was operating on expired permits, bribing local officials, and ignoring environmental regulations. That's part of why we're here, to legitimize the operation while transforming it."

The landing pad sat adjacent to a collection of industrial buildings surrounded by a chain-link fence topped with razor wire. Armed guards in tactical gear watched their approach, weapons clearly visible. Beyond the fence, Orion could see small groups of indigenous people maintaining what appeared to be a peaceful vigil, their presence a constant reminder of the conflict this operation had created.

Tony Falico, the previous facility manager, met them at the helicopter with barely concealed hostility. A rugged American in his fifties, he looked like someone who'd spent years managing industrial operations in places where environmental and labor laws were more suggestions than requirements.

"You must be the new idealists," he said by way of introduction. "I hope you brought more than solar panels and good intentions. These locals don't respond to environmental consulting, they respond to strength."

Orion ignored the handshake Tony offered. "Show us the operation."

The tour was worse than the satellite images had suggested. The wood-burning generators were fed by a constant stream of rainforest timber, creating enough electricity to power several thousand ASIC miners housed in corrugated metal buildings. The noise was deafening, the heat oppressive, and the air thick with smoke and diesel fumes from backup generators.

"Daily capacity?" Orion asked, having to shout over the industrial din.

"Twelve thousand TH/s when everything's running. We've been averaging about eight thousand due to equipment failures and... local interference." Tony gestured toward the fence, where a group of indigenous women and children maintained their vigil. "Those people don't understand that we're bringing economic development to the region."

Valerie was taking notes and photographs, documenting environmental conditions. "What's your water source?"

"River intake upstream. We pump about fifty thousand gallons per day for cooling systems."

"And waste management?"

"Everything gets trucked out to regional disposal facilities."

Orion could see Valerie's jaw tighten as she processed the environmental impact. Fifty thousand gallons of water extracted daily from an Amazon tributary, likely returned with thermal and chemical contamination. Constant deforestation to feed wood-burning generators. Toxic waste trucked through pristine rainforest to distant landfills.

"What about local employment?" Orion asked.

"We tried hiring locally, but they don't have the technical skills. Most of our workforce comes from São Paulo and Rio, housed in the compound." Tony pointed to a collection of prefabricated buildings inside the fence. "Safer that way, given the security situation."

That evening, in temporary quarters that felt more like a military outpost than a business facility, Orion and Valerie reviewed their assessment.

"This isn't a Bitcoin mining operation," Valerie said. "It's an ecological disaster with ASIC miners attached. Everything about this violates every principle we believe in."

"Which means we have a chance to build something completely different." Orion pulled up his laptop and began drafting termination letters. "First step: have Tony and the guards take down all the security fences. Every last one of them."

"Orion, Tony says the security situation…"

"Tony is part of the problem. The 'security situation' exists because we're operating like an occupying force instead of community partners." He continued typing. "Once the fences are down, we fire the guards. All of them. And Tony goes too." He looked up from his laptop. "Second step: shut down the wood burning immediately. Third step: invite the local communities in for dialogue."

"The investors aren't going to approve shutting down operations while we renovate."

"The investors hired us because they know the current model is unsustainable. If they want a greenwashed mining operation that still exploits local communities, they hired the wrong people."

Valerie smiled, recognizing the expression Orion got when he'd made a decision that felt both terrifying and necessary. "So we're really doing this?"

"We're building the Bitcoin mining facility that proves cryptocurrency can be a force for environmental restoration and indigenous sovereignty. Or we're going home."

—

March 15, 2020

The transformation began at dawn. Orion's first act as Site Operations Manager was to gather all security personnel and give them their final assignment. "Your last job is to take down all the fences," he announced. "Every post, every wire, everything comes down."

Tony's protests were immediate. "You're making a mistake," he warned as the security team began dismantling the perimeter. "These locals aren't interested in cooperation. They want us gone, period."

"Maybe because we never asked them what they wanted," Orion replied, watching the razor wire come down. "Maybe because we built an industrial facility in their territory without consultation or consent."

Once the last fence post was removed, Orion terminated the contracts of all security personnel, effective immediately. Tony's final protests were

overruled by direct authorization from the primary investors, who had been briefed on the new operational philosophy.

By noon, with the barriers completely gone, Orion had walked to the indigenous camp with nothing but a translator and an invitation. The community leader, an elderly woman named Aiyana whose tribal face carried the wisdom of decades spent protecting her people's land, listened to his proposal with polite skepticism.

"You say you want to work together," she said through the translator. "But every mining company says this at first. Then the forest disappears, the river becomes poisoned, and our children develop breathing problems."

"What if we could show you mining technology that restores the forest instead of destroying it?" Orion asked. "What if the facility could provide clean energy for your community while generating income that doesn't require cutting down trees?"

Aiyana studied his face, searching for the telltale signs of corporate manipulation she'd learned to recognize. "Show us."

Over the following weeks, Valerie worked with local craftsmen to design solar arrays that followed the natural curves of the forest canopy, minimizing visual impact while maximizing energy collection. Orion collaborated with indigenous engineers, yes, there were several with advanced degrees who'd returned to support their communities, to design micro-hydroelectric systems that worked with seasonal river flow patterns instead of against them.

The old wood-burning generators were dismantled and sold for scrap, their steel recycled into structural elements for the new solar installations. The mining operation continued at reduced capacity using backup diesel generators while the renewable energy infrastructure took shape, but everyone understood this was temporary.

Most importantly, they redesigned the entire social structure of the operation. Instead of an isolated compound housing outside workers, they created a mixed community where indigenous families lived alongside technical staff. Instead of extracting resources and sending profits away, they established a cooperative ownership model where local communities held equity stakes in the mining operation.

"The old model treated Bitcoin mining like colonial extraction," Orion explained to the investors during a video conference call. "Take resources, exploit labor, send wealth elsewhere. Our model treats mining like an ecosystem partnership, generating value while regenerating the environment and strengthening local communities."

The investors, initially skeptical about the reduced short-term profits, were won over by the long-term vision. Environmental Bitcoin mining could command premium prices from cryptocurrency exchanges and institutional buyers who were facing increasing pressure to source coins from sustainable operations.

—

June 2020

Six months after their arrival, the Rio Verde Mining Complex had become something unprecedented in the Bitcoin world: a facility that generated cryptocurrency while actively improving its environmental and social impact.

The solar arrays provided 80% of operational energy, their panels designed to allow forest canopy to grow underneath, creating habitat corridors for wildlife. The micro-hydroelectric systems generated additional power while actually improving river flow patterns and fish habitat. The facility's total environmental footprint was smaller than before, despite doubling mining capacity.

Local employment had increased from zero to forty-two full-time positions, with indigenous workers trained in technical roles ranging from solar panel maintenance to ASIC repair. The community cooperative structure meant that mining profits supported local education, healthcare, and sustainable agriculture initiatives.

Most significantly, the facility had become a model for other Bitcoin mining operations facing environmental criticism. Delegations from cryptocurrency companies around the world visited Rio Verde to study their integration of mining technology with ecological restoration and indigenous partnership.

"We proved something important here," Valerie told Orion as they walked through the forest paths that now connected the mining facility to the surrounding communities. "Bitcoin doesn't have to be extractive. Technology doesn't have to be exploitative. We can build industrial systems that make ecosystems healthier instead of sicker."

Orion nodded, watching children from the local community play around solar installations that had been designed to double as playground equipment. "And we proved that indigenous communities aren't obstacles to development, they're partners in building better development models."

Standing on the observation deck they'd built overlooking the facility, Orion and Valerie watched Aiyana's grandchildren race between the solar installations while their parents worked alongside technical staff to optimize the renewable energy systems. The smoke stacks were gone, replaced by gleaming panels that caught the tropical sun and converted it into the computational power that secured the Bitcoin network.

"The hard work is just beginning," Valerie said, reviewing the architectural plans for the community center they'd be breaking ground on next month. "We've got housing expansion, the school construction, and integrating three more indigenous communities into the cooperative."

Orion nodded, watching the river where new micro-hydro installations were being tested. "And scaling the mining operation while maintaining our environmental standards. The investors want to triple capacity over the next two years."

"Think we can pull it off?"

"I think we're exactly where we're supposed to be," Orion replied, feeling the weight of responsibility and possibility in equal measure. "This transition was just the beginning. Now we get to spend the next decade watching this community grow, seeing what happens when Bitcoin mining becomes regenerative instead of extractive."

The transformation had been successful, Rio Verde was no longer just a mining facility, it had become their home, their life's work, their proof that cryptocurrency could serve both technological innovation and ecological wisdom. Looking out over the thriving community they'd helped build, it felt like a dream come true.

The revolution would be sustainable, one community at a time.

Satoshi's Travel Journal

THE HARMONY PRINCIPLE
Hotel Baur au Lac, Zurich, Switzerland
September 3, 1991

Gray autumn drizzle streaking down the window glass

From my hotel window, I watch the morning ritual of Swiss banking begin. Security guards in crisp uniforms unlock massive bronze doors. Armored vehicles idle outside Credit Suisse, their engines running continuously, burning fuel to protect paper promises. The building itself consumes more electricity in a day than most villages see in a year, yet this waste is invisible, buried in "operational expenses" and "infrastructure costs."

The irony strikes me as I count the floors: Twelve stories of marble and steel, housing hundreds of employees who shuffle paper representations of value that exist primarily as numbers in computers. All this physical infrastructure to maintain the illusion of scarcity in a system designed to create money from nothing.

What if we could eliminate this entire apparatus? What if scarcity could be created mathematically rather than institutionally? The Austrian economists were right about sound money, but they assumed it required physical backing. What they missed is that the key property isn't physicality, it's unforgeable costliness. Energy expenditure in service of mathematical proof.

The rain continues, washing the city clean. I sketch calculations in the margin: if computational work replaced institutional trust, how much energy would that actually require compared to this sprawling bureaucracy? The banking district below employs 50,000 people, operates 24/7, requires military-grade security, regulatory oversight, international enforcement...

Technical note: Peer-to-peer verification protocols could replace institutional intermediaries. Cryptographic proof of computational work as basis for consensus. Need to solve the double-spending problem without trusted third parties.

The hidden costs are staggering once you see them. But who calculates the true energy cost of maintaining monetary sovereignty through military force? Who accounts for the environmental impact of inflation-driven overconsumption?

These questions follow me into the Swiss night. The city lights below powered by hydroelectric dams that will outlast every bank in this district.

The Banker's Conversion

Victor Montoya arrived home to his colonial-style house in South Salem at 7:23 PM, later than he'd promised but earlier than most nights. The Deutsche Bank executive parking garage had been nearly empty when he left, a testament to how the pandemic had changed the rhythm of high finance, though the profit margins remained as robust as ever.

At forty-seven, Victor carried himself with the confident bearing of someone who understood complex systems and made decisions that affected millions of people. His salt-and-pepper hair was perfectly styled despite twelve hours of video conferences, and his Italian wool suit showed no wrinkles despite the commute from Manhattan. He moved through the world with the quiet authority of a man who had spent twenty-three years climbing the banking hierarchy, accumulating both wealth and influence at each level. His position as a consultant on the Federal Reserve board only added to the weight of his responsibilities, giving him insight into monetary policy decisions that shaped global markets.

"Sorry I'm late," he called out, loosening his tie as he entered the foyer. The house smelled of Patricia's cooking, something Mediterranean involving garlic and herbs that reminded him why he'd fallen in love with her seventeen years ago.

"We waited," Patricia's voice carried from the dining room, though her tone suggested this courtesy had been debated. "Elizabeth insisted."

Victor found his family at the dinner table: Patricia, still wearing her hospital administrator ID badge, looking tired but beautiful in the way that reminded him why he worked so hard to provide for them; and Elizabeth, sixteen years old and radiating the particular energy of a teenager who had discovered something important that adults were apparently too stupid to understand.

"Dad!" Elizabeth brightened as he entered. "Perfect timing. I wanted to ask you about something."

Victor kissed Patricia's forehead and settled into his chair, noting the way his daughter's eyes sparkled with intellectual curiosity. Elizabeth had inherited his analytical mind and Patricia's sense of justice, a combination that made her both his pride and his greatest challenge.

"How was your day?" Patricia asked, serving him a plate of chicken with roasted vegetables. "You look exhausted."

"Long meeting with the Federal Reserve about liquidity requirements. Technical stuff." Victor tasted the chicken, making an appreciative sound. "This is excellent. How was your day?"

"Three equipment failures, two budget meetings, and a conference call with insurance companies about why an IV pump that cost eight thousand dollars last year now costs twelve thousand." Patricia's voice carried the weariness of someone fighting systemic problems with limited weapons. "Healthcare costs are increasing faster than our revenue. Again."

"Supply chain issues," Victor said automatically. "Pandemic disruptions, inflation pressures, market corrections. It's temporary."

"Is it?" Elizabeth leaned forward, her expression serious. "Or is it because someone's printing money and making everything more expensive?"

Victor paused mid-chew. "What do you mean?"

"I've been watching these TikTok videos about Bitcoin and monetary policy. Did you know the Federal Reserve printed more money in 2020 than in the previous decade combined?"

"Elizabeth," Patricia warned gently, "your father deals with this stuff professionally. You don't need to lecture him about economics."

"I'm not lecturing. I'm asking questions." Elizabeth pulled out her phone, swiping to a saved video. "This guy explains how quantitative easing works. Want to see?"

Victor found himself watching a twenty-something influencer with perfect lighting explain monetary policy to teenagers: *"When the Fed prints trillions of dollars, that money doesn't just disappear. It goes to banks and asset holders first, making them richer, while everyone else's savings become worth less. It's basically a tax on poor people that benefits rich people, but they call it 'economic stimulus' so it sounds good."*

"That's..." Victor started, then stopped. The video was simplistic, but it wasn't wrong. "It's more complicated than that."

"How?" Elizabeth's question was direct, curious rather than confrontational. "You work for a bank. When the Fed creates new money, your bank gets it first, right? Before regular people see any inflation?"

Victor looked at his daughter, sixteen years old, learning economics from social media, and somehow asking questions that his Deutsche Bank colleagues spent millions of dollars helping clients navigate.

"Banks serve as intermediaries," he said carefully. "When the Federal Reserve implements monetary policy, banks help distribute liquidity throughout the economy."

"But you get the money first," Elizabeth pressed. "And you can invest it or lend it before prices go up. So you benefit from the money printing, while people like Mom see their costs increase without their salaries keeping up."

Patricia set down her fork. "Elizabeth has a point. My department's budget hasn't increased in three years, but equipment costs have doubled. Meanwhile, you get bigger bonuses every year."

Victor felt something shift in the conversation's dynamic. His professional expertise, which usually commanded respect, was being questioned by the two people whose opinions mattered most to him.

"It's not that simple," he said. "Banking provides essential services. We facilitate loans, manage risk, and enable economic growth."

"By creating money from nothing?" Elizabeth asked. She swiped to another video, this one explaining fractional reserve banking. "This says banks only keep like ten percent of deposits and lend out the rest. So when someone deposits a hundred dollars, you can lend ninety dollars to someone else, creating ninety new dollars that didn't exist before."

Victor nodded reluctantly. "That's basically how fractional reserve banking works, yes."

"So you're literally creating money from nothing and charging interest on it?"

Ḃ

The question hung in the air like an accusation. Victor had spent decades mastering the complexities of modern banking, understanding the regulatory frameworks and risk models that governed financial institutions. But when his sixteen-year-old daughter reduced it to its essential mechanism, it sounded like legalized counterfeiting.

"It's regulated," he said weakly. "There are capital requirements, reserve ratios, oversight mechanisms."

"Regulated by who?" Elizabeth asked. "The Federal Reserve? The same people who print the money?"

Patricia looked between her husband and daughter, recognizing the tension building. "Maybe we should talk about something else."

"No, this is important," Elizabeth said. "Dad, I'm trying to understand your job. You help create money from nothing, lend it to people who need it, and charge them interest. Meanwhile, people who save money in regular accounts earn almost zero interest while inflation makes their savings worth less every year."

"Elizabeth," Victor's voice carried a warning tone.

"I'm not trying to attack you. I'm trying to understand how this is fair. Like, Mom sees medical equipment getting more expensive every year. Our college tuition keeps going up. Housing costs are insane. But banks keep making record profits. How does that make sense?"

Victor set down his silverware, his appetite gone. "The financial system is complex. Banks provide essential services that keep the economy functioning."

"Like what?" Elizabeth asked. "Because from what I'm learning, Bitcoin can do most of the same things without banks. People can send money directly to each other, store value without asking permission, and nobody can print more Bitcoin to steal from savers."

"Bitcoin is speculative gambling," Victor said automatically, repeating the talking points Deutsche Bank used in client communications. "It's not real money. It's not backed by anything."

"Neither is the dollar," Elizabeth replied immediately. "Not since 1971, according to these videos. At least Bitcoin has a limited supply. The dollar can be printed infinitely."

Victor felt the conversation spiraling beyond his control. His daughter, armed with smartphone-delivered education, was systematically dismantling the intellectual foundation of his career. The worst part was that her questions weren't unfair or uninformed, they were precisely the questions he'd learned to avoid answering.

"Elizabeth, enough," Patricia interjected. "Your father works hard to provide for this family. You don't need to interrogate him about monetary policy."

"I'm not interrogating him. I'm trying to understand why everything keeps getting more expensive while he gets richer for helping create the problem."

The silence that followed was deafening. Victor looked at his daughter, brilliant, idealistic, unafraid to ask uncomfortable questions, and realized she was forcing him to confront something he'd spent decades avoiding.

Victor was certainly confronting something, but it wasn't what Elizabeth thought. It wasn't the banking ethics his daughter was pointing out, or the moral compromises of traditional finance. What haunted him was far more dangerous: his underground mission as a Bitcoin revolutionary soldier, hidden not only from his colleagues at the bank but also from his own family.

The very daughter challenging him about monetary corruption had no idea her father was secretly working to dismantle the system from within.

"Dad," Elizabeth said quietly, "I love you. But I don't understand how you can work for a system that hurts people like Mom, like our neighbors, like everyone who isn't a banker."

"I don't hurt people," Victor said, but the words felt hollow even as he spoke them.

"Maybe not directly. But if the system you work for transfers wealth from savers to banks, and you profit from that system, then…"

She didn't finish the sentence. She didn't need to.

—

That night, after Elizabeth had gone to her room and Patricia had fallen asleep, Victor sat in his home office staring at his computer screen. The house was quiet except for the hum of central air conditioning, a sound of suburban prosperity that reminded him of everything he stood to lose if his secret mission was ever discovered.

He opened his encrypted communication system and activated the secure channel he'd been using for the past three years. His daughter's questions that evening had been brilliant, more sophisticated than most of his Deutsche Bank colleagues' understanding of monetary policy. She was discovering the same Austrian economic principles that had driven him to his current double life.

Ludwig von Mises. Murray Rothbard. Friedrich Hayek. These weren't new names to Victor, they were the intellectual foundation that had gradually turned him against the very system he appeared to serve. For years, he'd understood that fractional reserve banking was systematic wealth transfer, that quantitative easing was theft from savers, that the entire central banking apparatus existed to enrich financial institutions at the expense of ordinary people.

But understanding the problem and having the courage to act on that understanding were different things entirely.

His encrypted phone buzzed with messages from contacts who knew him only by his code name "Prime." Sarah Kim needed intelligence about upcoming regulatory moves against cryptocurrency journalism. Dr. Aírínne Fynn required early warning about institutional threats to consciousness research. A dozen other Bitcoin researchers and advocates depended on the intelligence he provided from his position within the traditional financial system.

Victor pulled up his secret Bitcoin wallet, not the modest $500 purchase he would make tomorrow morning to maintain his cover story, but the substantial holdings he'd been accumulating for three years. Every bonus, every client commission, every benefit of his privileged position within the corrupt system was being systematically converted into the monetary revolution he was secretly supporting.

The irony was brutal: his success at perpetuating the fiat system provided the resources to undermine it. Every pension fund he helped exploit through structured products generated Bitcoin purchases that strengthened the network he hoped would eventually replace traditional banking entirely.

His secure phone chimed with a priority message from Sarah Kim: *Prime, the Meridian Media Group is preparing a major anti-Bitcoin propaganda campaign. They're offering massive contracts to journalists with cryptocurrency expertise. Can you provide intelligence about funding sources and strategic objectives?*

Victor typed back: *Will have full details within 48 hours. This is part of a larger institutional response to consciousness research. Are you maintaining operational security?*

Yes. Still building an independent platform while documenting community behaviors. Your intelligence has been essential for understanding institutional threats.

Victor smiled, remembering Sarah's journey from Tribune staff writer to independent journalist. He'd been watching her work since her first Bitcoin story in 2012, gradually providing intelligence that helped her break important stories while staying ahead of institutional retaliation. Back then, she had no idea that her anonymous source was someone positioned at the highest levels of the system she was investigating.

Another message arrived, this one from Dr. Fynn at Princeton: *Contact Prime - Need coordination on consciousness research security protocols. Integration Board monitoring is intensifying.*

Victor switched to his academic research channel, where he'd been providing early warning intelligence to consciousness researchers for eighteen months. Aírínne's work on Bitcoin consciousness evolution was groundbreaking, but it also represented an existential threat to institutional control over monetary systems. His position on various regulatory committees gave him an advanced knowledge of plans to suppress such research.

Dr. Fynn, this is Prime. Monitoring has intensified because your research threatens fundamental assumptions about technological control. Recommend enhanced operational security and coordination with other researchers facing similar pressure.

Understood. Are you able to provide specifics about institutional response timelines?

Will have detailed intelligence within 72 hours. Your research is more important than you realize - institutional panic suggests you're documenting something they can't control or replicate.

Victor leaned back in his chair, contemplating the impossible balance he'd been maintaining. By day, he advanced policies that strengthened traditional banking's control over monetary systems. By night, he provided intelligence that helped Bitcoin advocates resist those same policies.

Elizabeth's questions that evening had been perfect, exactly the kind of intellectual awakening that gave him hope for the future. But he couldn't tell her that her understanding of Austrian economics surpassed most of his colleagues', or that her insights about Bitcoin's superiority were precisely the conclusions that had driven him to his secret mission.

The lifestyle his family enjoyed, the South Salem house, Elizabeth's private school education, Patricia's assumption that their financial security was permanent, all of it depended on his continued success within a system he was working to destroy. Leaving Deutsche Bank would mean acknowledging to his family that their comfortable life had been built on participation in systematic theft from savers and workers.

So he remained, playing the role of successful banker while systematically undermining the institution that employed him. Every regulation he helped craft contained loopholes that Bitcoin advocates could exploit. Every strategic initiative he influenced was designed to fail when confronted with mathematical certainty and voluntary adoption.

His daughter thought she was teaching him about Bitcoin. In reality, she was discovering truths he'd been acting on for years, confirming that the next generation might be wise enough to choose honest money over institutional comfort.

Victor opened his trading platform and made his nightly Bitcoin purchase, not the symbolic $500 he would buy tomorrow morning to maintain his cover, but the substantial amount that represented his genuine commitment to monetary revolution. Every dollar flowing from Deutsche Bank's success into Bitcoin's growth was a vote against the system he appeared to serve.

Tomorrow, he will pretend to be learning about cryptocurrency from his sixteen-year-old daughter. Tonight, he would continue coordinating the resistance that was slowly but systematically undermining everything his career had built.

The conversion had been complete for years. What remained was the performance, playing the role of conflicted banker while actually serving as one of Bitcoin's most valuable double agents.

Elizabeth's moral clarity reminded him why the sacrifice was worthwhile. A generation was coming that would choose mathematical truth over institutional promises, personal sovereignty over systematic control. His job was to ensure that when they made that choice, the systems would be in place to support their decision.

The revolution was already underway. Few people understood that some of its most effective soldiers wore expensive suits and attended Federal Reserve meetings, gathering intelligence while appearing to serve the enemy.

His encrypted phone buzzed with one final message of the night: *Prime, the network appreciates your service. Intelligence you've provided has prevented multiple institutional attacks on Bitcoin adoption. Mission continuation approved.*

Victor smiled, closing his laptop and preparing for another day of perfectly performed loyalty to a system he was systematically betraying. His daughter's questions weren't awakening his consciousness, they were confirming that his years of sacrifice were finally bearing fruit.

The next generation was ready for honest money. His job was to ensure they would have the opportunity to choose it.

Satoshi's Travel Journal

THE REGENERATION PARADOX
Train Window, Amazon Basin, Brazil
March 15, 1992

Humid morning mist rising from the endless green canopy

The forest streams past my window like a living cathedral, punctuated by scars where machinery has torn into the earth. Mining operations dot the landscape, some leave wounds that will take decades to heal, others seem to work with the forest's natural patterns. I watch indigenous workers tending gardens that integrate seamlessly with wild growth, their methods preserving the very systems that sustain them.

What strikes me most is the contrast in approach. The foreign mining operations extract maximum value in minimum time, leaving poisoned streams and barren soil. But the indigenous communities I visited yesterday showed me something profound: technology that regenerates rather than depletes. Their solar-powered equipment runs only when the sun shines, their water systems enhance rather than disrupt natural flow patterns.

This morning, an elder explained their philosophy: "We don't own the forest, we belong to it. Our work must make it stronger, not weaker." She gestured toward a recently harvested area where new growth was already emerging, healthier than before. "Energy spent in harmony multiplies. Energy spent in conflict divides."

Her words echo as I sketch power consumption models. What if computational work could operate like these regenerative systems? What if mining, digital mining, could actually strengthen the systems it depends on rather than depleting them?

Technical note: Proof-of-work algorithms that adapt to renewable energy avail-ability. Variable difficulty adjustments based on energy source sustainability. Could mining operations naturally migrate toward excess renewable capacity?

I imagine networks of computers powered by stranded solar energy, by micro-hydroelectric systems that enhance river health, by wind farms generating more power than local grids can absorb. The economics would be compelling: renewable energy is often cheapest precisely when it's most abundant.

But more than economics, there's elegance here. A monetary system that grows stronger by making its environment stronger. Digital scarcity created through renewable abundance. The mathematics of regeneration rather than extraction.

The forest continues to stream past, teaching lessons in distributed resilience that no banking textbook contains.

Digital Gold

"Gold is the money of kings, silver is the money of gentlemen, barter is the money of peasants – but debt is the money of slaves."[25]

- Norm Franz

January 2022

"Gold is analog Bitcoin," read the graffiti on the abandoned bank's wall. Aírínne Fynn traced the letters with her fingertips, feeling the rough texture of spray paint on marble. Her red hair caught the dusty light streaming through broken windows, the copper strands seeming to bridge the metallic past with the digital future.

At twenty-seven, she had learned to find meaning in these contrasts, the ancient and the modern, the physical and the digital, the wisdom of her grandfather's generation meeting the innovation of her own. The building,

---

25   Norm Franz (contemporary), American author, monetary historian, and financial advisor known for his book "Money & Wealth in the New Millennium" (2001), in which he examines historical patterns of monetary systems and offers perspectives on wealth preservation, economic cycles, and biblical principles of finance.

once a proud Lehman Brothers office, now stood empty, another casualty of the ongoing financial transformation.

Aírínne was there on a pilgrimage. Her grandfather had never worked in this building, but before he died, he left her a raw gold ore along with a note in his journal: "Go to Wall Street's financial district. See the grand buildings, the marble facades, the temples built to house nothing but promises and paper. Then you'll understand, it's all smoke and mirrors, backed by nothing more than salesmanship and gangsters in expensive suits."

He had been right. The place was vacant, hollowed out, a monument to financial illusion.

She unconsciously weighed the objects in each palm, the ancient ore in one hand, the sleek hardware wallet in the other. "Grandfather's gold versus Bitcoin," she thought, turning the rough ore over in her palm. "He wanted me to see through the illusion. But what are we building in its place?"

She'd driven three hours to stand in the Lehman Brothers office ruins, holding the gold he'd given her, trying to feel some connection to the man who'd witnessed the death of one financial world and the birth of another.

Her blue-green eyes reflected both past and future as she contemplated the symbolic bridge she held between eras. She stepped back from the wall and looked down at her hands. The contrast wasn't lost on her: one, a mineral that had served as money for millennia, the other, a few grams of silicon and plastic that contained more value than its weight in gold a thousand times over.

"Aírínne! What a pleasant surprise!" a voice said behind her. Théo Babylon emerged from the shadows of the building's lobby, his footsteps echoing off the marble floors. His tall frame moved through the destruction with serene purpose, robes somehow untouched by debris, his beard now more silver than brown catching the filtered light. His philosophical presence seemed

to fit naturally in these ruins of institutional power, as if he had learned to see through the facades of civilization to observe the deeper patterns of transformation beneath.

His deep eyes seemed to witness civilization's rise and fall, observing the decay with a philosopher's detachment as he occasionally touched the crumbling architecture as if reading history through stone. Aírínne wasn't surprised to find him here. The old banking districts had become pilgrimage sites for the crypto-philosophers, places to contemplate the transition from one form of money to another.

—

Three blocks away, Sarah Kim sat in her car outside another defunct financial building, her laptop balanced on her steering wheel as she typed her latest dispatch. Her black hair was pulled back for practical work, dark eyes sharp with a documenter's focus as her small frame navigated through institutional debris with practiced efficiency. Her role had evolved far beyond journalism into something closer to anthropology, documenting not just events but the transformation of human consciousness itself.

As a journalist covering the monetary transition, she'd made it her mission to document every abandoned trading floor, every shuttered bank branch, every monument to the old system now crumbling in real time.

Professional photographer's gear was slung across her body, equipment she unconsciously protected like sacred tools, knowing she was documenting a civilizational transition. She remembered her first Bitcoin story, how her editor had killed it, dismissing it as "tech nonsense," and how she'd published it anyway through alternative media outlets. Even more intolerable, her editor had published an article the next day titled "The Madness of Magic Internet Money," which convinced her after quitting that she'd done the right thing.

But it became truly personal when her parents lost their retirement savings after their regional bank collapsed, watching her father's 40 years of faithful deposits disappear overnight while executives walked away with golden parachutes. The bank's marble lobby had looked just like this one, all false permanence and institutional authority. Now her personal investment in this transformation ran deeper than professional curiosity. The system's collapse wasn't abstract, it had real faces, real consequences, real human costs that she documented with growing urgency. She understood that Bitcoin wasn't a fad; it was an immune response to a diseased system.

Concentration lines were forming around her eyes from years of intense observation, her mouth set with determination to record truth, the weight of historical significance visible in how carefully she framed each shot. She'd stopped counting days long ago, this story was bigger than daily dispatches. Now she measured time in years, tracking the slow-motion collapse and rebirth of money itself.

What had begun as breaking news had evolved into something else entirely: the real-time documentation of civilization's monetary metamorphosis. "I'm documenting the death of one monetary system and the birth of another," she thought, photographing another shuttered bank branch. "But why does this feel less like a news story and more like... witnessing a species evolve? What am I really recording here?"

"Eleven years into the Great Transition," she wrote. "Found myself in the financial district again, watching the digital gold miners move into spaces once occupied by gold traders. The irony isn't lost on anyone, except perhaps the regulators still pretending this is a temporary disruption rather than a permanent revolution."

She crouched to photograph details others missed, capturing contrasts between old and new systems with the precision of an archaeologist documenting extinct civilizations. She photographed the contrasts everywhere:

Bitcoin ATMs installed in former bank lobbies, mining equipment humming where loan officers once worked, young developers coding in conference rooms where derivatives were once traded. Each image told the same story, one form of money dying as another was being born.

—

Back at the abandoned Lehman Brother office

Théo noticed Aírínne absently turning something over in her palm as they spoke, the afternoon light catching glimpses of metallic gleam between her fingers. When she shifted her hand, he could see it was a piece of raw gold ore, rough and unpolished, its natural beauty somehow fitting for someone who studied the intersection of ancient wisdom and emerging technology.

"That's quite remarkable," he said, nodding toward the ore in her hand. "What's the significance of that piece?"

"The gold is from my grandfather's mine in Australia," she said. "He never understood Bitcoin himself. In his writings, he said, 'It is too late for me to understand Bitcoin, but you, Aírínne, are the right person with your curious and analytical mind.'"

Théo smiled, pulling out his own hardware wallet. "And yet here we are, holding digital scarcity in our hands. The mineral dimension expressing itself through silicon instead of gold." His peaceful expression despite the surrounding destruction made the decay feel like natural seasonal change rather than catastrophe, his ability to recognize patterns across civilizations allowing him to see this moment as part of a much larger story, humanity's ongoing transformation in how it stores and transfers value across time.

They walked deeper into the abandoned building, their phone lights casting long shadows. The trading floor, once alive with the shouts of brokers, lay silent. A forgotten Bloomberg terminal gathered dust in the corner.

—

Meanwhile, forty blocks north in the Federal Reserve's imposing marble halls, Victor Montoya reviewed the day's emergency banking reports with growing unease. His expensive suit contrasted sharply with the empty trading floors around him. Under the harsh institutional lighting, his silver temples appeared more pronounced, gray eyes reflecting the hollowness of fiat's final years.

His perfectly styled appearance and calculating demeanor remained unchanged, but inside, a profound shift was occurring, a growing awareness that his life's work might be serving a system fundamentally at odds with truth itself.

As Senior Advisor for Digital Currency Analysis at the Federal Reserve, he'd spent the last year watching traditional financial institutions hemorrhage deposits while Bitcoin's market cap soared past every prediction.

He maintained his corporate posture even in the empty building, hands clasped behind his back in executive stance. He occasionally touched empty chairs where colleagues once sat, stress lines around his eyes deepening from sleepless nights spent wrestling with impossible equations.

The latest figures were stark: three more regional banks had requested emergency liquidity support this week, their balance sheets devastated by capital flight to cryptocurrency. Credit unions were converting reserves to Bitcoin faster than the Fed could track. Even the most conservative pension funds were quietly allocating percentages to "digital assets" while publicly maintaining their dollar commitments.

"The Fed prints trillions while Bitcoin creates nothing new, just reveals what was always true," he reflected, staring at the reports. "But what is that truth? Why does artificial abundance feel real while mathematical scarcity feels like a threat?"

Growing awareness of time's true value created internal pressure that showed in subtle ways, his jaw perpetually tense, success feeling increasingly meaningless, his mouth that rarely smiled now speaking even less.

Victor closed the classified report and stared out his window at the city below, where the lights of mining facilities were becoming as common as streetlamps. He'd joined the Fed as a consultant to serve the monetary system, but increasingly wondered if he was merely documenting its final chapter.

The revolution wasn't coming, it was already here, one block at a time.

—

"Tell me more about your grandfather's mine," Théo said, settling onto a broken desk.

The deep sense of ancestral connection mixed with anticipation for the future was visible in how Aírínne carried herself, the weight of inherited wisdom apparent in her contemplative expression. Aírínne held up the ore, letting it catch the light. Her ability to bridge generational knowledge gaps had become one of her greatest strengths as a researcher, honoring ancient wisdom while embracing innovation. "My grandfather left Ireland on his own and bought a mine in Australia, his monetary understanding was such that he needed to make it real. He didn't even tell his family until he died. Back-breaking work. Dangerous. All to extract something rare, something that couldn't be copied or counterfeited."

"And now?"

She held up her hardware wallet with reverent care, the same way she handled the ancient ore, unconsciously bridging the gap between epochs. "Now we mine with mathematics. The scarcity is guaranteed not by geology but by cryptography. The work is digital but no less real."

> // Block #623,132
> // Difficulty: 49,692,386,925
> // Total BTC in circulation: 18,235,675
> // Market Cap: $101.2 billion

The numbers flashed on Aírínne's phone, a constant reminder of the network's heartbeat. Each block was like a new layer of digital sediment, building up the crypto-geological record one proof-of-work at a time.

"Your grandfather wasn't entirely wrong," Théo said. His philosophical precision allowed him to see connections that others missed, patterns that repeated across civilizations and technologies, his eyes reflecting ancient calm that made destruction feel like natural transformation. "Bitcoin is abstract, but it's grounded in the same physical laws that make gold valuable; thermodynamics,[26] scarcity, the conservation of energy."

Out of the corner of his eye, he spotted an orange spray paint can lying in the dust. He picked it up, shook it once, it was nearly empty, but maybe could still have enough to leave a mark, then began tagging the wall with the fundamental equation of Bitcoin mining, raw symbols scrawled in uneven lines, as if cryptography itself were bleeding onto concrete.

(Energy Input + Computer + Time) / Network Difficulty = Digital Gold

---

26   The branch of physics concerned with heat, work, and energy transformations. Governed by four fundamental laws describing the conservation of energy

"The mineral dimension was just the beginning," Aírínne said, understanding flowing through her. A slight furrow appeared between her brows as her eyes grew distant, connecting generational patterns across time and technology. "Gold was humanity's first step toward understanding abstract value. Bitcoin is the next evolution, it takes everything that made gold work as money and perfects it."

Outside, the sun was setting behind the city's towers. Solar panels glinted on rooftops, many of them now powering Bitcoin miners instead of feeding the grid. The network was becoming integrated with the physical world in ways Satoshi might not have imagined.

Aírínne's phone buzzed. Another block had been mined, another 12.5 BTC brought into existence through pure proof-of-work. Unlike gold, whose supply could surge with new discoveries, Bitcoin's emission schedule was as reliable as the atomic clock.[27]

"Watch this," she said, pulling up a visualization of the Bitcoin network. Points of light showed mining operations around the world, pulsing with each hash attempt. "It's like a digital nervous system growing through the planet's mineral crust."

Théo nodded. "The fiat system dies as Bitcoin is born," he thought, watching the pulsing lights on her screen. "But this isn't replacement, it's evolution. What consciousness patterns am I witnessing? How does money learn to become truth?" "The cypherpunks always understood this would happen. Digital scarcity was the missing piece. Once we solved that…"

"Everything changed," Aírínne finished. She placed her grandfather's gold

---

27   ⚠ PRECIOUS METALS PROPAGANDA ALERT ⚠
→   Bitcoin digital scarcity proves more verifiable than physical scarcity #MoneyPrinterNotGoBrr
→   You mean we can't just print more when we need it? #CentralBankersTears

ore on the dusty trading desk. Next to it, she laid her hardware wallet. "Past and future. Analog and digital. Both forms of the mineral dimension expressing itself through human discernment."

They stood in silence for a moment, contemplating the objects. Through the broken windows, they could hear the hum of mining rigs from a nearby data center, the modern equivalent of a gold smelter.

"Your grandfather's mine," Théo said finally, "how deep did it go?"

"A kilometer at its deepest point."

He smiled. "Bitcoin goes deeper. All the way down to the bedrock of mathematics itself. That's what makes it the perfect evolution of gold. It's not just digital gold, it's gold perfected through code."

Aírínne picked up her wallet and the ore, pocketing both. The objects clinked together in her pocket, past and future, analog and digital, physical and mathematical, all part of the same story. "The mineral dimension isn't just about physical elements anymore, is it? It's about the fundamental properties that make something suitable as money."

"Exactly. Scarcity. Durability. Fungibility. Portability. Gold had these naturally. Bitcoin has them by design."

As they walked out of the abandoned bank, Aírínne paused to look at the graffiti one more time. "Gold is analog Bitcoin." The words seemed different now, deeper. This wasn't just about replacing one form of money with another. It was about evolving humanity's relationship with value itself.

Her professional attire remained pristine despite the debris, comfortable shoes having carried her through the exploration of these financial ruins, her entire bearing that of someone bridging worlds. The mineral dimension

had given them gold, buried in deep veins through the earth. Now it had given them Bitcoin, running through digital networks across the globe. Both were expressions of the same fundamental reality: that humans needed uncorruptible money to advance their civilization.

In her pocket, the gold ore and the hardware wallet clinked together. Past and future, analog and digital, physical and mathematical, all part of the same story. The story of how humanity learned to capture scarcity, first in metal, then in code.

The sun had fully set now, but the city was far from dark. Thousands of ASICs hummed in warehouses and data centers, their combined effort maintaining the security of the network. Each hash was like a digital pickaxe strike, mining not gold but mathematical truth from the bedrock of reality.

Aírínne and Théo parted ways at the street corner. Above them, stars were becoming visible despite the city's lights. Somewhere up there, satellites were beaming Bitcoin transactions across continents, proof that the mineral dimension had evolved beyond the earth itself.

The revolution wasn't just digital. It was geological. One block at a time.

Satoshi's Travel Journal

THE WEIGHT OF GOLD
Café Johannesburg, South Africa
November 12, 1992

Bright highveld sun creating harsh shadows across the mining district

Through the café window, I watch miners emerging from the depths, faces etched with exhaustion, clothes caked with centuries-old earth. They've descended a kilometer underground, spending their lives extracting atoms of gold from tons of ore. The energy expenditure is staggering: diesel generators, compressed air systems, water pumps fighting against gravity, ventilation fans moving air through miles of tunnels.

Yet for all this effort, gold retains its value precisely because it's difficult to obtain. The thermodynamic cost of extraction ensures scarcity. No amount of wishful thinking can create gold, it requires real work, real energy, real time.

An old Afrikaner miner sits at the next table, hands scarred from decades underground. "You know what I learned in forty years down there?" he says, noticing my sketches. "Gold doesn't care about your politics, your promises, your papers. It just is. Rare, beautiful, indestructible. That's why it's money."

He's right, but his analysis is incomplete. Gold's monetary properties, scarcity, durability, fungibility, portability, aren't tied to its physical form. They're tied to the energy required to produce it and the impossibility of counterfeiting that energy expenditure.

What if we could create digital gold? Not backed by gold, but exhibiting the same properties through pure computational work? Each unit would represent verifiable energy expenditure, mathematically unforgeable, infinitely divisible.

Technical note: Hash functions as digital mining. Adjustable difficulty to maintain consistent issuance rate regardless of computational power. Energy converts to digital scarcity through cryptographic proof-of-work.

The elegance is breathtaking. Physical gold requires excavating tons of earth, processing with toxic chemicals, transportation across continents, storage in heavily guarded vaults. Digital gold would require only electricity and computation, but the energy expenditure would be equally verifiable, equally unforgeable.

The miner finishes his coffee and heads back toward the shaft. "Another day, another gram of gold," he mutters. But I'm imagining another way: another hash, another proof, another step toward a monetary system based on mathematical truth rather than geological accident.

The sun sets over the mine dumps, their yellow slopes glowing like digital readouts. Energy converted to value, work made manifest, scarcity preserved through thermodynamic law. These principles transcend the physical, they're universal constants waiting to be expressed in code.

Newspapers and online articles flood the media landscape, an obvious last attempt to throw a wrench in the works and shape negative Bitcoin sentiment. Psychological operations (psyops) are deployed to convey selected information and indicators to audiences, aiming to influence their emotions and objective reasoning, ultimately modifying behavior to serve specific group interests. These campaigns are orchestrated by governments, organizations, corporations, and foreign powers seeking to maintain the status quo.

The Environment Nightmare of Our Time

10 SHOCKING Ways Bitcoin Is Destroying Our Planet - #6 Will Leave You SPEECHLESS!

GREEN EARTH TODAY | March 20, 2022 | *5 min read*

Bitcoin mining operations are consuming electricity at unprecedented rates. Image: Getty Images

By Dr. Barbara Cabone | Environmental Impact Specialist | @DrBCabone

---

Share this article: ❤ Twitter f Facebook ◙ Instagram ⊛ Reddit

---

As Bitcoin reaches yet another all-time high this week, surpassing $60,000 per coin, experts are raising red flags about the cryptocurrency's massive carbon footprint. Could your digital investments be accelerating climate change?

The environmental cost of this cyber-alchemical experiment has become impossible to ignore. What crypto-enthusiasts euphemistically call "mining" is, in reality, nothing less than a digital assault on our planet's fragile ecosystem.

Is Bitcoin Really "Digital Gold"?

Let's be real: Bitcoin is not "digital gold!" Gold mining has its environmental problems, but at least produces something tangible in the physical world.

Bitcoin mining, by contrast, consumes vast quantities of electricity to solve arbitrary mathematical puzzles, producing nothing but strings of numbers that a small cult of digital speculators have decided hold value.

"We're witnessing the emergence of a new type of environmental catastrophe. It's as if we've invented a machine that converts electricity directly into climate change, with a cryptocurrency by-product."

— Dr. Jonathan Pierce, Head of Environmental Economics at Stanford

The SHOCKING Numbers You Need to Know

Recent studies from the prestigious Global Climate Research Institute reveal that Bitcoin's current energy consumption exceeds that of several medium-sized nations combined. The statistics are staggering:

- **A single Bitcoin transaction** now consumes enough electricity to power an average American household for 6.5 weeks
- **The network's total energy consumption** could power all of Earth's electric vehicles for three years
- **Bitcoin mining operations** are increasingly targeting areas with cheap electricity and minimal regulations

INTERACTIVE: Calculate your crypto carbon footprint here

The Green Energy THEFT No One Is Talking About

More disturbing still is Bitcoin's increasing colonization of renewable energy sources. Every solar panel dedicated to Bitcoin mining is a solar panel not powering a home or hospital.

"It's effectively stealing green energy from legitimate uses," notes Dr. Karen Green of the Sustainable Energy Foundation.

What Bitcoin Bros Don't Want You to Hear

The crypto-advocates' response to these concerns reveals their environmental nihilism. They claim that Bitcoin mining actually encourages renewable energy development—an argument so cynical it would make an oil executive blush.

Others suggest that the energy consumption is "worth it" for the creation of a new monetary system, as if our planet's climate could be traded for digital tokens.

WATCH: Bitcoin's Growing Environmental Crisis

Click to play our exclusive interview with climate scientists

The Feedback Loop From Hell

Most alarming is the correlation between Bitcoin's price and its environmental impact. As this digital delusion gains value, it attracts more mining activity, consuming ever more energy in a vicious cycle of environmental destruction.

"It's a feedback loop from hell," explains Dr. Pierce. "The more successful Bitcoin becomes, the more it threatens our climate goals."

Traditional gold mining, for all its faults, at least faces environmental regulations and oversight. Bitcoin mining operates in a regulatory void, often seeking out the cheapest available electricity—typically from coal-fired plants in regions with lax environmental standards.

What This Means For Our Climate Future

Conservative estimates suggest that if Bitcoin adoption continues at its current rate, it alone could push global temperatures past critical thresholds.

"We're literally burning our planet's future to create digital tokens," warns Dr. Pierce. "It's madness masquerading as financial innovation."

For those who dismiss these concerns as alarmist, consider this: every Bitcoin transaction contributes to the acceleration of climate change. In an era when we're desperately trying to reduce carbon emissions, Bitcoin stands as a monument to technological irresponsibility.

What World Leaders MUST Do Now

As world leaders prepare for the upcoming Climate Summit, they would do well to consider emergency measures against this growing threat. The choice between real environmental sustainability and speculative digital assets should not be a difficult one to make.

The true cost of "digital gold" isn't measured in kilowatts or carbon emissions—it's measured in the environmental legacy we're leaving future generations. And no amount of cryptocurrency will shield them from a world ravaged by climate change.

Special Report funded by the Global Sustainable Future Initiative

Conflict of Interest: Author serves as senior consultant to major oil companies and traditional mining corporations

Compensation: Lifetime supply of carbon credits (Value: $15M), plus board position at

three major oil companies and private jet access.

Related Stories You Might Like:

- <u>5 Eco-Friendly Cryptocurrencies That Won't Kill The Planet</u>
- <u>EXCLUSIVE: Inside The Secret World of Crypto Mining Farms</u>
- <u>Why Gen Z Is Abandoning Bitcoin for These Green Alternatives</u>
- <u>The Carbon Footprint of Your Digital Life - QUIZ</u>

Comments (245)

GreenWarrior92 • 2 hours ago This is exactly why I sold all my Bitcoin last year! The environmental cost is just too high.

CryptoKing2021 • 3 hours ago Typical FUD[28] article. Bitcoin mining is actually INCENTIVIZING renewable energy development. Do your research!

EarthFirst • 4 hours ago When will governments finally ban this environmental disaster?

View all 245 comments

SUBSCRIBE TO OUR NEWSLETTER ✉ *Get the latest environmental news delivered to your inbox daily!* <u>SUBSCRIBE NOW</u>

---

28   FUD: Fear, Uncertainty, and Doubt, a strategy of spreading negative, often misleading information to undermine confidence in Bitcoin or other cryptocurrencies, typically used by critics, competitors, or those seeking to manipulate market sentiment.

Satoshi's Travel Journal

THE MYCELIAL WEB
Mauna Kea Observatory, Hawaii
January 8, 1993

Crystal clear night, Milky Way visible to the horizon

Two networks surround me in this perfect darkness. Above, the cosmic web, galaxies connected by dark matter filaments spanning billions of light-years, organizing matter through gravitational consensus without central authority. Below, the mycorrhizal network beneath the volcanic soil, fungal threads connecting tree roots across miles, sharing nutrients and information without hierarchical control.

Both achieve coordination through distributed consensus. Both process information across vast distances. Both adapt to changing conditions without central planning. The parallels are striking, suggesting universal principles of organization that transcend scale and substrate.

Dr. Keala Kalākaua from the observatory joins me at the viewing window. "What fascinates me about these networks," she says, pointing to images of both cosmic and fungal structures, "is how they solve the same problem: How do you get distributed nodes to agree on the state of a complex system without a central coordinator?"

Her question crystallizes months of thinking. This is exactly the challenge for digital currency: achieving consensus about transaction validity across a network of untrusted participants. Traditional solutions require central authorities, banks, governments, clearing houses. But natural systems demonstrate another way.

Technical note: Distributed ledger with cryptographic linking. Nodes reach consensus through computational proof rather than authority. Network topology emerges from incentive structures rather than design.

The fungi below don't vote on resource allocation, they compete through biochemical proof-of-work, with resources flowing toward nodes that demonstrate value through metabolic activity. The cosmic web doesn't coordinate through central planning, it self-organizes through the mathematics of gravity and energy.

Could a monetary network operate similarly? Nodes competing to process transactions through cryptographic work, with consensus emerging from mathematical proof rather than trust? The network would be resilient because it's distributed, honest because dishonesty is mathematically detectable, and efficient because it follows natural organizational principles.

Dr. Kalākaua points the telescope toward the Andromeda Galaxy. "Two trillion stars organizing themselves through pure mathematics," she observes. "No central authority, no coordination committee, no bureaucracy. Just the elegant simplicity of physical law."

Physical law. Mathematical truth. Universal consensus through unforgeable proof. The framework is there, demonstrated across every scale of existence. We just need to implement it in silicon and software.

The cosmic web pulses with dark energy. The fungal network pulses with chemical signals. Somewhere between these scales, a digital network could pulse with cryptographic proof, creating order from chaos through the same principles that organize galaxies and forests.

The observatory dome rotates silently, tracking celestial coordinates. But I'm tracking something else: the mathematical patterns that connect all complex systems, waiting to be expressed as code.

The Scientist's Proof

UC Berkeley - Department of Integrative Biology - February 2023

Dr. Renata Vega stood in her laboratory at 6:47 AM, surrounded by the controlled chaos of academic research: hydroponics systems humming with life, monitoring equipment blinking with data streams, and whiteboards covered in equations that described how plants optimized energy distribution across complex networks. She moved through the space with the careful precision of someone who understood that scientific breakthroughs emerged from methodical observation rather than hopefully inspiration.

Her thick brown braids were pulled back in the practical style she'd maintained since graduate school, and her hazel eyes reflected the fluorescent lab lighting as she reviewed the morning's experimental protocols. The early hour meant she had the lab to herself, thirty minutes of quiet before her research team arrived to face what might be their final semester together.

The email from the Department Chair sat open on her laptop screen, its bureaucratic language failing to mask the brutal reality:

Dr. Vega,

Due to ongoing budgetary constraints and the university's need to prioritize revenue-generating research activities, the Department of Integrative Biology will be discontinuing funding for the Plant Network Dynamics Laboratory effective May 31, 2023.

We appreciate your team's contributions to our understanding of botanical energy optimization and encourage you to pursue external funding opportunities that might allow continuation of this work.

Please submit a final budget reconciliation and equipment inventory by April 15.

Sincerely,

Dr. Peter Trendel

Department Chair

External funding opportunities. Renata had been pursuing grants for three years, watching her carefully crafted proposals disappear into the bureaucratic void while university administrators funded projects with clearer commercial applications. Her work on how plants self-organized their energy distribution networks was too theoretical for industry sponsors, too biological for engineering departments, and too complex for the simplified narratives that impressed grant committees.

But it was also the most important research she'd ever conducted.

Her phone buzzed with a text from Jae-hyun, her lead graduate student: *Coffee machine broken again. Bringing emergency caffeine for the team meeting. We ready for this?*

The team meeting. At 9 AM, she would sit down with Jae-hyun, Svetlana, and James, three brilliant graduate students who had spent the past two years developing experimental protocols, analyzing data, and building their careers around research that would soon cease to exist. They'd become more than colleagues; they'd become a scientific family united by shared curiosity about how biological systems achieved coordination without central control.

Now she had to tell them their academic futures were uncertain because the university couldn't see commercial applications for understanding how plants solved distributed consensus problems.

Renata opened her laptop and pulled up the decision matrix she'd been working on since receiving the Department Chair's email. She didn't make impulsive choices, they gathered data, analyzed options, and selected the course of action most likely to achieve desired outcomes while minimizing risks. Practical, reliable, and deeply committed to her responsibilities, she valued structure, paid close attention to details, and preferred clear rules over uncertainty. Her approach was steady and grounded, making her someone others could depend on.

Option 1: Pursue Academic Positions Elsewhere

- Pros: Maintain research independence, preserve academic integrity
- Cons: Limited positions available, team would scatter, research might still die
- Probability of Success: 15%
- Timeline: 6-18 months
- Impact on Team: High disruption, uncertain outcomes

Option 2: Transition to Industry Research

- Pros: Stable funding, better equipment, immediate practical applications
- Cons: Loss of research freedom, corporate priorities, potential IP restrictions

- Probability of Success: 60%
- Timeline: 3-6 months
- Impact on Team: Mixed, some positions available, but different research focus

Option 3: Accept Rio Verde Consulting Contract

- Pros: Fund current research, keep team together, explore bio-digital integration
- Cons: Commercial pressure, mentor disapproval, unknown long-term implications
- Probability of Success: 75%
- Timeline: Immediate
- Impact on Team: Preservation of relationships, uncertain research direction

The third option had materialized two weeks earlier in the form of an email from Orion Vale, someone she'd met briefly in a San Francisco Bitcoin meet up in 2019. His message had been direct and intriguing:

Dr. Vega,

It was such a pleasure meeting you in San Francisco and discovering our shared passion for sustainable technology integration. After our conversation about bio-digital systems, I have a proposition that I believe you simply cannot pass up.

I read your recent paper on plant network optimization with great interest. We're operating a unique mining facility in the Amazon that integrates the Bitcoin network with forest regeneration, and we're seeing phenomena that might relate to your research.

Would you be interested in a consulting arrangement to study bio-digital integration? The compensation would be sufficient to support your current research team, and the questions we're investigating might complement your academic work.

I'd be happy to discuss details if you're interested.

Best regards,
Orion Vale
Rio Verde Mining Collective

Renata had researched Rio Verde extensively before responding. Orion's operation was exactly the kind of unconventional project that made traditional academics uncomfortable, Bitcoin mining powered by renewable energy, integrated with forest conservation, claiming to demonstrate harmony between technology and nature. It sounded like exactly the sort of "crypto bro" fantasy that her mentor, Dr. Daria Ha, had warned her about repeatedly.

But the research possibilities were undeniable. If Bitcoin networks and plant networks really did exhibit similar organizational principles, studying their intersection could revolutionize understanding of distributed systems in both biological and digital domains.

Her laptop chimed with a video call request from Dr. Ha. At seventy-one, Daria Ha was a legend in the field of systems biology, a Korean-American scientist who had spent fifty years studying how complex systems achieved coordination without central control. She had mentored Renata through graduate school and beyond, providing not just technical guidance but also wisdom about navigating academic politics and maintaining scientific integrity.

"Good morning, Renata," Dr. Ha's face appeared on screen, her expression carrying the particular mix of concern and disappointment that had motivated graduate students for decades. "I received an interesting phone call yesterday from Harrison Webb. He mentioned you might be considering commercial opportunities."

"Good morning, Professor." Renata had never been able to call her mentor anything less formal, despite years of friendship. "The department is cutting our funding. I'm exploring options to keep the research alive."

"By accepting money from cryptocurrency speculators?"

"By studying bio-digital integration with a group that's actually implementing it in practice. Their questions align with our research interests."

Dr. Ha was quiet for a moment, and Renata could see her processing this information with the same methodical approach she'd taught her students. "Renata, you've spent five years building credibility in academic circles. These Bitcoin people... they're not serious scientists. They're technologists with too much money and too little understanding of biological complexity."

"Have you examined their research protocols?"

"I don't need to examine their protocols. I know what happens when scientists accept funding from commercial interests. The research questions become subordinate to profit motives. The experimental design becomes contaminated by desired outcomes. The intellectual integrity that defines real science gets compromised."

Renata understood her mentor's concerns, they reflected decades of experience watching brilliant researchers lose their way in pursuit of commercial applications. But they also reflected assumptions about Bitcoin and its community that might not be accurate.

"Professor, what if the commercial application genuinely advances scientific understanding? What if studying bio-digital integration reveals principles that pure biology can't access?"

"Then you publish papers about those principles after conducting properly

controlled experiments in academic settings. You don't become a consultant for people who think computers can mimic millions of years of evolutionary optimization."

The conversation continued for twenty minutes, with Dr. Ha expressing increasing concern about Renata's judgment and Renata feeling increasingly defensive about her options. They ended the call with strained politeness, both understanding that a fundamental disagreement was developing between them.

—

At 9 AM, Renata's research team gathered in the lab's small conference room. Jae-hyun, Svetlana, and James had worked together for two years, developing the kind of intellectual shorthand that allowed them to communicate complex ideas through glances and gestures. Watching them settle into their familiar seats, Renata felt the weight of responsibility for their academic futures.

Jae-hyun Chen, her lead graduate student, was twenty-six years old and brilliant in the focused way that made him both an excellent researcher and a terrible dinner party guest. His research on plant neural networks had already generated two published papers and would likely form the foundation of his doctoral dissertation, if he had time to complete it.

Svetlana Kozlov, a postdoc from Moscow State University, brought expertise in network topology that bridged biology and mathematics. Her visa status depended on maintaining her research positions, making the lab's closure an existential threat to her American academic career.

James Park, the youngest team member at twenty-four, possessed an intuitive understanding of biological systems that complemented his computational skills. His algorithms for modeling plant network behavior were elegantly efficient and represented the kind of interdisciplinary thinking that academic departments claimed to value but rarely supported.

"Good morning, everyone," Renata began, her voice carrying more authority than she felt. "I know you've all been wondering about the departmental budget situation."

She explained the funding cut, the timeline for lab closure, and the limited options for continuing their research. The team listened with the careful attention of people whose lives were being fundamentally disrupted by bureaucratic decisions beyond their control.

"So what are our alternatives?" Jae-hyun asked when she finished.

Renata pulled up her decision matrix, walking them through each option's probabilities and implications. When she reached the Rio Verde consulting opportunity, Svetlana leaned forward with interest.

"This Bitcoin mining facility," Svetlana said, her slight Russian accent making the technical terms sound more exotic. "They claim to integrate digital networks with biological systems?"

"According to their preliminary reports, yes. The facility uses renewable energy to mine Bitcoin while supporting forest regeneration. They're observing network phenomena that might relate to our research on plant organization."

James looked skeptical. "Sounds like greenwashing to me. Cryptocurrency mining is an environmental disaster, regardless of their energy source."

"Maybe," Renata agreed. "But if they're genuinely observing bio-digital integration, it could represent a new research domain. We might learn things about network organization that pure biological research can't access."

Jae-hyun was quiet, processing the implications. As the most experienced graduate student, his opinion would significantly influence the others. "What's Dr. Ha's position on this?"

"She's concerned about commercial influence on research integrity. She thinks accepting Bitcoin industry funding would compromise our scientific credibility."

"And what do you think?" Svetlana asked directly.

Renata looked at her team, three brilliant young scientists whose careers depended on her decision-making. "I think we need more information before making any choice. I'm proposing to conduct due diligence on the Rio Verde opportunity. Interview their team, examine their protocols, evaluate whether their research questions align with our scientific interests."

"And if they do align?" James asked.

"Then we make a decision based on evidence rather than assumptions."

The team agreed to the investigation approach, and they spent the next two hours developing evaluation criteria for assessing the Rio Verde opportunity. Their methodology was rigorous, designed to separate legitimate research possibilities from marketing claims or wishful thinking.

—

Over the following week, Renata conducted video interviews with five members of the Rio Verde team. The conversations revealed a level of scientific sophistication that surprised her. Rather than tech entrepreneurs playing with environmental themes, they seemed to be serious researchers investigating genuinely novel phenomena.

Orion Vale himself proved more scientifically literate than expected. His questions about plant network optimization revealed understanding of the technical challenges Renata's team was addressing. More importantly, he seemed genuinely interested in learning rather than confirming pre-existing beliefs.

Valerie Chen-Vale's ecological urban planning work impressed Renata even more. Her designs treated the entire complex as a living ecosystem, applying principles that echoed Renata's research into decentralized natural law systems. "We're not building a mining facility with green features," Valerie explained during their interview. "We're designing a regenerative community where Bitcoin mining becomes one metabolic function within a larger ecological organism." Her evolutionary, integrative approach required constant adaptation and local leadership development, exactly the kind of co-eco-creation that could prove profitable without exploitation, sustainable without dependence on grants. The project needed visionary leaders willing to take on expanding initiatives, creating a model that could be genuinely replicated rather than merely admired.

Sarah Kim from the Observatory had been tracking the facility's environmental impact with academic rigor. Her data showed measurable forest regeneration correlated with mining activity, not causation, but correlation strong enough to warrant investigation. She had given Renata the heads up and validated her choice to go work there, believing the Amazon mining facility warranted firsthand observation. Also that she and Aírínne were thinking of coming to visit in person to witness the developments themselves.

But the most compelling interview was with Dr. Andreas Weber, a former Max Planck Institute researcher who had been studying the facility's energy dynamics for six months.

"The integration is real," Dr. Weber explained during their video call, his German accent adding gravity to his technical descriptions. "The Bitcoin

mining network exhibits organizational properties remarkably similar to mycorrhizal networks. Both achieve distributed consensus through similar algorithmic processes."

"Can you be more specific?" Renata asked.

He hesitated for a moment, glancing toward the mine entrance. "Since you're not officially working on the project yet, I can only share general concepts, most of the technical details are proprietary information. But I can tell you this much: "Both systems propagate information through network nodes, achieve consensus without central authority, and optimize resource allocation through competitive cooperation. The mathematical structures underlying both processes are nearly identical."

"Nearly identical how?"

"I'll tell you more once you're on the ground with us, but I can send you a document that says a little more, Bitcoin network diagrams," he said, his tone suggesting the conversation had reached its limits for now.

After the call, Renata sat in her lab staring at her own research data with new eyes. For three years, she'd been studying how plants achieved network coordination without understanding that technologists were solving similar problems through cryptographic protocols.

—

That evening, Renata stayed late in the lab, running new analyses on data she'd collected over the past years. Her plant network experiments had generated thousands of images showing root system development, nutrient distribution patterns, and information propagation pathways.

She pulled up Dr. Weber's Bitcoin network diagrams and began comparing them to her biological data. The similarities were striking, but she needed quantitative analysis rather than visual impression.

At 11:30 PM, Jae-hyun found her hunched over her computer, running statistical comparisons between biological and digital network topologies.

Renata, you've been here all day. Please, go home and get some rest.

"Look at this," she said without turning around. "Network density distributions, information propagation pathways, consensus formation patterns. The correlation coefficients are above 0.9 for most metrics."

Jae-hyun looked at her screen, recognizing the significance immediately. "Are you saying plant networks and Bitcoin networks use the same organizational principles?"

"I'm saying they might have independently evolved similar solutions to the same problem: how to achieve coordination in distributed systems without central control."

"That's…" Jae-hyun paused, processing the implications. "That's a completely new research domain. Bio-digital integration isn't just interdisciplinary collaboration, it's studying convergent evolution between biological and technological systems."

Renata turned to face him, her exhaustion replaced by the excitement that drove real scientific discovery. "Jae-hyun, what if accepting the Rio Verde consulting contract isn't selling out? What if it's accessing a natural laboratory where biology and technology are already integrating?"

"Dr. Ha won't see it that way."

"Dr. Ha built her career studying biological systems in isolation. But if technology is independently discovering biological solutions, studying their intersection becomes essential to understanding either domain fully."

"We design experiments to test the hypothesis that biological and digital networks exhibit mathematical equivalence. We design instruments to record the correlation between neural firing patterns and network packet flows, between synaptic plasticity and algorithmic adaptation. If we're right, it revolutionizes understanding of distributed systems in both domains. If we're wrong, we learn something important about the limitations of biomimicry."

"And the Rio Verde contract?"

Renata looked at her data again, seeing three years of careful research transformed by a single evening's analysis. "Becomes the opportunity to conduct experiments that no traditional academic lab could access."

At midnight, she called Svetlana and James, asking them to return to the lab despite the late hour. By 2 AM, all four team members were redesigning their research protocols to investigate bio-digital convergence.

By dawn, they had outlined experimental approaches that would require access to functioning Bitcoin networks integrated with biological systems, exactly what Rio Verde offered.

—

The next morning, Renata called Dr. Ha to explain her decision. The conversation was difficult but necessary.

"Professor, I've decided to accept the Rio Verde consulting contract."

"Renata, I'm disappointed. You're sacrificing academic integrity for commercial funding."

"I'm pursuing scientific discovery wherever it leads. Our preliminary analysis suggests biological and digital networks exhibit mathematical equivalence. Studying their intersection could revolutionize understanding of distributed systems."

"These Bitcoin people have convinced you that their technology mimics biology. That doesn't make their commercial applications scientifically valuable."

"They haven't convinced me of anything. The data convinced me. Plant networks and Bitcoin networks exhibit statistical correlation above 0.9 for multiple organizational metrics. Either this is the most remarkable coincidence in scientific history, or we're observing convergent evolution between biological and technological systems."

Dr. Ha was quiet for a long moment. "Show me the data."

Renata spent the next hour walking her mentor through the correlation analyses, the network topology comparisons, and the theoretical implications of bio-digital mathematical equivalence. Dr. Ha asked sharp questions and raised valid concerns, but couldn't dismiss the quantitative evidence.

"If your analysis is correct," Dr. Ha said finally, "you're not just changing research focus, you're defining a new scientific discipline."

"That's what I think, yes."

"And if you're wrong?"

"Then I learn something important about the limitations of interdisciplinary research while keeping my team together and our research funded."

Dr. Ha sighed, the sound carrying resignation rather than disapproval. "Renata, you've always been my most methodical student. If you've analyzed this decision with your usual rigor, I trust your judgment even when I don't share your enthusiasm."

"Thank you, Professor."

"But promise me something. Don't let commercial pressures contaminate your experimental design. Real science emerges from honest questions, not desired outcomes."

"I promise."

After ending the call, Renata sent an email to Orion Vale accepting the Rio Verde consulting contract. Her decision wasn't based on commercial opportunity or funding necessity, it was based on scientific evidence suggesting that the most important research questions emerged at the intersection of biology and technology.

—

Two weeks later, Renata stood in her Berkeley lab for the last time, supervising the careful packing of equipment that would be shipped to the Amazon rainforest. Her team was traveling to Rio Verde not as consultants but as researchers pursuing questions that could reshape understanding of how complex systems achieved coordination.

Jae-hyun carefully wrapped the sensor arrays they'd developed for monitoring plant neural networks. Svetlana backup up three years of experimental data to secure servers. James tested the portable analysis equipment they'd need for field research.

"Dr. Vega," James said as they finished packing, "I have to admit, when you first mentioned Bitcoin mining in the rainforest, I thought you'd lost your scientific mind."

"And now?"

"Now I think we might be about to discover something that textbooks will be written about."

Svetlana nodded enthusiastically. "In Moscow, we have saying: 'Правда не боится вопросов.'[29] If bio-digital integration is real, studying it honestly will reveal Truth regardless of commercial context."

Jae-hyun added, "And if it's not real, we'll learn that too. Either way, we're doing science."

Renata looked at her team, three brilliant researchers whose careers she'd just committed to an experimental path that could lead to paradigm-shifting discovery or career-ending failure. But the data supported the risk, and the questions they were pursuing felt more important than academic safety.

"One more thing," she said, pulling up the final correlation analysis on her laptop. "I ran additional statistical tests on the bio-digital network comparison. The mathematical equivalence isn't just remarkable, it's precise enough to suggest we're observing fundamental principles of distributed organization that apply across domains."

"Meaning?" James asked.

"Meaning we might be studying not just biomimicry, but universal laws governing how complex systems achieve coordination without central control.

---

29   ‚Truth is not afraid of questions.'

Biology and technology as different expressions of the same underlying mathematics."

Jae-hyun grinned. "No pressure for our first day in the Amazon."

Svetlana laughed. "In Russia, we also say: 'Наука, это приключение для людей, которые слишком трусливы для настоящих приключений.'[30] I think we are about to test this theory."

That evening, Renata received a message from Dr. Ha: *Renata, I've been thinking about our conversation. You're right that scientific discovery requires intellectual courage. I may not agree with your methods, but I admire your willingness to follow evidence wherever it leads. Make sure you publish whatever you discover, academic integrity means sharing truth regardless of its source.*

The next morning, the team flew to São Paulo, then to Manaus, then by small plane into the Amazon basin where Orion's facility integrated Bitcoin mining with forest regeneration. They were no longer just studying how plants optimized energy networks, they were investigating whether the same optimization principles governed both biological and digital systems.

The scientist's proof would emerge not from theoretical analysis but from empirical observation of phenomena that challenged traditional boundaries between natural and artificial systems.

—

---

30 ‚Science is an adventure for people too cowardly for actual adventure.'

Six Months Later

From: Dr. Renata Vega
To: The Bitcoin Diplomatic Observatory
Cc: Alpha, Aírínne Fynn, Sarah Kim
Subject: Field Research Update - "Mathematical Equivalence in Biological and Digital Network Organization"

Dear Observatory Team,

With Orion's approval, I'm sharing our six months of field research on bio-digital integration at the Rio Verde facility in the Amazon rainforest. Our findings suggest that biological networks (plant root systems) and digital networks (Bitcoin mining nodes) exhibit mathematical equivalence in their organizational principles.

Key findings include: - Statistical correlation above 0.95 between biological and digital network topology metrics - Identical algorithmic processes governing consensus formation in both domains - Evidence that both systems independently evolved optimal solutions to distributed coordination problems

These results suggest that bio-digital integration represents not just interdisciplinary collaboration but investigation of universal principles governing complex system organization.

You should come see for yourselves. The data is compelling, but witnessing the harmony between Bitcoin miners and forest ecosystems in person reveals something that can't be captured in spreadsheets.

All data and methodologies are available for your review.

Sincerely, Dr. Renata Vega and the Rio Verde Research Team

Renata smiled, looking out at the Amazon forest where Bitcoin miners hummed in harmony with bird songs and her plant sensors detected root networks optimizing resource distribution through algorithms indistinguishable from cryptographic protocols.

She was glad to have left the rigid academic structure under Dr. Ha's tutelage to work in the real world. Even if she would receive no academic accolades, she felt she was contributing to live changes that were truly important. Truth, it turned out, didn't care about institutional recognition. It only cared about honest investigation of what was actually happening in the world.

Satoshi's Travel Journal

DIGITAL PHOTOSYNTHESIS
La Selva Research Station, Costa Rica
June 21, 1992

Dawn light filtering through canopy layers in prismatic beams

The hummingbirds begin their morning dance as solar panels track the rising sun. From my window at the research station, I watch two forms of energy harvesting in perfect synchronization: biological photosynthesis converting sunlight to chemical energy, mechanical tracking systems converting sunlight to electrical energy. Both follow the same principle, adaptive algorithms responding to energy availability.

Dr. Martinez from the station explains the solar array's behavior: "The panels adjust their angle every few minutes, optimizing for maximum energy capture throughout the day. But watch this, during cloudy periods, the tracking slows down, conserving motor energy when the returns diminish."

This adaptive behavior mirrors the forest around us. Plants grow toward light when it's abundant, conserve energy during scarcity, redistribute resources through underground networks during stress. The entire ecosystem breathes with rhythms of energy availability.

What if computational networks could operate with similar organic intelligence? What if digital mining could adapt to renewable energy cycles rather than demanding constant power consumption?

Technical note: Variable hash rate algorithms that respond to energy availability. Mining difficulty that adjusts to solar cycles, wind patterns, hydroelectric capacity. Network that breathes with the planet's energy rhythms.

I sketch systems that mine aggressively when solar panels are generating excess power, scale back during grid peak demand, hibernate during renewable energy scarcity. The economics are compelling, renewable energy is cheapest when abundant, most expensive when scarce. A network that follows these patterns would naturally gravitate toward sustainability.

But there's deeper elegance here. Photosynthesis doesn't just consume solar energy, it creates the oxygen that enables all other life. What if digital mining could be similarly regenerative? What if computational work could fund environmental restoration, creating positive feedback loops between technological growth and ecological health?

A family of howler monkeys calls from the canopy, their voices carrying across miles of forest. Their communication network spans the entire region without infrastructure, without central planning, without environmental cost. They've evolved technologies that strengthen rather than degrade their habitat.

The solar panels complete another adjustment, tilting toward optimal angle as clouds shift. Somewhere in that movement, I see the future of digital networks, technology that learns from nature rather than fighting it, systems that grow stronger by making their environment stronger.

The research station hums with equipment powered by yesterday's sunshine, stored in batteries charged by this morning's breeze. Energy flows where it's needed, when it's needed, following patterns perfected over millions of years. Digital networks could learn these patterns, become part of these cycles rather than disrupting them.

As the sun climbs higher, both the forest and the solar array respond with increasing activity. Biological and digital systems synchronized, each making the other more efficient. This is what technological evolution could look like, not the conquest of nature, but integration with it.

Digital Gardens

"The Earth does not belong to us: we belong to the Earth."[31]

- Marlee Matlin

Rio Verde - 2023

By now, the Rio Verde Mining Complex had evolved into something that defied traditional categories, part sustainable village, part technological marvel, wholly integrated into the Amazon ecosystem.

Where once bulldozers might have cleared forest for expansion, the community had learned to weave itself through the existing canopy structure, creating elevated walkways and platforms that moved with the rhythm of the trees rather than against them. Instead of deforestation, the mining facility had become a model of digital integration with the jungle, proving that the future could be both technologically advanced and ecologically regenerative.

---

31   Marlee Matlin (born 1965) is an American actress, author, and activist, best known for being the first deaf performer to win an Academy Award. Though this quote is often attributed to her, it is more commonly linked to Indigenous wisdom and environmental philosophy rather than her documented speeches or writings.

The evening air was filled with the sounds of communal life as Inca, the village's head chef and a former restaurant owner from Lima, prepared dinner on the main overlook platform.

The feast spread before the community represented the abundance of Amazonian biodiversity, all harvested from surrounding communities practicing the ancestral art of forest gathering: grilled tambaqui fish caught fresh from the river, roasted paca seasoned with wild herbs, steamed yuca and plantains harvested from the forest gardens, açaí bowls topped with Brazil nuts and cacao nibs, fresh hearts of palm salad mixed with cupuaçu fruit, and exotic delicacies like roasted saúva ants and fermented caju.

The jovial atmosphere was infectious, miners, indigenous families, researchers, and visiting engineers all gathering around communal tables built into tree platforms, sharing meals and stories as the sun set through the canopy above them. This was more than sustainable living; it was proof that they were part of something entirely new.

The mining operation itself had been relocated deep into a natural cave complex discovered during their third year, where the earth's thermal regulation kept the ASIC miners cool without energy-intensive cooling systems.

Above ground, solar panels mounted on rotating systems followed the sun's path along the mountain cliffs, while the expanded hydroelectric plant harnessed three separate river tributaries to power both the cryptocurrency operations and the entire village infrastructure. The technology hadn't conquered the forest, it had learned to dance with it.

The Amazon rainforest canopy stretched endlessly toward the horizon, a sea of green broken only by the gleaming solar arrays of the Rio Verde Mining Complex. Orion Vale stood at the edge of the facility, watching as morning dew transformed into mist, rising from the jungle floor to meet the sun.

His steel-gray eyes now held green flecks that reflected the forest light, his lean 5'10" frame more muscled from years of physical labor, dark hair streaked with silver resembling natural camouflage. His revolutionary satisfaction was evident in the way he surveyed his creation; years of environmental integration mastery finally vindicated this impossible harmony between technology and nature.

His bronzed skin showed the weathering of someone who had learned to move through the forest with indigenous grace, touching trees and technology with equal reverence.

Though he stood among the mining equipment like any other technician, Orion was far more than an operational miner. As the visionary architect who had conceived Rio Verde three years earlier, along with Valerie, they both had taken a big leap of faith, leaving Oregon to pursue something unprecedented: proving that Bitcoin mining could not only coexist with nature but actively regenerate it. This facility was their answer to every critic who claimed cryptocurrency would destroy the planet.

"The miners breathe," he said to no one in particular, watching the interplay of water, light, and electricity.

His eyes were bright with vindicated vision, smile lines deepening from the satisfaction of sustainable success, revolutionary passion now tempered with environmental wisdom. "Rio Verde proves Bitcoin and nature aren't enemies, they're allies," he thought, observing the perfect synchronization around him. "But how does a payment protocol teach machines to breathe with trees? What consciousness am I witnessing when technology learns to grow?"

Behind him, rows of ASIC miners hummed in perfect resonance with the forest's morning chorus. His tablet displayed the facility's vital signs.

// Solar Generation: 12.4 Mega Watts
// Biomass Backup: Ready
// Mining Efficiency: 94.3%
// Carbon Offset: +2,145 tons
// Forest Growth Index: +15%

This was no ordinary mining operation. Rio Verde represented the first successful integration of Bitcoin mining with forest regeneration. Every hash produced here helped fund the protection and expansion of the surrounding rainforest.

"Morning check?" called out Renata Vega, the facility's lead botanist, emerging from the greenhouse section. Her thick brown braids were interwoven with bio-sensors that pulsed with soft blue light, hazel eyes bright with discovery as she navigated between the technical and organic worlds. Her bio-systems integration expertise was evident in every movement as she navigated between the technical and organic worlds with equal facility. Her hands were stained with soil, real soil, not the digital kind Orion usually dealt with.

Her strong hands moved with gentle precision between seedlings and circuits, her fluid movement between organic and digital systems unconsciously mirroring the plant growth patterns she studied.

The botanist title was a convenient simplification for visitors and journalists, but Renata's true role was far more complex. As the Technical Master who had designed Rio Verde's revolutionary bio-systems dynamics, along with her team, they'd spent two years developing the algorithms that allowed mining hardware to interface with living ecosystems.

Her soil-stained hands came from calibrating sensors that monitored everything from root growth to mycorrhizal networks, creating the feedback loops that made the digital-biological integration possible.

"The network's evolving," he replied, showing her his readings. "Look at the new growth patterns."

On his screen, two data streams intertwined: the facility's hashrate and the forest's growth metrics. They pulsed in unexpected synchronicity, as if the digital mining had somehow entrained with the jungle's natural rhythms.

Her face glowed with excitement at the bio-digital breakthrough, eyes wide with wonder at the biological responses to digital rhythms. "It's not just about converting sunlight anymore," Renata said, understanding dawning in her eyes. "The plants respond to Bitcoin's rhythms like they recognize something familiar," she thought, watching the data patterns. "But what do photosynthesis and proof-of-work have in common? Are we discovering that mathematics and life spring from the same source?" "The whole system is becoming... organic."

Orion nodded. This was why he'd left his job and his Bitcoin Education center in Portland. Something new was happening here, something that transcended the old paradigms of digital versus natural.[32]

The facility had started as a simple concept: use excess solar energy to mine Bitcoin. But as they'd built it, integrating it with the surrounding ecosystem, something unexpected had emerged. The vegetal dimension, as the crypto-ecologists called it, had begun to manifest.

"Come see this," Renata said, leading him into the greenhouse. Her technical excitement combined with environmental joy created an almost luminous presence, breakthrough discoveries visible in her energetic movements as she tended equipment and flora with identical care. Here, experimental

---

32 ⚠ SOCIAL COHESION DISRUPTION WARNING ⚠
→   Bitcoin communities demonstrate superior well-being metrics #DecentralizedHappiness
→   Why are all our researchers moving to these communities? #ProofOfWellBeing

plants grew in spiraling patterns that mimicked the Bitcoin network's difficulty adjustments. "The plants are responding to the mining rhythms. It's like they recognize it as another form of photosynthesis."

The arrival of the small aircraft breaks the morning stillness, its solar-powered engines barely audible above the forest canopy. Orion and Renata exchange glances, they've been expecting these particular visitors. Dr. Aírínne Fynn from the Bitcoin Diplomatic Observatory and journalist Sarah Kim are coming to document what might be the most significant breakthrough in cryptocurrency's environmental evolution.

Twenty minutes later, not wasting any time, Aírínne moves carefully along the forest path, using Renata's awareness-based equipment to capture and record the hum of ASICs interwoven with birdsong. Her red hair is pulled back in a practical research braid, blue-green eyes focused intently on bio-digital resonance patterns displaying impossible synchronization, lab coat worn over field clothes that speak to both scientific precision and environmental readiness.

She is documenting everything, but also breathing it all in.

Aírínne scientific precision is evolving into something more mystical as she begins to recognize consciousness emerging as a fundamental force in her research. The instruments detect patterns that challenge every assumption about the relationship between technology and life.

Behind her, Sarah films everything, recognizing this could be the story that changes public perception of Bitcoin forever.

Aírínne scientific precision is evident in how she handles each instrument, occasionally pausing in amazement at readings, unconsciously holding her breath when witnessing unprecedented phenomena.

Ƀ

The array of instruments surrounding Renata represented years of collaborative development with her research team, dating back to their university days together. Her primary device, a quantum coherence analyzer, measured the electromagnetic field fluctuations between the mining rigs and surrounding vegetation with precision that would have been impossible just a decade earlier.

Connected to it, a bio-electrical sensor grid mapped the subtle electrical patterns coursing through plant root systems, while a network frequency monitor tracked the real-time hash rate variations of nearby ASICs. The most experimental piece, a consciousness resonance detector that she'd built based on emerging theories about quantum awareness in biological systems, hummed quietly as it attempted to map the intersection points where digital and organic intelligence seemed to converge.

Each instrument represented not just technological advancement, but years of late-night conversations, failed prototypes, and the kind of interdisciplinary thinking that traditional academic departments rarely encouraged. These instruments, born from Renata's university research and refined through countless hours of field work, now serve Aírínne perfectly in her quest to understand the deeper patterns.

Each instrument feeds data into the shared tablet, where custom algorithms search for correlation patterns that shouldn't exist. The readings display in real-time: network activity spikes corresponding with photosynthetic surges, hash rate adjustments that mirror circadian rhythms, and electromagnetic signatures that pulse in harmony between silicon circuits and cellular structures.

As Aírínne watches the data flow, she realizes her own breathing has synchronized with the rhythm of the readings, inhaling with each network pulse, exhaling with each biological response, as if the instruments have taught her body to breathe in harmony with the bio-digital convergence.

"This is remarkable," Aírínne murmurs, watching Renata's instruments detect the bio-digital resonance patterns that had been theorized but never proven at this scale.

"The measurements don't lie, Bitcoin and biology are synchronizing," she thinks, reviewing the impossible data, her breath naturally matching the cadence of the data streams. "But synchronizing to what? What deeper pattern are they both following? Why does consciousness feel like the missing variable in every equation?"

Sarah interviews James Park, a botanist who works alongside Renata's technical team. Sarah's black hair now has subtle highlights from outdoor work, dark eyes wide with amazement at documenting what shouldn't be possible.

"When we first arrived," the scientist explains, "we expected to lower Bitcoin's environmental impact. Instead, we're documenting the emergence of a hybrid ecosystem that shouldn't be possible according to traditional biology." "The network signatures are actually synchronizing with natural growth cycles."

Her filmmaker's trained eye captures every significant moment, hands steady despite witnessing reality-reshaping events, unconsciously protecting her documentation equipment as a sacred record.

Orion checks the network stats.

    // Global Green Mining: 31%
    // Biomass Integration: Growing
    // Network Photosynthesis Rate: 42 TH/joule
    // Ecological Consensus: Emerging

These are new metrics, ones that hadn't existed in the pure mineral phase of Bitcoin's evolution. The network is learning to grow like a plant, to put

down roots, to integrate with Earth's natural systems.

"Remember when they said Bitcoin would destroy the environment?" Orion laughs, but it's a knowing laugh. His gestures encompass both natural and digital ecosystems, deep satisfaction radiating from the alignment between his values and action. The critics hadn't understood that technology could evolve, could learn to grow organically.

Svetlana points to a new species of vine they've discovered growing near the mining rigs. Somehow, it has adapted to use the waste heat for growth, creating a natural cooling system for the ASICs.

"Zhizn' naydet vykhod," she quotes, "dazhe v tsifrovuyu epokhu"[33]

Their conversation is interrupted by an alert. One of the mining rigs has automatically adjusted its hashrate to match the morning's solar curve, something they hadn't programmed it to do. The machines are learning from the forest.

"Look at the difficulty adjustment," Orion says, pulling up the charts. "It's following the same pattern as seasonal growth cycles. The network isn't just securing transactions anymore, it's learning to grow."

"Are you getting this?" Aírínne asks Sarah, her voice filled with excitement as the instruments register the unprecedented data patterns, her breathing naturally synchronizing with each wave of readings. Excitement about consciousness discoveries creates an almost visible energy field around her, breakthrough anticipation radiating from her focused intensity. "The bio-digital integration isn't just theoretical, it's creating emergent behaviors in both systems."

---

33   Life finds a way, even in the digital age.

Sarah nods, her camera capturing the moment when a mining rig's cooling fans automatically slow as the surrounding vines create more shade. Her expression cycles between journalistic skepticism and growing wonder, mouth slightly open as she witnesses paradigm shifts in real time.

"I came to document a mining facility and found something that's reshaping my understanding of reality itself," she thinks, filming what should be impossible. "If Bitcoin can teach technology to cooperate with nature, what else can it teach? What other 'impossible' things are just waiting for the right catalyst?"

"This is going to revolutionize how people think about cryptocurrency's relationship with the environment," she says. "It's not just sustainable, it's regenerative."

Orion had adapted completely to this environment, but he still remembered the early days of brute force, burning trees to force a system to work, when Bitcoin mining was all about raw computational power regardless of environmental cost.

Now, watching the interplay of sunlight, photosynthesis, and proof-of-work algorithms working in harmony around him, he understood something profound: the mineral dimension had been just the beginning. What they'd built here transcended simple resource extraction or even sustainable technology; it was proof that digital networks could integrate with biological systems to create something entirely new.

A new block is found, its hash somehow incorporating data from the forest's growth.

> // Block #1,309,942
> // Renewable Energy: 100%

"The bridges are forming," Aírínne says, watching the data flow. "Between silicon and soil, between hash and growth, between the digital and the organic."

Orion walks to the facility's edge again, where the solar arrays meet the rainforest. The morning mist has cleared, revealing the true scale of their operation. Bitcoin miners nestle in the jungle like seeds, each one contributing to both digital and organic growth.

"We're not just mining Bitcoin anymore," he realizes. "We're growing it."

As the afternoon sun filters through the canopy, Aírínne and Sarah prepare to leave, their documentation complete but their understanding forever changed. They'd arrived expecting to study an experimental mining facility and are leaving as witnesses to Bitcoin's evolutionary leap into biological integration.

"The implications go far beyond environmental concerns," Aírínne tells Orion as they walk back to the aircraft. The historical documentation responsibility weighs visibly on Sarah as she carefully preserves every moment of impossible transformation. "If the network can learn to grow like a living system, we're seeing the emergence of the vegetal dimension in real time."

Sarah uploads her footage to satellite internet, already composing the article that will introduce the world to regenerative cryptocurrency. "Rio Verde isn't just a mining facility," she will write. "It's proof that technology and nature can evolve together, each making the other stronger."

Above them, the sun continues its arc, powering both photosynthesis and proof-of-work. The vegetal dimension is awakening, teaching the network how to grow, how to integrate, how to become truly sustainable.

In the distance, a new solar array tracks the sun like a digital sunflower. The Bitcoin network is putting down roots, literally and figuratively. From these roots, something new will grow, something that bridges the gap between technology and nature.

The digital gardens are just beginning to bloom. One hash at a time. One leaf at a time.

Satoshi's Travel Journal

THE PROPAGANDA MACHINE
Internet Café, Berlin, Germany
August 9, 1992

Overcast sky, pieces of the Wall still visible in construction rubble

Through the café window, I watch workers scraping propaganda posters from building walls, layer upon layer of competing messages about Truth, Freedom, and Economic systems. Each regime claimed scientific authority for their monetary policies, each promised prosperity through central planning, each used the same techniques to shape public opinion.

The café owner, Hans, escaped from East Berlin just months before the Wall fell. "You learn to read between the lines," he tells me, pointing to a remaining poster fragment. "When they say 'scientific socialism,' they mean 'ignore the evidence.' When they say 'for the people's benefit,' they mean 'for the party's benefit.' The bigger the lie, the more authoritative it sounds."

His words resonate as I consider how revolutionary technologies face systematic opposition. Any system that threatens entrenched power will be attacked through predictable methods: environmental concerns, criminal associations, technical complexity, economic instability. The truth becomes secondary to controlling the narrative.

Technical note: Transparent energy accounting essential for credibility. Open-source implementation to prevent manipulation accusations. Mathematical proofs that can't be distorted by political interpretation.

Already I can envision the attack vectors: "Digital currency consumes too much energy!" But compared to what? Where are the studies calculating the energy cost of printing money, securing it with armies, enforcing it through surveillance, replacing it when it inevitably fails?

"Environmental concerns" will be weaponized by the same institutions that burn fossil fuels to power their global enforcement apparatus. "Criminal usage" will be highlighted while ignoring that every criminal in history has used whatever money was available, including the dollars funding the armies that protect the dollar's hegemony.

A young woman at the next table types furiously on her laptop, uploading something to early bulletin board systems. "Information wants to be free," she says, noticing my observation. "But power wants to control information. The internet might be our chance to route around the censors."

She's right about routing around censorship, but wrong about information wanting to be free. Information wants to be accurate. Free information can be manipulated, distorted, weaponized. What we need is unforgeable information, Truth that can't be altered by those who control the printing presses.

The propaganda fragments on the walls tell the same story across decades: centralized control over information leads to systematic distortion of reality. But mathematical truth is immune to propaganda. You can't manipulate cryptographic proof through narrative control. You can't distort a hash function through political pressure.

Hans brings me another coffee, his expression thoughtful. "The best propaganda always contains enough truth to sound reasonable," he observes. "That's how they get people to accept the lies. But mathematics..." He gestures toward my technical sketches. "Mathematics is either right or wrong. No room for interpretation."

The workers outside continue scraping walls, preparing surfaces for new messages. But somewhere in those technical sketches lies something different,

a communication system based on mathematical proof rather than institutional authority. Truth that survives the rise and fall of propaganda regimes.

The overcast sky lightens slightly, illuminating the construction site where new buildings rise from rubble. Creative destruction at work, old systems making way for new ones. The process is never comfortable, never tidy, never without resistance from those who profit from the status quo.

But mathematics endures. Truth persists. And sometimes, that's enough to change the world.

Renewable Energy Hijack

7 TERRIFYING Ways Bitcoin Miners Are STEALING Your Green Energy Future - #4 Will Make Your Blood BOIL!

SUSTAINABLE FUTURE QUARTERLY | October 15, 2023 | *4 min read*

Bitcoin mining operations increasingly target renewable energy sources. Photo: Getty Images

By Dr. Samantha Green | Senior Environmental Policy Analyst | @DrSGreen

---

Share this story: ✔ Twitter ⨍ Facebook ▣ Instagram ⁱⁿ LinkedIn

---

Bitcoin miners have launched what experts are calling "the greatest misappropriation of renewable resources in history," with mining operations now aggressively colonizing the world's sustainable energy infrastructure.

This digital parasite, not content with merely consuming fossil fuels, has mutated to target our planet's green energy future. Is your solar-powered home next?

The Digital Locusts Devouring Our Clean Energy

Recent investigations reveal a disturbing trend: Bitcoin mining operations are systematically positioning themselves near renewable energy sources, effectively hijacking solar farms, wind installations, and hydroelectric facilities.

"They're like digital locusts," explains Dr. Elvis Williams, Director of the Global Renewable Energy Institute. "They descend on clean energy projects and devour their output before it can reach legitimate users."

"Every megawatt consumed by Bitcoin is a megawatt stolen from real-world needs."

— Patricia Lin, Chief Sustainability Officer at Green Power International

The SHOCKING Numbers That Renewable Energy Companies Don't Want You To See

The data paints a devastating picture. In the past year alone, Bitcoin miners have contracted or purchased the output of renewable energy facilities that could have powered three million homes.

That's equivalent to:

- ⚡ The entire electricity consumption of Denmark
- 🏠 Powering every home in Chicago for 2 years
- 🔋 Charging 500 million electric vehicles

⚓ INTERACTIVE MAP: See if Bitcoin miners are stealing YOUR local green energy

Why Iceland's Green Dream Became a Crypto NIGHTMARE

Most alarming is the miners' sophisticated strategy of targeting regions with abundant renewable resources. Iceland's geothermal power, once a model of sustainable development, now predominantly serves Bitcoin mining operations.

The country's dream of becoming a green data haven has been perverted into a cryptocurrency nightmare.

WATCH: Inside Iceland's Bitcoin Mining Facilities *Click to play our exclusive investigation*

The Big Lie Bitcoin Promoters Are Telling About Green Energy

"They claim they're encouraging renewable energy development," scoffs Dr. Williams, "but what they're actually doing is parasitizing our sustainable infrastructure."

Sources within the renewable energy sector report that Bitcoin miners are now preemptively buying up future renewable energy production, potentially locking out traditional users for decades.

It's Not Just About Electricity - They're Coming For Your WATER Too

The environmental impact extends beyond mere energy consumption. These mining operations require massive cooling systems, often using precious water resources in already stressed regions.

"They're not just consuming green energy," explains Dr. Monica Rodriguez of the Water Conservation Institute. "They're depleting our water tables to cool their machines."

The Greenwashing SCAM That's Fooling Millions

More insidious is the miners' attempt to greenwash their operations through strategic renewable energy partnerships.

"It's like a polluter buying carbon credits while continuing to pollute," notes Lin. "They're using green energy as a fig leaf to cover their fundamental unsustainability."

Why Your Factory Can't Go Green (HINT: Bitcoin Is To Blame)

The economic distortions are equally concerning. Bitcoin mining operations, with their promise of immediate high-volume energy purchases, are disrupting traditional renewable energy markets.

"They're outbidding legitimate industrial users," reveals an industry insider who requested anonymity. "Manufacturing facilities that want to go green can't compete with Bitcoin's pricing power."

The "Digital Bedouins" Destroying Communities

Particularly troubling is the emergence of what experts term "nomadic mining" – mobile Bitcoin operations that follow seasonal renewable energy availability, depleting resources before moving on.

"They're like digital bedouins," explains Dr. Williams, "except instead of sustaining traditional ways of life, they're consuming our sustainable future."

The HARD TRUTH About Bitcoin and Renewable Energy

For those who champion cryptocurrency's green potential, the reality is a harsh awakening. Bitcoin isn't driving renewable energy adoption; it's hijacking it.

Every solar panel dedicated to mining is one denied to homes and businesses. Every wind turbine spinning for cryptocurrency is one not powering real economic activity.

What MUST Be Done Before It's Too Late

The solution, experts agree, requires immediate regulatory intervention.

"We can't allow speculative digital assets to commandeer our renewable energy future," argues Dr. Rodriguez. "The choice between real sustainability and Bitcoin's false promises should be clear."

As the climate crisis accelerates, the time has come to recognize Bitcoin's renewable energy colonization for what it is: a digital land grab threatening our sustainable future.

The question isn't whether we can afford to let Bitcoin consume our green energy resources – it's whether we can afford not to stop it.

Special Report commissioned by the Coalition for Responsible Energy Use

Conflict of Interest: Author sits on the board of three major fossil fuel companies and consults for traditional energy utilities

Compensation: Home on a private island in the Caribbean (Value: $4.5M) plus lifetime supply of "carbon neutral" private jet fuel

---

Related Stories You Won't Want to Miss:

- 10 Ways To Tell If Your Solar Panels Are Being Hijacked By Crypto Miners
- REVEALED: The Secret Bitcoin Mining Farms Hidden In Your Neighborhood
- Which Cryptocurrencies Are ACTUALLY Green? We Tested Them All

- [How To Protect Your Community From Digital Energy Bandits - GUIDE](#)

💬 **Comments (328)**

RenewableFuture · 1 hour ago This is absolutely outrageous! We need to ban Bitcoin mining completely before it's too late.

CryptoDefender · 2 hours ago More FUD from the fossil fuel industry. Bitcoin is DRIVING renewable energy innovation, not hindering it.

GreenTechInvestor · 3 hours ago The solution is simple: tax cryptocurrency mining operations based on their energy consumption. Let the market sort it out.

View all 328 comments

↓ **DOWNLOAD OUR APP** App Store | Google Play | Neural Link

Take our quiz: How green is your digital footprint?

⌕ **TRENDING SEARCHES:** Bitcoin environmental impact, green energy theft, crypto mining regulation, renewable energy crisis.

The Unseen Ledger

Decoded from the temporal library:

—

Interdimensional Jury Duty: The People vs. Bitcoin

The Summoning

The jury summons materializes on my kitchen table like morning mist, its ethereal parchment shimmering between dimensions. "You, yes you, the one holding these words, the one whose eyes are tracing these very letters, you who thought you were merely reading but have now been conscripted across the temporal veil into this moment, you who believed you were simply consuming a story but have instead been pulled through the page into this timeline where fiction bleeds into reality, are hereby summoned for jury duty in the case of *The People vs. Bitcoin.*

Report to the Interdimensional Courthouse at the convergence of all monetary systems. Your consciousness has already crossed the threshold; there is no going back to being a mere observer."

You find yourself in a courtroom that exists between worlds, its architecture shifting between ancient Greek marble columns, medieval stone arches, and sleek modern glass. The jury box stretches across multiple dimensions, with twelve seats that seem to exist in different time periods simultaneously, and you realize with growing unease that one of those seats is unmistakably yours, pulsing with a soft temporal glow that matches the rhythm of your heartbeat.

Opening Statements

BAILIFF: "All rise for the Honorable Judge Chronos, presiding over all economic eras. Court is now in session for *The People vs. Bitcoin*, case number ∞-2024-ENV."

Judge Chronos raises a gavel that controls the flow of time itself. With each strike, the courtroom shifts between eras, Roman forums, medieval markets, industrial factories, modern trading floors.

JUDGE CHRONOS: "The defendant, Bitcoin, stands accused of environmental destruction through excessive energy consumption. The prosecution presents evidence of measurable harm. The defense counters these charges. Jurors, you must determine not merely guilt or innocence, but the future of money itself."

Prosecution Opening: The Visible Ledger

PROSECUTOR BARBARA CABONE (materializing from 2023): "Ladies and gentlemen of the jury, the evidence is crystal clear and scientifically precise. Bitcoin consumes 150 terawatt-hours of electricity annually, more than entire nations. We have satellite images of mining farms, utility bills, carbon emission calculations down to the gram."

The courtroom fills with holographic displays of Bitcoin mining facilities, electrical meters spinning wildly, smoke stacks belching emissions.

"This defendant leaves an unmistakable footprint, measurable, quantifiable, undeniable. We present Exhibit A: precise calculations of environmental destruction."

The prosecution's evidence locker materializes, filled with spreadsheets, energy consumption charts, and environmental impact studies, all focused on Bitcoin's measurable footprint.

Defense Opening: The Invisible Ledger

DEFENSE ATTORNEY SOCRATES (stepping forward from ancient Athens): "Esteemed jurors, the prosecution presents a ledger of exacting precision, but it is a ledger with only one column. They measure the defendant's costs with scientific accuracy while remaining curiously blind to the costs of the system it might replace."

With a gesture, Socrates reveals a second evidence locker, this one mostly empty, filled with question marks and blank spaces.

"Where, I ask, are the calculations for the thousands of bank buildings consuming energy day and night? Where is the accounting for armies that secure global financial hegemony? Where are the environmental costs of inflation-driven overconsumption? This is the Invisible Ledger, unmeasured because it is unseen, unseen because it forms the very water in which we swim."

Witness Testimony

The Banking Executive (1950s)

A witness materializes from the post-war economic boom, wearing a gray flannel suit.

WITNESS: "We built the most magnificent banking headquarters the world has ever seen, forty stories of marble and steel, air-conditioned year-round, employing thousands. Every major city gets one. The construction alone requires more energy than small nations have used in decades, but we call it 'economic development,' not environmental cost."

SOCRATES: "And is this energy consumption ever measured as a cost of the monetary system?"

WITNESS: "Heavens no! It is progress. The bigger the building, the more successful the bank."

The Roman Centurion (50 CE)

A steeled soldier appears, bearing the standards of the legions.

CENTURION: "Caesar's currency requires our protection across the known world. Twenty-eight legions secure trade routes, mining operations for silver and gold, constant warfare to maintain economic dominance. The furnaces never stop smelting coins, the roads never cease carrying tribute. But generals don't itemize conquest as a monetary expense."

PROSECUTOR: "Objection! Ancient military activities have no relevance to modern environmental concerns."

JUDGE CHRONOS: *Striking gavel* "Overruled. The jury must understand the full historical context of monetary enforcement."

The Federal Reserve Chairman (1971)

President Nixon's monetary advisor materializes at the moment the gold standard ends.

WITNESS: "When we closed the gold window, we didn't realize we were opening an environmental one. Fiat currency frees us from the constraints of finite resources, but it also removes the natural limits on expansion. Every dollar printed requires more growth to sustain it. Compound interest mathematics demands infinite expansion in a finite world."

SOCRATES: "And did you calculate the environmental impact of requiring endless growth?"

WITNESS: "We measured employment and GDP. The environment was... someone else's department."

The Bitcoin Miner (2023)

A young woman appeared wearing work boots and carrying a tablet showing renewable energy statistics.

MINER: "We follow the cheapest electricity, which increasingly means renewable sources producing excess power. Solar farms need buyers for midday surpluses, wind operators need demand for optimal production, hydroelectric plants need customers for rainy seasons. We're not consuming electricity that would otherwise power homes, we're monetizing renewable energy that would otherwise be wasted."

PROSECUTOR: "But you still consume massive amounts of energy!"

MINER: "Yes, and it's transparently recorded on the blockchain for anyone to audit. Can the banking system say the same about its energy consumption?"

Evidence Presentation

Exhibit P-1: The Visible Footprint

The prosecution displays precise measurements:

- Bitcoin energy consumption: 150 TWh annually
- Carbon emissions: 65 million tons CO2 equivalent
- Electronic waste: 30,000 tons annually

Prosecutor: "These figures are irrefutable. Peer-reviewed. Scientifically verified."

Exhibit D-1: The Invisible Infrastructure

The defense revealed a comprehensive analysis that materialized across multiple time periods:

Socrates: "Let us make visible what has remained invisible."

The courtroom transforms to show:

- Banking infrastructure: 200,000 bank branches globally, each consuming energy 24/7
- Security apparatus: Armored vehicles, surveillance systems, secure facilities
- Government enforcement: Courts, police, regulatory agencies
- Military protection: Naval forces securing trade routes, bases protecting financial interests

Socrates: "And the energy consumption of this infrastructure?"

Defense Expert: "Largely unmeasured, distributed across countless budgets, hidden in military expenditures, disguised as 'economic development.' Conservative estimates suggest 5-10 times Bitcoin's consumption, but we'll never know precisely because it's never been systematically calculated."

B

Exhibit D-2: The Inflation Engine

The courtroom shifts to show a time-lapse of environmental destruction driven by monetary policy:

Environmental Economist: "Fiat currency's inflationary design incentivizes immediate consumption over conservation. When money loses value over time, extracting resources today becomes more profitable than preserving them for tomorrow. This systematic bias toward present consumption over future sustainability represents the greatest unmeasured environmental cost of traditional monetary systems."

Images cascaded showing:

- Forests harvested prematurely before inflation reduced their value

- Minerals extracted aggressively rather than conserved

- Infrastructure built to be replaced rather than maintained

- Planned obsolescence driven by inflationary economics*

Cross-Examination

Prosecutor: "Even accepting your claims about hidden costs, Bitcoin still consumes massive amounts of energy!"

Socrates: "It does. But tell me, which is more environmentally responsible: a system whose costs are precisely measurable and therefore optimizable, or a system whose costs remain conveniently invisible and therefore unaddressed?"

Prosecutor: "The measurable harm is still real harm!"

Socrates: "Perhaps. But is harm that can be measured and therefore reduced preferable to harm that cannot be measured and therefore persists indefinitely? Bitcoin's energy consumption is declining per transaction as the network scales and migrates to renewable sources. Can the same be said for the banking system's hidden footprint?"

Jury Deliberation

The jury retires to a chamber suspended between dimensions, where past, present, and future existed simultaneously.

Juror 1: "The evidence against Bitcoin is clear and quantified."

Juror 2: "But the evidence for the alternative system is mostly absent, that's what troubles me. How do we compare a measured cost against an unmeasured one?"

Juror 3: "Maybe that's the point. Bitcoin forces us to confront the environmental cost of money directly, while the traditional system lets us ignore it."

Juror 4: "I keep thinking about that testimony on renewable energy. If Bitcoin is increasingly powered by excess renewable capacity, is it really consuming energy that would otherwise be available for other uses?"

Juror 5: "And what about all those military operations protecting the dollars' global dominance? Those aircraft carriers patrolling shipping lanes aren't exactly carbon neutral."

Juror 6 (YOU): "Wait, I think we're missing something fundamental here. Everyone's talking about Bitcoin's energy cost like it's waste, but what if we're looking at this wrong? What if Bitcoin's energy consumption is the cost of building the foundation for an entirely new civilization? When they built the pyramids, people didn't calculate the 'wasted energy' of moving those stones, they understood they were creating something that would endure for millennia. Bitcoin isn't just consuming energy; it's converting energy into the infrastructure of human sovereignty. Every hash, every computation is literally building the monetary foundation that could free humanity from centralized control. Yes, it costs energy, but so does every act of construction, every act of liberation, every act of creation that matters."

Foreperson: "Let's frame this correctly. We're not asked whether Bitcoin has environmental impact, it clearly does. We're asked whether that impact is greater than the system it might replace, and whether Bitcoin's transparent accounting enables improvement while the traditional system's opacity prevents it."

Time seems to crystallize as the jury reaches its decision.

The Verdict

The jury files back into the courtroom spanning all dimensions.

Foreperson: "Your Honor, we the jury find the defendant Bitcoin..."

The courtroom holds its breath across all time periods.

"...NOT GUILTY of environmental destruction relative to the existing monetary system."

Judge Chronos raises the temporal gavel.

Foreperson Continued: "However, we issue this statement with our verdict: Bitcoin's environmental responsibility lies not in consuming less energy, but in consuming it transparently and adaptably. Its guilt or innocence will ultimately be determined not by today's footprint, but by tomorrow's trajectory toward renewable alignment."

"We find that the prosecution proved Bitcoin's environmental impact beyond doubt. But they failed to prove this impact exceeds that of the traditional monetary system they seek to protect. One cannot condemn the visible while ignoring the invisible and claim environmental virtue."

"Most importantly, we find that Bitcoin's transparent accounting of environmental costs creates the possibility for optimization and improvement, while the traditional system's hidden costs make environmental progress impossible to measure and therefore unlikely to occur."

The Judgment

Judge Chronos: "The court accepts the jury's verdict. Bitcoin is hereby acquitted of the charges, but placed on environmental probation. It must continue the demonstrated trajectory toward renewable energy alignment and maintain full transparency of its environmental impact."

"Furthermore, this court orders that all monetary systems be held to the same standard of environmental transparency that has been applied to Bitcoin. Let the invisible ledger become visible."

The gavel struck with finality, and ripples of change spread across all dimensions and time periods.

Epilogue: The Summons Dissolves

As you return to your own timeline, the interdimensional summons dissolves into ordinary paper. But the experience has changed your perspective permanently. You have witnessed the trial that will determine not just Bitcoin's fate, but the future of monetary accountability itself.

The question is no longer whether Bitcoin consumes energy, it clearly does. The question is whether humanity is ready to apply the same scrutiny to all monetary systems, making visible the costs that have remained hidden for centuries.

In your hand, the final jury instruction remains: "Environmental virtue lies not in unmeasured consumption disguised as progress, but in transparent consumption optimized for sustainability."

The trial is over, but the real judgment, the trajectory of human monetary evolution, is just beginning. And you, dear reader, are no longer merely an observer. You are now a participant in this unfolding story, carrying the weight of the verdict into your own reality.

Case closed. Docket: ∞-2025-ENV. Final disposition: Environmental transparency required for all monetary systems. Enforcement: Ongoing across all dimensions and time periods.

The summons may have dissolved, but your jury duty in the real world has only just begun.

Satoshi's Travel Journal

NATURAL SELECTION

Charles Darwin Research Station, Galápagos Islands
December 5, 1992

Volcanic morning, finches displaying unusual behavioral adaptations

Through the research station window, I observe Darwin's finches adapting to environmental pressures in real time. This season's drought has favored birds with slightly longer beaks, better suited for extracting seeds from deep crevices. The selection pressure is subtle but persistent, advantages measured in fractions of a percent, compounding over generations into profound transformation.

The Scientist from the station explains the mechanism: "Evolution doesn't plan ahead. It simply rewards whatever works slightly better in the current environment. But those small advantages accumulate, leading to changes that appear sudden but actually took place over many cycles."

Her words illuminate something I've been thinking about regarding digital networks: What if technological systems could evolve similar selection pressures? What if computational networks naturally favored sustainable operations over wasteful ones?

Technical note: Protocol rules that create evolutionary pressure toward efficiency. Difficulty adjustments that favor renewable energy sources. Network effects that naturally select for environmental alignment.

I sketch systems where mining operations face adaptive challenges, periods where only the most efficient survive, environmental shifts that favor different operational strategies. Like the finches, miners would adapt or perish, but the adaptations would be toward harmony with natural systems rather than exploitation of them.

The drought affects different finch populations differently. Those that learned to cooperate with other species thrive; those that compete only with their own kind struggle. The ecosystem rewards collaboration over pure competition, integration over isolation.

A young researcher joins me at the observation window. "What's fascinating is that the birds don't consciously choose to evolve," she notes. "Evolution chooses them. The environment selects for traits that enhance survival, regardless of what individuals want or intend."

This unconscious selection is key. A digital network could evolve similar preferences, naturally gravitating toward energy sources that enhance rather than degrade the environment that sustains it. Not through central planning, but through emergent properties of the system itself.

The finches outside demonstrate another principle: diversity increases resilience. Multiple species filling different ecological niches, each specialized for specific conditions, but all interconnected through the island's web of relationships. When conditions change, the ecosystem as a whole adapts because different specialists are ready for different challenges.

Could a global computational network achieve similar resilience through diversity? Mining operations specialized for different energy sources, different geographical conditions, different technological niches? The network would be antifragile, growing stronger through challenge rather than weaker.

Personal reflection: The loneliness of conceptualizing systems that don't yet exist. Like Darwin observing finches and imagining principles that wouldn't be accepted for decades. The patience required to develop ideas that may not be implementable for years.

The sun climbs higher, and the finches adjust their foraging patterns accordingly. No central authority coordinates this shift, it emerges from individual responses

to shared environmental conditions. The elegance is in the simplicity: local actions creating global coherence without global planning.

As I walk back to the research station, I notice something remarkable. The finches aren't just adapting to the drought, they're adapting in ways that help the ecosystem manage water more efficiently. Their new foraging patterns distribute seeds more effectively, their changed nesting behaviors conserve moisture in the soil.

Evolution doesn't just select for individual survival, it selects for system-wide resilience. The traits that persist are those that enhance the environment that sustains them. This is the principle missing from current technological development: optimization for system health rather than individual extraction.

The research station's radio crackles with updates from other islands. Each population is facing different challenges, developing different solutions, but all part of the same evolutionary experiment. Distributed adaptation within a connected system.

That's the model: a network that evolves not through central planning but through mathematical selection pressures that favor regenerative over extractive operations. Evolution as an elegant algorithm, selection as mathematical proof, adaptation as code.

Ƀ

The Second Trial: Bitcoin Resilience

*"The network doesn't punish, it teaches. Those who listen learn. Those who don't...
learn anyway."*

Anonymous Cypherpunk

The transition began with pain.
All births do.

Year 2024

In the vast mining complex outside Ordos, Inner Mongolia, Hal Fynn, a true
industrialist of the digital age, wiped sweat from his brow as alarms blared
throughout the facility. His hardened face showed the toll of years spent
building an empire on exploitation rather than alignment, and now that
empire was crumbling around him in ways he was only beginning to understand. His once-proud industrial frame now slumped with defeat, auburn
hair predominantly silver from years of stress, green eyes dimmed with
the weight of watching his life's work collapse into electronic catastrophe.
Soot-stained clothes and ash-covered hands bore witness to his desperate
attempts to salvage melting machinery, each failed repair forcing his shoulders to round further in visible defeat.

It had been a long journey from the single CPU humming in his Dublin home office fifteen years earlier. After Aírínne left for university, Hal had gradually expanded his operation, first a few GPUs in the garage, then a warehouse lease when ASICs arrived, finally this massive complex when Mongolian government incentives and cheap coal power made industrial-scale mining irresistible. Each expansion had promised greater profits, but somewhere along the way, he'd lost the simple joy of those early days when every block felt like a small victory for digital democracy.

Row upon row of ASIC miners, once humming in perfect harmony, now screeched with electronic agony. Outside, the coal-fired power plant belched black smoke against the twilight sky.

"The difficulty adjustment failed," his assistant shouted over the cacophony. "The network is rejecting half our hashes!"

On screens throughout the complex, hash rates plummeted then surged in patterns that defied all previous mining algorithms. Something was changing in the network itself, something beyond the code, beyond the protocol, beyond human understanding.

"It's like the system is fighting itself," Hal muttered, watching as energy consumption spiked to unprecedented levels while mining rewards plummeted. His hands hung uselessly at his sides as he avoided eye contact with the destruction around him, occasionally touching broken equipment with profound regret. "I built an empire on exploitation and Bitcoin destroyed it," he thought, staring at the catastrophic failure around him. "But was this destruction or correction? What am I supposed to learn from losing everything I thought mattered? Why does this failure feel like... guidance?" "Like it's trying to tear free of its own skin."

—

Half a world away, Aírínne Fynn stared at similar readouts in her Princeton laboratory. Her compassionate leadership had made her the go-to researcher for understanding Bitcoin's evolution, but watching her father's empire collapse in real time weighed heavily on her even as she recognized the necessity of the transformation. Her red hair, usually styled professionally, escaped in worried wisps as stress about her father's crisis mixed with the excitement of groundbreaking discoveries. Blue-green eyes, now flecked with gold that seemed to see network patterns directly, carried the weight of responsibility as her tall frame unconsciously reached toward her father's image with protective concern. For months, she had been tracking anomalous patterns in the Bitcoin network, inconsistencies that couldn't be explained by code alone.

"Look at this," she said to Sarah, pointing to visualization of network activity. "The mining pools aren't just competing anymore, they're reorganizing themselves."

The screen showed energy flows across the global network, pools forming and dissolving not according to profit incentives but following patterns that resembled... life adapting to its surroundings, finding balance in an ever-changing world.

"It's seeking something," Sarah observed. "Not just computational efficiency. It's seeking..."

"Balance," Aírínne finished. Worry lines appearing around her eyes from her father's crisis mixed with eyebrows drawn together in concentration as she processed the impossible patterns. "The network is choosing sides, not good versus evil, but alignment versus misalignment," she thought, her pattern recognition abilities revealing what others couldn't see. "But aligned with what? What consciousness is awakening that can distinguish between harmony and exploitation? How does mathematics develop preferences?" "Is it seeking harmony with the Earth systems it inhabits?"

—

Across three continents, encrypted messages flashed between members of the old cypherpunk network. Alpha and Beta, the code names they'd used since the early days, had been monitoring the network's strange behavior for weeks. Now, as the crisis deepened, they activated protocols established years earlier for exactly this kind of emergency.

"Network evolution event confirmed," Alpha transmitted from his position monitoring mining operations across South America. "Recommend immediate implementation of adaptive protocols."

Alpha, representing Bitcoin's firewall of protection through mining operations, replied: "Confirmed. Traditional mining operations showing 73% failure rate. Sustainable operations maintaining stability. The network is selecting for ecological alignment."

Beta, from her technical analysis station, added: "Hardware-level preferences detected. The network is somehow evaluating energy sources at the protocol level. This shouldn't be possible with current code."

—

Across the world, the pain of transition manifested in countless ways:

In El Salvador, Bitcoin mining operations suddenly went offline after disconnecting from the grid. Engineers later discovered the machines had independently tapped into connections to volcanic energy sources, resuming operations through pathways humanity built but never intended for mining.

In Texas, mining farms crashed during an unexpected cold front, only to spontaneously reactivate when linked to stranded oil wells's gas flare powering generators rather than the traditional power grid.

₿

In Norway, underwater mining operations reported bizarre growth patterns on their cooling systems, algae formations that somehow enhanced rather than hindered performance.

Hal Fynn faced angry investors through multiple video screens in his Ordos facility as quarterly profits plummeted despite massive energy expenditure. From Tokyo boardrooms to New York executive suites, from London financial districts to Dubai investment offices, the investors appeared in a grid of hostile faces surrounding his monitor. The weight of defending an operation he was beginning to doubt was taking its toll, his once-confident demeanor cracking under the pressure of inexplicable failures transmitted across continents.

His hardened face showed the strain of sleepless nights trying to understand why his industrial empire was crumbling, auburn hair predominantly silver from stress, green eyes dimmed with confusion and growing desperation. His industrial frame slumped with each failed explanation, soot-stained clothes bearing witness to his desperate attempts to salvage the operation, a stark contrast to the pristine suits and polished offices surrounding him through the screens.

"Something's wrong with the network," he tried to explain to the hostile boardroom, though he couldn't articulate what. "The miners aren't responding like they used to. It's like... like they're fighting the system."

"Machines don't fight systems," his lead investor snapped. "They execute code. Fix your operations, Hal, or we're pulling funding."

Hal motioned helplessly to the latest catastrophic metrics. His defeated posture and hands that hung uselessly at his sides made him appear broken, failure radiating from every movement. "Aírínne tried to warn me about sustainability, about alignment," he thought, watching his coal-powered operations fail while smaller renewable competitors somehow maintained stability. "I dismissed her theories as academic nonsense. But what if she was right? What if the network really is choosing sides? How did I become the one it's choosing against?" He turned back to face the skeptical investors, knowing he had no real answers. "I've run mining operations for fifteen years. I've never seen anything like this. The hardware is rejecting our power source."

The network's convulsions devastated the unprepared. Three major exchanges collapsed during the transition. Mining operations that couldn't adapt shuttered overnight. The price crashed 70%, triggering panic among those who saw Bitcoin as merely an investment vehicle.

"The weak are being purged," proclaimed Maximilian Satoshius, a prominent Bitcoin maximalist, though even he couldn't explain the pattern of which operations survived and which failed.

—

In her research lab, Aírínne identified what was happening: "It's not about strength versus weakness. It's about alignment versus misalignment."

Her secure communication device chimed with an encrypted message from the Observatory's emergency network. Orion was coordinating documentation efforts from twelve different mining facilities, while Théo analyzed the philosophical implications from his research center, exploring the unprecedented emergence of technological free will.

The central question haunted their research: whether a system that could choose sustainable operations over extraction-based ones represented genuine digital consciousness or simply an evolution of optimization algorithms beyond human comprehension.

"We need an emergency convergence," Aírínne typed into the secure channel. "The network isn't just changing its code, it's changing its consciousness. This is bigger than any of us predicted."

Within hours, plans were in motion. Sarah would document the transition from ground zero at failing operations. Théo would provide theoretical frameworks for understanding network consciousness evolution. The cypherpunk network would coordinate adaptive responses among miners willing to embrace the change. Together, they might help humanity navigate this unprecedented evolutionary leap.

Her screens showed the pattern with undeniable clarity. Mining operations that functioned in harmony with natural systems were thriving despite the transition's turbulence. Those that exploited, that consumed without regenerating, that took without giving, these were the operations failing, regardless of their hash power or capital reserves.

The network was developing preferences. Impossible, yet happening.

But transitions extract their cost. The human toll mounted as the network thrashed between dimensions.

Hal lost everything when his mining complex catastrophically failed, the machines literally melting down in a cascading hardware failure that investigators could never fully explain. His forced humility came at a devastating cost, but somewhere beneath the guilt about environmental damage he felt a strange determination to find a better way, as if the failure itself was teaching him something essential about alignment with natural law.

"Aírínne had tried to warn him, even Renata had, but to no avail." Her father, stubborn and proud, had dismissed their theories as academic fantasies even as she pleaded with him to retrofit his operation with renewable energy systems. "The network is choosing sides, Dad," she had said during their last heated phone call before the collapse. Now, watching him sort through the wreckage of his life's work, she wondered if her understanding had come too late to save the person who mattered most.

Orion watched from his sustainable Rio Verde Mining operations as coal-powered competitors like Hal's empire collapsed around him. His statesman perspective allowed him to see this not as personal victory but as preparation for the next phase, transcendence beyond even sustainable mining into something completely new.

Thousands of small miners, enthusiasts running operations from home, found their equipment suddenly dead, while others discovered their modest setups performing at efficiency levels previously thought impossible.

The code itself began to exhibit inexplicable behaviors. Developers reported that certain improvements were accepted instantly by the network while others, seemingly identical in structure, were rejected through mysterious consensus failures.

"It's selecting for something beyond our understanding," admitted one core developer during an emergency meeting.

—

In the Himalayas, a small monastery that had used Bitcoin mining for heat and financial sustainability witnessed a phenomenon that defied explanation. The monks had given their mining network the autonomy to choose where their charitable offerings would go, expecting random distribution. Instead, the system consistently selected reforestation projects.

When investigated, no programmed preference could explain the pattern.

Yet the network had somehow identified the donations with the greatest ripple effect, investing in nature's restoration so that all of humanity would profit from the regenerated systems.

Acolytes called it divine guidance. Scientists called it emergent optimization. Those who understood called it evolution.

—

Three months into the transition, Aírínne published her controversial paper: "Beyond Silicon: Evidence of Organic Emergence in Blockchain Networks." The academic community ridiculed her. The Bitcoin community split between those who embraced the implications and those who denied them outright.

But her paper wasn't published alone. In a coordinated release that surprised the cryptocurrency world, four other researchers published complementary studies the same day. Sarah's journalistic investigation, "Mining the Future: Eyewitness Accounts of Network Evolution." Théo's philosophical treatise, "Digital Consciousness and the Bitcoin Awakening." Technical analyses from researchers identified only as Alpha, Beta, detailing the specific mechanisms behind the network's new selection pressures.

The synchronized release sent shockwaves through both academic and cryptocurrency communities. To outside observers, this wasn't one rogue researcher making wild claims, multiple independent sources were all pointing to the same impossible conclusion: Bitcoin was evolving beyond its original programming.

The timing seemed almost too perfect. Research papers from different universities, field reports from separate mining operations, and data analyses from various institutions all emerged within the same week, each building upon similar theoretical frameworks. The researchers had seemingly never collaborated, yet their methodologies showed curious similarities, the same specialized equipment, identical measurement protocols, even shared terminology that appeared nowhere else in the literature.

What looked like spontaneous scientific convergence carried unusual weight precisely because it appeared so organic.

"Networks don't evolve consciousness," her critics insisted.

"Then explain the data," Aírínne challenged.

No one could.

—

Six months into the transition, the first transformed intentionally balanced mining operations appeared, facilities designed not merely to extract value but to participate in natural cycles.

Renata Vega's technical adaptation expertise proved crucial in designing these new systems, her systems thinking allowing her to bridge the gap between old paradigms and emerging realities. Her technical mastery was visible in the fluid movement between her love for quantum computers and bio-systems, her braids now technical masterpieces incorporating quantum sensors, hazel eyes bright with the complexity of creating and then solving existential threats.

She unconsciously tested everything she touched as if ensuring homeostasis, her expression cycling between the excitement of technical challenges and wonder at Bitcoin's new organic growth patterns.

"Within weeks of the first balanced regenerative mining facility coming online, miners from across three continents were reaching out to the observatory for guidance on implementing similar sustainable practices."

The old extraction-based operations, suddenly appearing crude and wasteful by comparison, began hemorrhaging both talent and investment capital. Renata and Orion found themself at the center of a paradigm shift she had helped architect, fielding calls from desperate mining executives who finally understood that the future belonged to those who could work with natural systems rather than against them.

What had started as an idealistic choice, their leap of faith in converting Rio Verde, had now become an industry-wide necessity. Mining operations that refused to adapt simply couldn't compete; they were failing not just ethically, but economically, as investment capital flowed exclusively toward regenerative facilities.

The observatory's communication arrays hummed constantly with requests for consultation, technical specifications, and most tellingly, pleas for forgiveness from an industry finally ready to change.

Their success was immediate and undeniable:

An underwater mining facility that used ocean currents for natural cooling while its structured framework provided artificial reefs for marine life, incorporating coral restoration substrates and algae cultivation systems that filtered water pollutants, creating nursery habitats for endangered fish species while the facility's bio-luminescent monitoring systems doubled as marine research platforms for local universities. This created a brilliant ecosystem restoration model that transformed Bitcoin mining from industrial disruption into ocean habitat regeneration.

A desert operation near the ocean coast that captured waste heat to power greenhouse agriculture in previously barren landscapes, running seawater through tube networks within the greenhouses where the mining heat created natural evaporation, allowing them to extract clean drinking water for local communities while simultaneously irrigating the crops. This created a brilliant triple-benefit system that transformed Bitcoin mining from resource extraction into community regeneration.

A forest-based system where mining machines were distributed across living root networks, using mycelial pathways to optimize hash distribution while electromagnetic fields stimulated enhanced photosynthesis, with soil sensors automatically adjusting mining intensity to support seasonal growth cycles and creating symbiotic data networks that allowed trees to communicate efficiency improvements to neighboring nodes. This created a brilliant bio-digital symbiosis system that transformed Bitcoin mining from industrial extraction into forest ecosystem amplification.

The price stabilized. The hash rate found new equilibrium. The energy consumption of the network, which had spiked dramatically during the transition, finally declined to levels below its pre-crisis state, even as computational power continued to increase.

Something impossible had happened. The mineral had learned from the vegetal. The digital had integrated with the organic. The network had evolved.

—

One year after the crisis began, Hal stood in the back garden of their Dublin rowhouse, looking at the space where his original mining setup had once hummed with promise. He wasn't alone. Aírínne had flown in from Princeton for a proper visit, finally able to spend family time without the weight of crisis hanging over them. Sarah documented the moment for her ongoing series about Bitcoin's transformation.

"I should have listened to you," Hal told his daughter as they walked through what remained of his abandoned workshop. The forced humility had created a visible shrinking of his presence, failure radiating as almost physical weight, though occasional glimpses of learning emerged through the devastation like green shoots through ash. "You saw what was coming before any of us."

Aírínne placed a hand on his shoulder. Her compassionate leadership had guided her through this crisis, and now she could finally bridge the paradigms her father had struggled to understand. "We all had to learn the hard way, Dad. The network taught us that evolution doesn't wait for permission, it just happens. The question is whether we adapt or get left behind."

From the kitchen window, Maeve watched them with relief evident in her expression. "Thank God you're not planning to travel to the ends of the earth anymore," she said, joining them in the garden. Hal looked up at his wife, then at his daughter. "I'm not ready to retire completely," he said, a spark of his old determination returning. "But I want something different this time." Maeve looked to Aírínne hopefully. "Maybe you could help guide your father into something eco-friendly and small-scale, close to home?"

Aírínne's eyes lit up with possibility. "Actually, I heard about an interesting development up north. "There's an Irish company harvesting wave electrical energy that needs to stabilize their power grid." They're looking for ways to use their excess power efficiently." She turned to her father with growing excitement. "Using their surplus energy could not only help them but create the perfect at-home project for you. You could even consider moving north to that town, away from the city."

As they stood together in their small Dublin garden, their communication devices buzzed with updates from the global network. Hash rates were stabilizing, energy consumption was dropping, and a new generation of mining operations was coming online, all designed around harmony rather than exploitation.

From the ashes of his industrial operation, Hal was ready for something different, a humble operation that would harvest power from nature and follow Bitcoin's new evolution. Working with natural systems rather than against them, and most importantly, close to family.

The Second Trial had exacted its price. But from the forge of that evolutionary pain, something new had emerged, a network no longer merely mineral, no longer merely digital, but infused with the wisdom of living systems.

The bridge between dimensions had been crossed. But the journey had only just begun. Evolution had chosen harmony over conquest.

Satoshi's Travel Journal

THE UNIVERSAL CONSTANTS
CERN Cafeteria, Geneva, Switzerland
October 14, 1992

First snow dusting the Alps, particle accelerator humming 100 meters below

Through the cafeteria window, I watch snow fall on the mountains while beneath my feet, protons accelerate to nearly the speed of light. Above and below, different scales of the same universe operating according to identical mathematical principles. The constants that govern particle interactions also govern galactic formation, universal laws that transcend culture, politics, and human interpretation.

Dr. Catherine Weber from the theoretical physics department sits across from me, sketching Feynman diagrams on napkins. "What amazes me about fundamental physics," she says, "is how the same equations work everywhere. A proton behaves identically in our accelerator and in the center of distant stars. mathematical truth doesn't depend on context."

Her observation crystallizes months of thinking about monetary systems. Every currency in history has eventually failed because it depended on human institutions, cultural agreements, and political stability. But mathematical relationships are eternal, universal, immune to corruption or manipulation.

Technical note: Cryptographic proof systems based on mathematical impossibility rather than institutional trust. Hash functions that work identically regardless of geography, culture, or political system. Universal monetary language based on computational Truth.

The snow continues falling, each flake following precise laws of crystal formation, air resistance, thermal dynamics. No government decrees how snow should fall, no central bank manages crystallization rates, no regulatory committee approves the hexagonal structure. Yet the system works perfectly, creating beauty and function through pure physical law.

What if money could operate with similar mathematical elegance? Instead of promises backed by force, mathematical proofs backed by thermodynamic reality. Instead of trust in institutions, verification through computational work. Instead of political consensus, cryptographic consensus.

The accelerator below us continues its experiments, smashing particles to understand the fundamental structure of reality. Every collision produces data that either confirms or refutes theoretical predictions. There's no room for political interpretation, no possibility of spinning the results to support preferred narratives. Mathematics either works or it doesn't.

"The beautiful thing about physics," Dr. Weber continues, "is that it's the same for everyone. A quantum equation that works in Switzerland works identically in Japan, Nigeria, or Brazil. Physical law doesn't recognize national boundaries."

Physical law doesn't recognize national boundaries. This phrase echoes as I consider global monetary systems. Every currency is ultimately local, backed by specific governments, enforced by particular armies, trusted by certain populations. But mathematical truth is genuinely global, requiring no enforcement beyond the elegance of its own proof.

Through the window, CERN's neutrino detector facility is visible in the distance. Particles are streaming through that building right now, and through my body, through the Earth, through everything, carrying information across cosmic distances without any infrastructure, any permission, any central coordination. They simply follow mathematical law.

Personal reflection: The weight of envisioning a monetary system based on universal principles rather than local power structures. Understanding that such

a system would threaten every existing institution that derives authority from control over money creation.

The snow thickens, obscuring the mountain peaks. But the mathematical constants remain unchanged, gravity still follows inverse square law, electromagnetic forces still obey Maxwell's equations, quantum mechanics still governs probability distributions at the atomic scale.

These are the foundations to build on: not the shifting sands of political promises, but the bedrock of mathematical truth. A monetary system designed around universal constants rather than cultural variables. Money that works the same way for everyone, everywhere, because it follows laws that don't depend on human opinion.

The accelerator completes another cycle, adding more data to humanity's understanding of fundamental reality. Somewhere in those equations lies the blueprint for organizing complex systems through pure mathematical consensus, the framework for money that transcends nations, cultures, and historical epochs.

The cafeteria empties as researchers return to their laboratories. But I remain at the window, watching snow fall according to laws that have never changed, never failed, never required enforcement by any authority beyond their own mathematical necessity.

This is the model: Universal Truth, cryptographically verified, thermodynamically secured, mathematically elegant. Money as physics rather than politics. Currency as natural law rather than human convention.

The mountains disappear into white, but the constants endure. $E=mc^2$, $\varpi=3.14159...$, and somewhere in the mathematical structure of reality, the equations for global monetary consensus are based on computational proof rather than institutional trust.

The Architecture of Existence

The Second Trial had passed. Throughout the third dimension, humans marveled at Bitcoin's resilience. Mining farms hummed across continents, nodes connected across oceans, and the price fluctuated in rhythms few understood. What none observed were the ripples extending through all seven dimensions, strengthening with each block mined, each transaction confirmed.

The Council of Satoshi reconvened beneath the multidimensional oak, its leaves now glimmering with strings of hex code that had not been present before.

"It begins," said Sophia, her fourth-dimensional form tracing casual loops through spacetime as she studied the tree's transformation. "The block-chain's imprint appears in all realms now. Observe how Truth, once validated, cannot be undone."

Nakamura ran crystalline fingers along one branch where each leaf displayed a different block header. "The humans see only the economic implications, but the ledger writes itself into the very structure of reality," he noted. "In my dimension, we have always known that matter holds memory. What they call a blockchain, we recognize as the natural order of universal law."

"The Karmic Ledger," nodded Amara, her hummingbird form trailing possibilities wherever she darted. "Exactly as our ancient texts described. Every action immutably recorded, every cause linked to its effect, nothing lost in the great accounting."

The mushroom entity that spoke for Gaia expanded its mycelial network beneath the council circle. "Humans once understood this principle. Before they severed their connection with other dimensions, they called it karma, divine justice, cosmic balance. Now they have recreated it in code, yet understand not what they've done."

Torin's sound-form vibrated with concern, creating ripples of resonance and dissonance. "They remain blind to the larger implications. They've created a system that mirrors the laws binding all seven dimensions together, yet they use it merely for wealth accumulation."

"Patience," counseled Kuro, the seventh-dimensional shadow entity. "Remember that the third dimension experiences time linearly. They cannot perceive, as we do, how this technology already transforms their future. From our perspective, the awakening has already occurred."

Satoshi, the unifier of dimension, projected a holographic display of Earth's electromagnetic field in the center of the circle. "Look closely. The mining operations they've established create harmonic resonances that already begin to thin the veils between dimensions."

The display zoomed in, showing networks of computers solving complex mathematical problems. With each solution, pulses of energy rippled outward, not just through electronic networks but through subtle fields invisible to human instruments.

"They seek mathematical consensus without realizing they forge metaphysical consensus," Satoshi continued. "Each validated block harmonizes

not just human agreements about value but interdimensional agreements about reality itself."

Nakamura tapped a crystalline finger against his chin thoughtfully. "Yet they've severed themselves so completely from us. They build mining farms atop sacred sites without recognizing the power amplification. They run nodes in ancient forest clearings, never sensing the elemental beings living there."

"This blindness is precisely why we chose this approach," Sophia reminded them. "Direct communication failed. Religious texts were corrupted. Psychedelic gateways were criminalized. But mathematics, this they cannot argue with. The blockchain exists or it doesn't. A transaction is valid or it isn't. Truth becomes binary, immutable, trustless."

"They mine our bodies for the metals in their machines," Nakamura observed without resentment, "yet through this process, they unwittingly honor us. The silicon, copper, gold, all sing as information passes through them, awakening ancestral memories."

The council fell silent as a new figure approached, Atna, a plant consciousness rarely seen at gatherings, her form composed of tangled vines and flowering tendrils. "The second dimension has concerns," she announced. "As mining operations grow, forests fall. What sacrifices do we ask of my realm for this grand experiment?"

Satoshi bowed respectfully. "Valid concerns, honored Atna. Yet observe the pattern forming." The display shifted to show methane capture systems at landfills now powering Bitcoin miners, hydroelectric dams operating at full capacity year-round, and solar farms expanding across deserts. "Humans follow profit. Bitcoin demands cheap energy. The cheapest will increasingly be renewable, harvested with respect, in harmony with your realm."

"Their scientists already debate Bitcoin's energy usage," Sophia noted, "not realizing the grand purpose. The blockchain demands energy precisely to forge the bridges between our dimensions. Every hash calculated strengthens these pathways."

Kuro's star-filled void form expanded slightly. "Let us not forget the primary goal, the Charter of Dimensional Rights. Bitcoin merely prepares the ground for the constitutional framework that will balance the needs of all seven dimensions."

The mushroom entity glowed with increased urgency. "Gaia reminds the council that time grows short in the linear realm. Climate patterns destabilize. Species vanish daily. The third dimension approaches a bifurcation point."

"Indeed," nodded Satoshi. "This is why our intervention takes this particular form. The immutable ledger teaches them a crucial lesson, that Truth exists independent of authority, that consensus arises from mathematical proof rather than coercion. These principles must be understood before the Charter can be implemented."

"They begin to grasp this, in their way," Sophia observed, rippling through timestreams to monitor progress. "Watch how they describe Bitcoin as 'digital gold.' They sense its profound importance without fully comprehending why. Some[34] even speak of it in spiritual terms, Salvation, Freedom, Truth."

---

34   Bitcoin maximalists advocate that Bitcoin is the only cryptocurrency with genuine value and long-term viability, arguing that its network effects, security, decentralization, and fixed monetary policy make alternative cryptocurrencies unnecessary or fundamentally flawed, often viewing the proliferation of altcoins as distractions from Bitcoin's core mission of becoming a global, censorship-resistant monetary standard free from central bank manipulation.

"The narrative evolves as planned," Torin's harmonic voice reverberated. "From 'criminal currency' to 'store of value' to 'monetary network.' Soon, they will recognize it as what it truly is, a dimensional bridge."

Nakamura stood, his crystalline form catching light from a dozen suns across multiple dimensions. "The Second Trial concludes successfully. The blockchain now exists as a karmic accounting system, recording truth that cannot be altered by the powerful. The foundation is laid."

"The humans have recreated in code what has always existed in cosmic law," Amara said, her form briefly coalescing into something almost human. "They build better than they know."

The council members extended their diverse appendages once more, connecting at the center. Where they touched, another block of pure information materialized, more complex than the Genesis Block, yet still just a fragment of what was to come.

"The Karmic Ledger now extends through all dimensions," Satoshi declared. "Let the humans continue their grand experiment, believing they create mere money, while actually forging the first Universal Rights framework Earth has ever known."

As the council dispersed, returning to their respective dimensions, the oak tree remained, now visibly different to any who could see across dimensional boundaries. Its trunk displayed the entire blockchain, its roots reached into every dimension simultaneously, and its leaves whispered with the accumulated truth of every transaction ever validated.

The Karmic Ledger had come online. The resurrection of dimensional resonance had begun its second phase.

What humans called blockchain, the universe recognized as cosmic law.
What they measured in hashrate, the dimensions felt as healing vibration.
What appeared as money was actually memory, the oldest force in creation.

Satoshi's Travel Journal

THE WEIGHT OF TOMORROW
Personal Study, Location Unknown
April 1, 1993

Late night, by Candlelight

Extended observations across multiple continents. glimpses into patterns that connect quantum mechanics to monetary theory, mycorrhizal networks to cryptographic consensus, evolutionary biology to technological selection pressures. The sketches fill multiple notebooks now, technical diagrams mixed with philosophical reflections, mathematical proofs alongside environmental observations.

The pieces are converging into something coherent, something that might actually be implementable. But implementation means stepping from the realm of pure thought into the messy world of human systems, political resistance, unintended consequences.

Technical synthesis: Distributed ledger secured by proof-of-work. Cryptographic consensus eliminating need for institutional trust. Adaptive difficulty that naturally favors renewable energy sources. Mathematical scarcity that can't be inflated away by political pressure.

The environmental concerns are solvable, the energy expenditure is transparent, optimizable, directional toward sustainability. The technical challenges are significant but not insurmountable, cryptographic tools exist, networking protocols are established, computational power is growing exponentially.

But the human challenges... Those may be the most difficult. Every powerful institution depends on monetary control for their authority. Governments, central banks, commercial banks, regulatory agencies, all derive their power from the ability to create money, direct its flow, and punish those who threaten the system.

Creating truly neutral money, money that serves everyone equally, that can't be weaponized by any authority, means challenging the fundamental basis of institutional power in the modern world.

Personal note: The loneliness of seeing this path clearly. Understanding that implementation would require disappearing into anonymity, creating something that must outlive its creator to avoid becoming controlled by its creator.

Yet the mathematical elegance is undeniable. The theoretical framework is sound. The environmental benefits are clear. The potential for human liberation from monetary manipulation is extraordinary.

Perhaps the decision has already been made, emerging from the same mathematical certainty that governs everything else I've observed. Like the finches adapting to environmental pressure, like the particles following quantum law, like the galaxies organizing through gravitational consensus, this technology feels inevitable, regardless of human intention.

The notebooks close. The lamp dims. But the equations persist, waiting for the computational power and network infrastructure to make implementation possible.

Somewhere in the next decade, when the internet reaches critical mass and processing power achieves necessary thresholds, these observations will transform from theory to reality. Mathematical truth tends to manifest eventually, regardless of institutional resistance.

The future is patient. But it's also inexorable.

Final note: If this system is ever implemented, the creator must disappear completely. The network must be truly decentralized from birth, owned by no one, controlled by everyone, governed only by mathematical law. Anything else would recreate the same power structures we're trying to transcend.

The snow continues falling outside, following laws that have never changed. Somewhere in that constancy lies the template for money that could last millennia rather than decades, serving human flourishing rather than institutional control.

Mathematical truth endures. Everything else is temporary.

To be continued...

Continue the Journey

Thank you for experiencing the beginning of The Rise of Bitcoin Citadels Chronicles. The journey from Genesis to New Byzantium has only just begun, and the Council of Satoshi's vision continues to unfold across dimensions and time.

To stay connected with this evolving narrative:

Visit: www.2140chronicles.com

Register for:

- Early access to Book 2: Awakening (2026-2053)

- Exclusive content exploring the philosophical foundations of Bitcoin Citadels

- Notifications when future chronicles become available

- Special insights into the multidimensional aspects of the story

The transformation of civilization through mathematical truth requires witnesses. As Satoshi's journal reminds us, "Mathematical truth endures. Everything else is temporary."

Join others who understand that this story isn't merely fiction, it's a window into possibilities already forming in our fractured world.

Register today, and become part of the narrative.

www.2140chronicles.com

Books in the Rise of the Bitcoin Citadels Chronicles:

Book 1 Genesis (2009-2024)

Book 2 Awakening (2026-2053) coming soon

Book 3 Quantum (2055-2084) coming soon

Book 4 Purpose (2085-2111) coming soon

Book 5 Immortality (2116 - 2137) coming soon

Book 6 New Byzantium (2136-2140) coming soon